THE CAUSE

Further Titles by Alan Savage from Severn House

THE COMMANDO SERIES

COMMANDO

THE CAUSE

THE SWORD SERIES

THE SWORD AND THE SCALPEL

THE SWORD AND THE JUNGLE

THE SWORD AND THE PRISON

STOP ROMMEL!

THE AFRIKA KORPS

THE CAUSE

Alan Savage

This first world edition published in Great Britain 2000 by
SEVERN HOUSE PUBLISHERS LTD of
9–15 High Street, Sutton, Surrey SM1 1DF.
This first world edition published in the USA 2000 by
SEVERN HOUSE PUBLISHERS INC of
595 Madison Avenue, New York, N.Y. 10022.

British Library Cataloguing in Publication Data

Savage,   Alan
    The cause. (The Commando series ; bk. 2)
    1.   World War, 1939-1945 - Fiction 2.War stories
    I.   Title
    823.9'14 [F]

    ISBN 0-7278-5555-7

F
1327357

Typeset by Hewer Text Ltd.,
Edinburgh, Scotland.
Printed and bound in Great Britain by
MPG Books Ltd, Bodmin, Cornwall.

Contents

To set the Cause above renown,
To love the game beyond the prize,
To honour, while you strike him down,
The foe that comes with fearless eyes:
To count the life of battle good,
And dear the land that gave you birth.
And dearer yet the brotherhood
That binds the brace of all the earth.

Sir Henry John Newbolt

This is a novel. Except where they can be historically identified, the characters are invented, and are not intended to portray real persons, living or dead. Many of the incidents did actually happen.

Part One
Torch

O how comely it is, and how reviving
To the spirits of just men long opprest,
When God into the hands of their deliverer
Puts invincible might.

John Milton

The Assignment

C aptain Harry Curtis, First Commandos, leaned back in his deckchair and looked up into a clear blue sky at two aircraft circling high above his head. They were too far away for him to make out their markings, but he had no doubt they were RAF machines on a training flight. With the Luftwaffe in this summer of 1942 so heavily engaged in Russia there were few raids over England nowadays, certainly not in daylight, and definitely not as far north as Worcestershire. Seated in the garden of his parents' house in the village of Frenthorpe, only a few miles from Worcester itself, it was difficult to believe there was a war on anywhere.

But for the memories.

Harry wondered if he was, actually, shell-shocked, or in some way traumatised by the catastrophe at St Nazaire. The raid, only five months ago, had been intended to rob the Germans of a base both for U-boats and, possibly, the giant battleship *Tirpitz*, supposing she ever abandoned her defensive duties in the Arctic for a raid into the Atlantic. And it had achieved its objective, in the destruction of both the docks and the U-boat pens.

But at what cost? He supposed not more than half-a-dozen of the thousand-odd Commandos and sailors who had made their way up the Loire had escaped. He was one of the lucky ones. Or perhaps he was just more ruthless than other men.

Oddly, he had never thought of himself as ruthless, or savage. Yet when he found himself in action, he apparently became a controlled killing machine. This pleased his superiors – they had

3

spent a small fortune teaching him, and others, the art of killing, and destroying, as quickly and efficiently as possible.

And others, he thought. Some seven hundred Commandos, each as highly trained as himself, had gone into St Nazaire, to their deaths or to captivity.

Had they been betrayed? Certainly the Germans had been waiting for them, in more strength than they had been told was possible.

It was not something he wanted to think about, because the traitor could only be someone known to him, perhaps even a friend. Perhaps even more than that. But he had shot his way out, and then escaped, using the Resistance route, through Vichy France to the Spanish border, then across an essentially hostile Spain into Portugal, and thence home. It had taken him more than two months. He had reached England again in June, and been given extended recuperative leave, to bask in the summer sunlight of Worcestershire.

He wasn't sure that had been a good idea. He had been allowed too much time to think, and not only about St Nazaire. About the whole war. As an eighteen-year-old officer in the Guards he had been badly wounded on the beach at Dunkirk. While still in hospital, but mending well, he had been invited to volunteer for a new, special fighting force which would carry the fight to the enemy in a way not yet possible for the full strength of the British army. Well, the Commandos had done that, with a fair amount of success, until St Nazaire. His exploits had earned him a captaincy at an unusually early age, and the Military Cross.

And an even earlier retirement from active service? He was beginning to fear that might be so for he had been left in Frenthorpe for two months, while the war seemed to be going from bad to worse. The Germans were resuming their advance into Russia, having cleared the British out of the Balkans; Rommel was tearing up the desert, had retaken Tobruk, and was generally accepted as being on the verge of throwing the British entirely out of Egypt and the Japanese seemed to be running wild in the Pacific. The only gleam of light was the US Navy's great victory at Midway, a couple of months ago, but in an ocean so large, and peppered with islands each of which was a Japanese strongpoint, it was difficult to see how much progress could be made. Certainly not while all else was falling apart.

Jupiter, the huge black Newfoundland who had been asleep under Harry's chair, gave a half-snort, half-bark, which indicated that he had been disturbed by some noise. Harry sat up, and looked at the conservatory door, in which his mother had just appeared.

In contrast to her tall, well-built son, Alison Curtis was a small, neat woman. Only the fair hair – greying in her case – and the handsome features indicated their close relationship. She also looked vaguely apprehensive, as always when confronting Harry. She remembered too well the eager schoolboy receiving his commission just three years before. That he had survived Dunkirk had been a miraculous deliverance. Since then . . . she knew he had become a Commando, and she knew theirs was a secret and brutal war. More than that she did not know, but she could understand that the eighteen-year-old schoolboy had gone forever, that this twenty-one-year-old captain was far older than his years, that an invisible curtain had been pulled down between him and his family, perhaps between him and the whole of humanity. It was a curtain she did not know how to penetrate and she was not sure she would ever dare risk attempting it.

But there were some who seemed able to do so. "Captain Forester is here, Harry," she said.

Another reason for apprehension. Alison Curtis had never been sure about Harry's relations with women. As a mother she had had his domestic future all mapped out with marriage to the daughter of their close friends the Clearsteds. A neat family enclave growing up together . . . but Harry had never taken to Yvonne Clearsted and their engagement had been brief and bitter because the army had already been taking over his life. Then there had been that Norwegian woman who had been far too good-looking, and who had mysteriously disappeared, and now this female soldier who kept appearing – and Harry was apparently always pleased to see her.

As now. "Belinda!" he cried, getting up, and only then remembering to stand to attention – in terms of service Belinda Forester was his superior officer and, as adjutant to both their superior officer, the woman who gave him his orders. That alone would have made him glad to see her, after two months of doing nothing. But their personal relationship was even more important. Short and slim, with piquant features and wearing her black hair cut just below her ears, she was a most attractive woman, especially in uniform. He flattered himself that he was her *favourite* man, which was not to suggest that he was her *only* man – they had in fact only shared a bed on half a dozen occasions in the two years he had known her. Sex for Belinda was something to be indulged in, and enjoyed, when there was nothing more important to do. As personal assistant to a colonel in the Commandos there was usually a great number of things that were more important. But Harry always looked forward to the next time.

"Harry," she said and, as she was in uniform, held out her hand.

"You'll stay for lunch, Captain?" Alison suggested.

"That would be very nice, Mrs Curtis," Belinda said, "but we must be away immediately after."

"We?" Alison asked. She might no longer be sure of how to handle her son, but she did like to have him at home, where at least there was no chance of his being killed or seriously wounded again.

"We?" Harry asked, more enthusiastically.

"I'm afraid so," Belinda said. "Presuming you are fit?"

"I am fit," he assured her.

"Well, then . . ." – she glanced at Alison – "I wonder if . . .?"

"You wish to speak with Harry in private," Alison said. "Of course. I'll see to lunch."

She bustled into the house.

"I sometimes feel she thinks I am a messenger from the Devil,"

Belinda remarked, and stooped to hug Jupiter, who had got to his feet. "Hello, old fellow. You like me, don't you?"

"I'm sure Mother will too, when she gets to know you better." Harry indicated the second deck chair. "But right now . . ."

"Whenever I appear you disappear," Belinda agreed, sitting down and taking off her cap. "We've had a catastrophe."

"Another one?"

"This one makes St Nazaire look like a tea party. Dieppe."

"What was worth raiding at Dieppe?"

"This wasn't a raid," Belinda said grimly. "It was a rehearsal for the invasion. We're not talking about a few hundred men and one old destroyer. This was six thousand strong."

Harry gave a low whistle. "I didn't know we had that many."

"We don't. Most of them were Canadians. They had back-up. Thirty tanks and most of the RAF. But the German defences were simply too strong. They got themselves pinned down on the beaches, lost all the tanks, and were just cut to pieces. Something like two-thirds went, including well over a thousand dead. The rest were taken prisoner."

"Shit," Harry commented. "And I didn't know."

"Why should you have known?" Belinda asked. "You weren't involved. And this was top secret. It still is, for the time being."

"Yes," Harry said thoughtfully. "But the RAF . . .!"

"That was even worse," Belinda said. "In addition to proving that an invasion is a practical possibility – and that has been put back at least a year, now – the secondary idea was to draw the German air defences into the battle and hopefully destroy them. We put up sixty squadrons. They probably put up more."

"Don't tell me they won?"

"They certainly didn't lose. We're claiming a hundred and thirty-odd kills, but the Germans are saying they lost only forty-eight, and the Resistance people on the ground are going with the German claim. While we are admitting a hundred losses."

"What a foul-up. What does Lightman say about it?"

"Colonel Lightman," Belinda said, very quietly, "took part in the assault. He has not been heard of since."

7

They gazed at each other. Major Lightman, as he had then been, had been the officer who had inducted Harry into the Commandos, who had overseen his early training, who had remained a father figure ever since. That he had also been Belinda's immediate superior, and that they had been lovers, had brought him even closer, even if perhaps the Colonel had been unaware of it.

"I'm sorry," he said. "Very sorry."

Belinda gave a little shrug. "He was a good soldier."

"But not a good man?"

"Are there many of those about?"

She was separated from her husband, he knew, and, while not in the least feminist, was entitled to have a jaundiced view of the opposite sex.

Including him?

"Yet you slept with him," he remarked, probing.

"He was the boss."

"Ah. Just as you are my boss."

She gave a quirky smile. "Not any more. You've been promoted to Major. That's pretty good going, at twenty-one. The way things are, if you can hang about, *if*, you could be a colonel at twenty-five. Sir."

"Don't be a noodle, Linda. I'm not sir to you."

"You are, when we are in uniform. Or," she added, regarding his civilian clothes, "even one of us. You are also to get the VC."

"Good God! For what?"

"I imagine, for saving Harbord's life under enemy fire, as reported by Jon Ebury."

Harry had actually forgotten about that. "So what happens now?"

"Well, as you can imagine, even if, as I say, the whole thing is being kept a deadly secret – you must not even mention it to your parents – everyone is pretty shook up. Quite apart from the fact of having lost so many good, and well-trained, men, the question is again being raised by those, shall I say, more regular senior officers, as to just what good, if any, we are doing. First

8

Commandos has a new colonel, Peter Bannon." She paused, waiting.

"Peter Bannon?" Harry cried. "He was my company commander in the Guards."

He long ago 1940 seemed.

"I had no idea he'd joined us."

"Quite recently. But he has the seniority. He wants to see you. And not only for old time's sake. Trained officers are a little thin on the ground, right this minute. It is also important for us to do something, anything, to restore the confidence of our superiors."

"Right," Harry said. "This afternoon, is it?"

"It'll be this evening before we reach London," Belinda pointed out.

The train was, as always, crowded. Harry and Belinda spent most of the journey standing in the corridor, pressed against each other by the mass of bodies all around them.

"I've waited all summer to be in this position." He bent his head to whisper into her ear. "Or are you in mourning?"

"I told you, for a soldier, yes."

He straightened, looked down at her. She was, he supposed, a product of both the war and the position in which she had found herself, coming on top of the frantic thirties, when women had been seeking to implement the increasing freedom they had obtained, in dress and employment as much as moral attitudes, since the equalising process of the Great War. But he couldn't help but wonder if she was as hard-bitten as she liked to pretend.

"How long have you known Bannon?" he asked.

She tilted her head to look up at him. "Just over a week."

"Ah."

She wrinkled her nose. "He's not my type."

"They do say that the size of a man's nose is an indication of other things. Peter has a big one. Nose, I mean."

"Maybe I like them small and active."

"Touché," he agreed. "So where do I spend tonight?"

9

"Where do you think? It's been a pretty empty summer for me, as well."

"Harry!" Peter Bannon was tall and heavily built, with matching features, in which his nose, as Harry had reminded Belinda, was prominent. "Good to see you. I've been hearing nothing but good reports."

"Thank you, sir."

"Sit down, man, sit down." Bannon indicated the chair in front of the desk. There was no other furniture in the small office other than a filing cabinet. The closed window did little to shut out the noise of the London traffic. "Forester has brought you up to date?" He glanced at Belinda, standing to attention just inside the door.

"Yes, she has. Rather a bad show."

"That's one way of putting it. It was a bloody disaster. The only good thing about it is that it has proved a point we have been making for some time, that our re-entry into Europe is not going to be a simple matter, or even a practical one, for the foreseeable future. Our new allies don't see it that way at all. Their idea is, all right, you guys, we're in the war now, so let's get it over and done with. Forget the Pacific. They have mobilised an army of nearly a million men to fight the war in Europe. They are assuming that it will be merely a matter of transferring those troops to England, assembling them, and sweeping across the Channel. I imagine that idea would make Hitler's day. Anyway, they're now having to reappraise the situation. But they still have those million-odd men, all, so we are told, raring to go. Now Roosevelt's Chief of Staff, Marshall, has come up with an alternative idea. The poor Brits are being bashed everywhere. Rommel will be in Cairo by the middle of next month, so we're told. So, the Seventh Cavalry or whatever will ride to the rescue of the Eighth Army just as if they were fighting the Indians in Arizona."

"The Americans are sending an army to help defend Egypt?"

"In a manner of speaking"

10

"But it'll take them months to get to Egypt. They dare not risk passing through the Mediterranean."

"Oh, quite. No, no, their idea is to land in Morocco and Algiers. They reckon the French will come across to them. The Americans and the French have a long history of mutual assistance: Lafayette, the Statue of Liberty, and all that."

"It's an idea," Harry said. "But I don't see how landing in Algiers is going to help our troops in Egypt."

"Yes," Bannon said drily. "Some of these military planners look at maps and forget to check the scale. Landing in Algiers to help relieve pressure on Egypt is rather like landing in San Francisco to relieve pressure on Washington. However, this is their intention. Top secret, of course. They've named it Operation Torch. It's scheduled for some time in the next couple of months. Now frankly, we're not unhappy with this. We're hoping to be able to sort Egypt out before the Yanks get ashore: the last thing we want is them crowing that they rescued the Eighth Army. But at the same time, we have to co-operate with them, because let's face facts, over the next few years they are going to have a bigger input that we possibly can. So, they have asked for assistance, and we are going to give it to them. As I say, they are sure that, on the whole, the French in North Africa would rather be on our side than Germany's. But there is a problem: the Commander-in-Chief of French Forces in Morocco and Algiers is Admiral Darlan. Do you know anything of him?"

"Only that he is also Commander-in-Chief of the French Navy."

"He was. But that is an important point. He was Commander-in-Chief of the French Navy when we virtually destroyed it, following their surrender back in 1940. Most French sailors bear a grudge for that, he has a bigger grudge than most. He is also a fervent Vichy man, perhaps for that very reason. So, while the Americans feel the French may wish to come across, they are quite sure Darlan won't, and he is the boss on the ground."

"Can't de Gaulle help?"

"They don't want de Gaulle to be involved, at any level. He is

Alan Savage

not even being told about Torch until it is carried out. They have a point. To many Frenchmen, de Gaulle is a traitor, and the Americans feel that his presence may harden resistance to them, or even begin a civil war. So, no de Gaulle, until after North Africa has been secured."

"Which cannot happen until Admiral Darlan has been taken out."

Bannon stroked his nose. "Or, shall we say, hopefully persuaded to change sides."

"I see," Harry said, seeing all too well.

"You are a trained parachutist," Bannon remarked.

"Yes, sir."

"You speak French, fluently."

"Yes, sir."

"You are also experienced at working behind enemy lines."

"I've done it once or twice."

"Quite."

"What exactly are my orders, sir?"

"You will lead a small body of Commandos which will be dropped in North Africa at an appropriate time to co-ordinate with the American landings. The night before the landings, you will enter Algiers, proceed to Admiral Darlan's headquarters, and place him under arrest."

"Just like that."

"I accept that it would be simpler just to shoot the place up, and the Admiral with it, but the Americans would like him taken alive, if possible."

"As you say, sir, they do tend to confuse the possible with the impossible. How big a squad am I being given?"

"We think eight will be about right. More than that would be difficult to move about. You will hand pick them yourself."

"And the Americans seriously suppose that eight men in British Army uniforms can simply stroll into Algiers without being arrested immediately?"

"Ah . . . you will be wearing French uniforms."

Harry stared at him.

12

"Oh, quite. This means that if you are captured you will be shot. However, I should point out that after the St Nazaire Raid Hitler issued an order of the day that any British Commando taken prisoner shall be shot, immediately, whether in uniform or not. Naturally we are protesting against this order, but I'm not sure we will have any success, especially after this Dieppe business."

"Are you saying that all those prisoners, I believe more than two thousand of them," – he glanced at Belinda – "are going to be shot?"

"We're working on that. We hold quite a few German prisoners ourselves, who are a bargaining counter. However, there it is. I understand this is a very dangerous mission. You have every right to decline it, Harry. But we do need a most experienced man to carry it out, and right this minute you are just about our most experienced officer. There is also the saving grace that even if you are arrested to be tried as spies, the Americans should be ashore, if everything goes according to plan, before you can be executed."

"If everything goes according to plan," Harry agreed. "Of course I am not going to decline, sir. You say I am to be allowed to pick my own team. How much can I tell them?"

"It would be best if you were to tell them nothing, save that they are going on a very dangerous mission behind enemy lines."

"Very good. Have we any people on the ground already?"

"Yes, we have some agents in Algeria, and indeed in Algiers."

"Am I allowed to contact any of these people? They may be very necessary."

"We are organising that now. We would hope to have an agent who knows the ground and the people fly in with you. I will come back to you on this. Now, you have two months, just, to find your people, and make sure they are up to scratch. And, incidentally, bring yourself up to scratch as well."

"Yes, sir."

"The old training camp in Scotland is still available. Use it. When you have your team together, move them down to the

jump training area. Obviously we cannot reproduce desert conditions here in England, but we will do the best we can."

"Thank you, sir."

"I wish for weekly reports. One sheet of paper will do."

Harry nodded.

"Captain Forester will organise your French gear and docu-
ments."

"Yes, sir."

"Well . . . good luck, Harry. But I will see you again before
you go."

Harry saluted, and left the room. Belinda followed him.

"Jesus," she remarked.

"Yes. It could work."

She looked at her watch. "It's nearly seven. Let's go have a
drink."

London, Harry reflected, had taken on a timeless air. When he
had first come here, in the autumn of 1940, just out of hospital
and looking for a good time, it had still been a huge, sprawling
and yet tightly-packed city. Oddly, his first night in London, 7th
September 1940, had been the first night the German bombers
had attacked the capital. Right in the middle of his good time!
Actually, the bombs had added to the excitement of his first
sexual encounter, so much so that he had almost fallen in love
with the "nightclub hostess" who had become his partner for the
night, for all that she had undoubtedly been old enough to be his
mother.

Perhaps he had a weakness for older women: Belinda was
several years his senior. In the event, his callow adoration of Niki
– he had never learned her last name – had ended almost
immediately. When next he had returned to London, a newly
trained Commando, brimming with the self-confidence of having
just learned how to kill, Niki, and her club, had both been mere
holes in the ground, courtesy of the Luftwaffe.

There had been quite a few holes in the ground, and collapsed
buildings. Then there had been more and more. Now, as he and

14

The Cause

Belinda made their way to the nearest pub, in the twilight the city
looked like what it had become, a bombsite. The absence of any
artificial light, even in the buildings that still stood, added to the
impression, even if this was because of the blackout.
It was impossible to decide whether London would ever recover. Or, for that matter, Warsaw or Amsterdam or Moscow or
Singapore. This was warfare on a scale and non-battlefield
intensity that had not been seen before. As for human
relations . . .
He had then learned that *knowing* how to kill, an essentially
abstract matter, was poles apart from *wanting* to kill, which is
very personal and, indeed, consuming. Niki's disappearance into
chaotic disintegration had made so much else that had seemed
important become absolutely irrelevant. Especially pure and
proper young women like Yvonne Clearsted, to whom a kiss
was an emotional milestone. Presumably, being still only nine-
teen, he should have gone all the way with his parents' wish that
he marry the girl. He had proposed in the safe knowledge that as
a very junior Army officer there was no prospect of his being
allowed to marry for some considerable time, but any chance the
relationship might have had to develop had been ended by the
appearance of Veronica Sturmer.
He had not known what to make of Veronica Sturmer. He still
did not. She had been lovely, sensual, eager . . . but though half-
Norwegian, her other half had been German, and he had never
been sure which half had predominated. But she had saved his
life, at the cost of her own.
There had been just emptiness, after that. In the two months he
had spent at Frenthorpe since St Nazaire, he had made no
attempt to contact Yvonne, who had apparently joined the
ATS and wasn't there most of the time, anyway. In that time,
there had not even been Belinda . . . who was now looking at him
past her gin and tonic, quizzically.
"Who's in a brown study, then?" she asked.
"Sorry. I just drifted off."
"I don't blame you. What a shitting awful assignment."

15

"I've had worse. Like the man said, the Seventh Cavalry should arrive before I can actually be tried and shot."

"And what about going in?"

"Natural hazard."

She gave a little shudder, and finished her drink.

"Another?" He had been nursing his beer.

She watched the bar filling up, with people still uncertain whether or not they would be alive come morning, however the German raids had diminished in frequency.

"I'd rather go home," she decided. "There's gin there as well."

For all the odd hotel rooms they had shared in the past, Harry had only once ever been invited to Belinda's flat. That had been just two months before, when he had finally arrived back in England, after his escape from France. He had supposed this the ultimate accolade, even if he had understood that he was really being offered psychiatric assistance in recovering from the deaths of so many of his friends and comrades, and at that time had had no doubt it was a flat that had been visited often enough by David Lightman.

He would not have been human had he not wondered just what he was being offered now.

Belinda closed and locked the door behind them. "You *do* drink gin? If not, there's some beer."

She went into the bedroom.

Harry was overwhelmingly aware of neatness. But then, she was a neat person. The bottles waited on a small sideboard. There was even an ice bucket, although there was no ice.

"Where do you start?" Belinda asked from beyond the bedroom door.

"With some names I have in mind."

"I thought all your names were dead, or prisoners."

"Not quite all. There's still Harbord."

He poured, and she emerged from the bedroom door.

"I thought he was a no-no."

"He was, when he began. But then, I imagine I was too."

16

"Not you," she said. "Never you. You were a natural." She took the glass from his hand, sipped. "I knew that, the moment I laid eyes on you."

"You could have fooled me."

He took the glass from her hand, put it on the table beside his own, held her in his arms. "Anyway, a natural what?"

"A natural born killer." She kissed him. "Do you have a weakness for undressing women in uniform?"

"Doesn't everyone?" he asked.

They lay together on her bed, entwined with contentment, passion momentarily spent. Although she kept the light on – she liked to see what was happening – with the blackout curtains drawn the bedroom was utterly isolated from the rest of the city, and thus they were also utterly isolated from the rest of humanity.

Harry could imagine no better position to be in, than utterly isolated with Belinda Forester. If her flat was neat, she was even neater. Everything about her was perfection, except for her breasts, which were a shade large. But that was another aspect of perfection.

Now she pushed herself up the bed, to reach for her half-consumed gin and tonic. His head rested on her stomach.

"How's your divorce coming along?"

"In fits and starts. There's a war on. Why?"

"Ah . . ." He sat up as well. They had discarded the sheet.

"Don't tell me you're looking to the future? I don't think you can afford to do that. Anyway, me? You know too much about me. I'd never make a good wife."

"Because the last time didn't work?"

"Because," she said, and put down her empty glass, "there is so much I want to do, which doesn't necessarily include a husband. Can you understand that?"

"I think so."

"Well, then . . ." – she turned on her knees, putting one leg across both of his to straddle him and sit on his thighs – "there

17

are one or two things about me you probably don't know. Like for instance, I speak fluent French."

"I didn't know that," he agreed.

"I have also received parachute training," she added.

The Squad

"Oh, no," Harry said. "Oh, no, no, no."

She pouted. "I think your attitude is absurd. I can shoot, too."

"The Commandos are a male organisation," he told her.

"You wouldn't be an organisation at all if I hadn't spent the last two years organising you," she pointed out.

"That's entirely different. Anyway, can you imagine what Bannon would say? Or the big boys in Whitehall? Or the press, when they got hold of it?"

"But you'd like to have me along," she suggested, "all things being equal."

"All things are never equal. And no, I would not like to have you along. You cannot operate successfully if you have to keep looking over your shoulder to make sure someone else is all right." He held her shoulders to bring her down to him. "Sitting where you are has got me going again."

Next morning Harry caught the train to Glasgow and thence Fort William. As ever, after a night with Belinda, he felt relaxed, at ease with himself and the world. Which was not to say the world was at ease with him.

Was he afraid of what he had been ordered to do? Fear was not a word in his vocabulary. Apprehension, certainly, but as to whether his mission would be a success rather than fear of any personal mishap. He had been quite seriously wounded twice, but each time had made a full recovery. Both incidents had happened in the thick of battle and, as is the way with wounds, entirely without warning. When he died, as he understood was possible every time he went into action, that too, he hoped, would be entirely without warning.

And this mission? It contained the element of daring irrationality that was so important a part of Commando operations, but he did not suppose it would be as dangerous as the assault on St Nazaire.

Providing they weren't betrayed again.

He reached the Commando training camp the next day, was shown in to Colonel Lewton, who was now in command.

"Harry Curtis!" Lewton, a small man, shook hands. "I've heard a lot about you. What brings you up here?"

"Two things, actually," Harry said, sitting before the desk. "I've been out of action for the past couple of months, and I need to get back to full training as rapidly as possible."

Lewton nodded. "We can do that. And the other?"

"I wish to recruit seven men for a special mission. They must be trained parachutists, and they must be the very best."

Lewton looked thoughtful. "And French speaking?"

"Yes."

Lewton grinned. "Well, I won't ask you more than that, Major. I'll check with my people and let you have a list. You understand that just about all the people here now are recruits?"

"Yes. I lost all my people at St Nazaire. What about Harbord?"

"He was wounded on that caper, wasn't he? He hasn't been returned to duty yet. There is some doubt as to whether he ever will be. Mental rather than physical. I'm sorry. Was he a close friend?"

"No," Harry said. "But we shared a few experiences."

Harry commenced training immediately to regain that special level of fitness required by the Commandos and, more especially, a Commando officer, who could not require any member of his squad to go anywhere, or do anything, that he was not about to do himself.

The training was useful mentally, too. He had had doubts about his own capacity, after St Nazaire. Returning to full physical fitness and combat readiness was restorative. It was also exhausting, and left him little time for reflection before he fell asleep at night. The men with whom he trained were of course well aware who he was, that he was a major, and that he was as experienced a fighting man as anyone in the British army. Perhaps they had not expected him to be so young. But while they treated him with a cool reserve in the beginning, they very soon accepted him for what he was – the very personification of what they hoped to become.

And he studied them – especially those whose names were on the list given him by Lewton – as they went on twenty-mile jogs, crawled through assault courses and climbed sheer cliffs, fired their tommy-guns, and practised how to creep up on a man and kill him, silently, and quickly, whether by knife thrust, wire round the throat, or their bare hands. There were some forty of these, recruits who had shown more talent than the norm, who had had parachute experience, and who spoke French. But they dwindled with alarming rapidity when he started interviewing. Obviously, he had to have a second-in-command, and he started with a lieutenant only a year younger than himself, fresh-faced and eager.

"Simmons, is it?" Harry asked. "Sit down."

He had been given an office next door to Lewton's, and Simmons sank into a chair, somewhat nervously.

"I am recruiting for a special mission," Harry explained. "It will have to be a matter of volunteering."

"Yes, sir. I volunteer."

"Not so fast. *Comment allez-vous?*"

"Sir?"

"It says here you speak French."

"A little."

"Hm," Harry said. "Thank you, Mr Simmons."

"I can brush it up, sir."

"That would be a good idea. I'll talk to you again in a few days."

No lieutenants, he thought regretfully. Sergeant Le Boule,

however, *was* French. "What on earth are you doing in the Commandos?" Harry asked him.

"I volunteered. My mother is English," Le Boule said.

He was a short, heavy-set man with a small moustache.

"Would you care to volunteer again?" Harry asked.

Slowly he built up his group, and eventually had five French-speaking privates to go with the sergeant. There remained Simmons, the only possible officer. He had gallantly spent his spare time taking French lessons, and although his accent remained unacceptable he would at least understand what was being said to him.

He presented his list to Lewton, who nodded as he scanned the names. "Seems sound enough. Do they know where they are going?"

"Not yet. But they know they are going to have to jump. So with your permission, sir, I will take them south for final training."

"You have it. And good luck. Are you going to bring any of them back?"

"It's my intention," Harry said.

He spent a good deal of time considering just how he was going to carry out the mission. Much would, of course, depend on the quality of the guide Bannon produced. But he didn't doubt they could get into Algiers and indeed reach Darlan's headquarters. Getting back out again was the difficult bit, as he had told the Colonel. But he had some ideas about that too, if the timing was right.

He took his squad south and put them through some intensive dropping practice. But they had all jumped before, and seemed to know what they were doing.

They were more concerned when they were measured up for French uniforms. But the uniforms themselves, when completed, were placed in a separate carry-all, which was padlocked: Harry had the key. Whether they actually fitted well or not was not really relevant – they would only be worn for a brief period.

"Can you tell us whereabouts in France we'll be going?" Simmons asked.

"No," Harry said.

"But . . . will we get out?"

Harry frowned at him. "You volunteered."

Simmons flushed. "It's just that, well . . . I have this girl . . ."

"I know," Harry said, sympathetically. "But she'll have to wait till you get back."

If that happens, he thought.

To his great relief, Belinda arrived the next day.

"How's it going?"

"As well as can be expected."

"You have a team?"

"Just."

"Happy?"

"Not altogether. But it's the best I can do at such short notice."

"It's a rough world. The boss wants to see you."

He left Simmons in command. The squad, of course, could not be allowed leave. As far as their nearest and dearest were aware they were still in Scotland, training. Harry felt rather guilty about gallivanting off to London, with Belinda at the end of it, while they were left without any creature comforts whatsoever. Well, he supposed, he could always recommend them all for medals when they got home.

"This is Mustafa Le Blanc," Bannon explained.

Which appeared to be a contradiction in terms, Harry thought, as he shook hands with a short, slim, and disturbingly young man. Le Blanc had a swarthy complexion, a handsome face, liquid eyes, and was very nervous, judging by his perspiration.

"Monsieur Le Blanc's mother lives in Ghardaia," Bannon explained. "Which is the nearest town to where you will be dropped."

"I see. And his father?"

"My father, *pouf*!" Le Blanc commented.

"It appears he ran off," Bannon said. "You have never seen him, have you, monsieur?"

"He lives in Paris," Le Blanc said. "If I ever see him, I cut his throat."

Here we go again, Harry thought, fervently hoping M. Le Blanc senior remained in France.

"The point is," Bannon said, "that M. Le Blanc was born in Ghardaia. He knows the area like the back of his hand."

"Show me," Harry suggested,

Belinda spread a map on the desk.

"It is two hundred and fifty miles from Ghardaia to Algiers," Harry said.

"I will guide you," Le Blanc said. "I will take you in, and I will bring you back out."

"With whoever you happen to have with you," Bannon added.

"Why?" Harry asked.

"Eh?"

"Why is he going to take this risk?"

Bannon looked at Le Blanc.

"I hate the French," Le Blanc said, and added hastily, "the Vichy French."

"Hm," Harry commented. "I assume he can jump," he said to Bannon.

"He has received training, yes."

"Well, that's something. Thank you, M. Le Blanc."

Le Blanc looked at Bannon uncertainly, and the Colonel asked Belinda, "Perhaps you could make him a cup of tea."

"Of course," she said. "If you'll come with me, M. Le Blanc."

The French-Algerian followed her from the room.

"I assume you're not afraid she'll be raped," Harry remarked, when the door had closed.

"Do I gather you do not like M. Le Blanc?"

"Did you see the way he was looking at her? And I wouldn't trust him further than I could kick him, and I was never very good at football."

"Yes. Unfortunately, beggars can't be choosers. He comes

24

with the recommendation of the Foreign Office, who seem to have obtained him from the Gaullists."

"Who you tell me do not know what is going on."

"Neither does he."

"What *does* he know?"

"That a group of Commandos need to be parachuted behind enemy lines in Algeria to disrupt enemy communications."

"Forgive me for asking, sir," Harry said. "I suppose we are actually at war with Vichy France?"

"In a manner of speaking," Bannon said. "They broke off relations with us after we destroyed their navy."

"But we have never actually engaged each other, on the ground?"

"Well, no, there's been no proximity."

"Quite. Now, as I see it, Ghardaia is some thousand miles from our present position at El Alamein in Egypt, as the crow flies. But my people are to be put down there to, as you put it, disrupt enemy communications. Rather remote from the battle area, isn't it? What I am trying to say is, M. Le Blanc, who whatever his personal habits must be quite bright, surely can work out that there has to be more than just disruption of communications involved. I mean, if we blow up a single train in Algiers, is that going to assist General Auchinleck in the slightest? Or even interest him? Or, come to think of it, Rommel."

"Alexander," Bannon said absently.

"Say again?"

"Auchinleck has been relieved of his command and sent to India. Alexander commands in Cairo."

"Shit!" Like most professional solders, Harry reckoned the Auk, as the Field-Marshal was known to his men, was one of the best fighting soldiers in the army. On the other hand, he had to remember, as he had been personally involved, that General Alexander had been the last man off the beach at Dunkirk.

"I do take your point, Harry," Bannon went on. "Le Blanc is employed to take you into northern Algeria, hide you amongst his people, and guide you to wherever you wish to go. He may well have his own opinions about this, but as he is now under military guard there is no way he can communicate those opinions to anyone. Equally, we have been assured that his hatred for the Vichy Government is genuine. And as I said just now, he is all we have. He happens to have close contacts with a Free French cell in this place, Ghardaia, family, in fact, and they are apparently prepared to help us."

"And if he, or one of his associates, betrays us?"

"If he behaves in any way that is to you suspicious, you have my permission to shoot him."

Harry grinned. "I always knew you were on our side, Peter."

"Now," Bannon said. "Let's get down to business. As we agreed, this whole business has to be a matter of timing. We really can't afford another foul-up."

"You mean the powers that be have still not forgiven us for Dieppe?"

"Unfortunately, there has been another cock-up. It was decided that before Montgomery – he's Alexander's field officer, commanding the Eight Army – launched his attack on Rommel's position at Alamein, it would be of inestimable assistance if we could regain possession of Tobruk, both from a supply point of view and because it would be a sword cut across Rommel's lines of communication."

"Makes sense. It didn't work?"

"It was a disaster. It had to be a combined Navy/Commando operation, of course, as that was the only way in. Unfortunately, the Luftwaffe had complete command of the air. Several of our ships were sunk by the dive-bombers, the whole force was thrown into confusion, and I'm afraid the only Commandos who got ashore did so as prisoners."

"Shit," Harry said again. "When did this happen?"

"The middle of last month. Oh, nobody knows about it, except the top brass and those who were there. But still, it raised another question about if we were ever going to get it right."

"And presumably it put back this chap Montgomery's plans even further."

"I don't know about that. My information is that he is going as planned, next week. Churchill is obviously very anxious that we should gain a victory, on our own, before the Americans take over the show."

Harry nodded. "I appreciate that."

"Now, and this is the most secret piece of information you will ever be given, Harry, the American landing is timed for 8th November."

Harry did a quick calculation. "Sunday fortnight."

"That's right. The fleet is already at sea, and it's a damned big one. Your date with Darlan therefore has to be either the previous Thursday or Friday. That will give you time to remove the Admiral into the desert, and persuade him where his future lies."

"Do we have somewhere to go?"

"Le Blanc has arranged a base for you."

"But he doesn't know who we're going to put in it. What do you think his reaction will be when he finds out?"

"He may well wish to execute Darlan, if his claims about hating the Vichy regime are true. It will be up to you to restrain him. Now, we reckon you have to be on the ground at Ghardaia a week before you make your move, that will be Thursday 29th October. That is, Thursday after next. This is to allow you to reconnoitre the ground, make your plans, and allow for any last minute hitches."

Harry stroked his chin. "Every minute we're on the ground longer than necessary increases the risk of discovery or betrayal."

"It is a risk, of course. But I'm afraid we simply have to trust this fellow Le Blanc. And his associates."

"Cheer me up," Harry muttered.

"Now," Bannon went on. "We still have to get you there. The direct route isn't really on, because it isn't direct. We can get you as far as Portugal without trouble, but once you leave there, as the French are liable to shoot down any unidentified aircraft without asking questions, you will have to go Gibraltar, Malta, Alexandria. Once we get you into Egypt, there are enough long-

27

range aircraft to fly you south of the battle zone, over the French Sahara, which is largely controlled by the Free French, and thence up into Algeria, out of the desert, for a drop at Ghardaia."

Harry scratched his head. "Forgive me for asking, but don't the Germans also make a habit of shooting down unidentified aircraft over the Mediterranean? Or even identified ones, if they're not their own."

"You will have fighter protection and, making, as you will be, two jumps, as it were, you will be able to move at night. There is also the point that if Montgomery starts on time, which is supposed to be on Friday night – full moon and all that – the Germans, on the ground, on the sea, and in the air, will be totally concentrated against him, not aircraft flying around outside the battle zone."

"One further point. Should Montgomery lose this battle, we are liable to arrive in Alexandria to find Rommel already in possession."

"In which case you will give him your name, rank, number and date of birth, and sit out the rest of the war in comparative comfort. So we're told."

"We are Commandos. Will we not be shot on sight?"

"Hardly if captured in a British base. Any further questions?"

"When do we leave?"

"Tomorrow night."

"Are you telling me he didn't even attempt to pinch your bottom?" Harry asked Belinda, as she made tea in the privacy of her flat.

Le Blanc had remained, under guard, at the headquarters office.

"Not once," Belinda said. "Do you regard that as a problem?"

"No so long as he hates the Vichy French more than he likes me, or any of my people," Harry said.

"What would you do?" she asked, interested. "I mean, if he made an advance."

The Cause

"I would remind him that I'm his superior officer, that we are operating in a war situation, and that I would be fully entitled to shoot him."

"And leave yourself without a guide? He knows you wouldn't do that."

"You'd be surprised what I can do," Harry told her. "Thanks for the tea. Well, it's another of those good-byes."

"Oh? Aren't you going to stay the night? You don't leave for another twenty-four hours."

"I've seven rather anxious men waiting for me in Uxbridge. I really think I need to be with them."

"Seems to me that was what you said before St Nazaire."

"Absolutely."

"Duty," she sighed. "And what did I say to you before St Nazaire?"

"Something like, try to come back, in one piece. And I did, didn't I?"

"By a whisker," she said. "Come and give me a hug and a kiss, you big lug."

"Why am I treated so?" Mustafa asked, as they were driven down to Uxbridge.

"How, so?" Harry asked.

"Like if I am a prisoner. I am an ally. I am Free French. I have met de Gaulle," he added proudly.

"You're one up on me there," Harry said. "You are not being treated as a prisoner, Mustafa. But this is a highly secret operation, and we cannot take a chance on a careless word."

Mustafa considered this. Then he asked, "What do we do in Algiers?"

"I'll tell you when we get there."

"When is this? Soon, eh?"

"Soon," Harry promised him.

The rest of the squad weren't very happy with Mustafa either.

"Do we really have to have this dago along, sir?" Simmons asked.

"We do, Lieutenant. And I should point out that while he may be of mixed blood, he is a member of the Free French, and is risking his life, and the lives of his family, to help us."

"Yes, sir," Simmons said uncertainly. "You don't think he's . . . well . . ."

"They make good fighting men," Harry assured him.

He was more concerned with Mustafa's jumping ability, and spent most of the next morning putting him through his paces. But Mustafa had been well-trained, and was totally competent. He was also an excellent shot, at least on a range.

"You could grow on me," Harry said. "Not too quickly," he added hastily, as the young man smiled his appreciation.

It was after lunch that he told them they were leaving that night. "It's a long flight," he told them. "But there will be stops."

The aircraft was blacked-out, and they flew into nowhere. Simmons kept looking at his watch. "We'd be over Paris, by now," he remarked. "Odd there's been no flak. When do we reach the jump zone, sir?"

"We're not jumping tonight," Harry said. "I can tell you now that we're on our way to Gibraltar."

"Gibraltar?" they asked together.

"Just think about it," Harry advised.

Obviously they did. Gibraltar – but they had been picked for their ability to speak, or at least understand, French.

They touched down just before dawn.

"Get some sleep," Harry recommended.

He was himself hurried off to see the local Operations Officer. "Ah, yes," said Major Connolly. "We were expecting you, Major Curtis. En route to Malta."

"That's the idea."

"Tomorrow night."

"Eh? Why not tonight?"

"My orders are tomorrow night," Connolly said.

"What do we do until then?"

"Have a look at the Rock."

"I should point out that we are on a top secret exercise."

30

"Isn't everyone," Connolly said. "I'm sorry, old man, I have my orders and there it is. You're welcome to take it higher, but I don't think it'll get you anywhere."

Harry knew he was right, and he learned the reason for the delay next morning, when Connolly told him that Montgomery had commenced his assault on the Axis positions before El Alamein.

"I suppose they didn't want you flying into that," Connolly said.

"We're only going as far as Malta," Harry reminded him – two could play at the secrets game.

His people were remarkably relaxed, even Mustafa. It was a first time in the fortress colony for all of them, and they found much to interest them. Harry supposed it didn't matter if they did chat up the locals, as they themselves didn't know the object of the mission. In fact, only Mustafa actually knew they were bound for Algeria.

Harry himself spent most of the two days either sleeping or playing billiards in the officers' mess, and trying to think ahead. Or standing on the dock and staring out at the Atlantic. It was an awesome thought that somewhere out there was an armada of several hundred ships, laden with men, racing towards North Africa . . . and no one in North Africa knew it was there!

Certainly no one was supposed to.

"I thought Jerry controlled the Mediterranean," Simmons remarked, as they took off that evening.

"As you may have heard, Jerry has problems," Harry told him. But he was fairly anxious himself and went forward to be with the pilots. They were indeed being escorted, a fighter on each wing, but he did not suppose they would be terribly useful if they suddenly ran into a squadron of Messerschmitts. Nor was there anywhere to hide; it was a magnificently clear night, and beneath them the moon sparkled on the water.

"You lot must be pretty important," the pilot remarked. "We don't usually have an escort."

"But you've made this flight before?"

31

"A few times. Life expectancy is short. You going to have another go at Rommel?"

"It would be a good idea, don't you think?" Harry asked.

As before, they were on the ground before dawn, and Harry found himself with another Operations Officer.

"How are things going at Alamein?" he asked.

"Haven't a clue, old man," Major Onslow said. "He didn't wait for you, eh? Haw haw haw. I'd say you're going to miss the whole show."

"Not if we get there tonight," Harry suggested.

"Can't be done. You're down for tomorrow."

"What did you say?"

"Here's my command sheet."

"For God's sake . . ." Harry made a hasty calculation. It was Sunday morning. He was due on the ground at Ghardaia on Thursday. And he had not even got to Egypt yet.

"Sorry, old man," Onslow said. "There is a war on, you know. There have to be priorities."

"So what does one do with one's Sunday in Malta?"

"Well, you know, old man, one could always go to church. That's what the locals do."

This time Harry did take it higher, and that afternoon obtained an interview with the Governor, who was also the overall military commander. He had actually met Lord Gort, who had been commander-in-chief of the BEF in France before the debacle that had led to Dunkirk. And the Field-Marshal remembered him.

"Harry Curtis," he said. "A major, eh? You're doing well. And now you're with this hush-hush combined operations business, eh? What brings you to Malta?"

"Actually, sir, I am trying to get to Alexandria," Harry explained. "Just as rapidly as possible, with my squad."

"Something to do with Monty, eh?"

"Ah . . . indirectly, sir. But it really is most urgent. And I'm told there is no aircraft available until tomorrow night."

"That is probably right. Monty needs everything we have. But if he knows you're coming he won't mind a slight delay."

"Sir, I have got to be out of Egypt by Thursday morning," Harry said urgently.

Gort frowned at him. "Are you seriously trying to tell me that this mission, or whatever it is you're on, is more important than the battle being fought at Alamein?"

"It could well turn out to be, sir."

The Field-Marshal studied him for some seconds. "And of course you're not allowed to tell me what it is."

"I'm afraid not, sir. I can only say that if I do not reach my destination on time the whole course of the war may be changed. For the worse."

"That," Gort said, "almost sounds like an ultimatum. Very well, Major Curtis. You will fly out of Malta tonight. I will wish you good fortune."

"Some flap," the pilot remarked. "Look over there."

He was, very wisely, keeping well out to sea, but to the aircraft's right there was what appeared to be a gigantic thunderstorm, a melange of flashing lights and rumbling explosions which almost rose above the noise of the engines.

"Are we winning?" Harry asked.

"Well, I don't see how we can possibly lose," the pilot said, "seeing as how we outnumber Jerry by at least two to one, in aircraft and tanks as well as men, not to mention petrol – he doesn't have any. But it's not proving as easy as some of us expected. He's a tough bastard."

And he doesn't have a clue what is about to hit him in the backside, Harry thought.

Major Ash was actually on the tarmac at Alexandria to meet them. "Thought you weren't going to make it," he said.

"Join the club," Harry said, watching his weary men disembarking. "All I want to hear from you is that we are on schedule."

"Ah. Well, as I'm sure you understand, we're short of aircraft—"

"Don't give me that twaddle," Harry said. "One is to be supplied."

"Yes. Well, you know, old man: London proposes and the general on the spot disposes. Depends on how the battle goes. But I should think we'll manage something in a day or two."

"Will you billet my men?" Harry asked. "They need to get some sleep. And fix me an appointment with General Alexander."

Someone else Harry had actually met, in France, two years before.

"Curtis," he remarked. "I remember. You were one of the last men off the beaches."

"But not the very last, sir," Harry said, hating himself for such a blatant piece of flattery – but he needed all the help he could get.

"Yes," Alexander said drily. "and now you're a Commando, eh?"

His tone was disparaging. He was, of course, an ex-Guards officer himself, but he had stayed with the regiment until field rank.

"And a major," he remarked, more disparagingly yet. "Aren't you a little young?"

He had himself been regarded as the outstanding young British officer to have survived the Great War, but he had been in his middle twenties when that had begun.

"The fortunes of war, sir," Harry suggested.

"Yes," Alexander agreed, again drily. "I assume you appreciate that it's dashed awkward your turning up here in the middle of a most important battle and demanding the use of one of our aircraft."

"I was under the impression that it had all been arranged, sir."

"Possibly it was, but that was before the battle began. Now . . . things aren't going as well as we had hoped. There is still a long struggle ahead of us. We need everything we have, here!"

Harry took a deep breath. "Does the name Torch mean anything to you, sir?"

Alexander stared at him, brows slowly drawing together. Then he said, "Close the door."

Harry obeyed, returning to his seat before the desk.

"That is absolutely top secret," Alexander said.

"Yes, sir."

"But you know of it."

"Yes, sir. My mission is to do with it."

"Codename?"

"Illicit, sir."

"No doubt very appropriate." Alexander picked up his phone. "Carpenter, get me the file named Illicit. Yes, I know it is top secret. Let me have it immediately." He replaced the phone. "So you are trying to get to Morocco, by the most roundabout route imaginable."

"Algiers, sir. Morocco would have been reasonably straight-forward."

"I'm sure." He looked up as his adjutant placed the file on his desk, and then stood to attention. Alexander opened the file, which contained only two sheets of paper, and scanned them both very rapidly. "Why wasn't this brought to my attention before?" he asked.

"Well, sir," the adjutant said. "What with everything that was going on . . ."

"Very good," Alexander said. "Have a long-range aircraft made ready to transport Major Curtis and his people to . . . wherever they want to go. What would that be?"

"A Dakota, sir. It is not an armed aircraft."

Alexander looked at Harry.

"I'm not proposing to fight anyone in the air, sir."

"What is its range?"

"Well, sir, three thousand miles."

"At?"

"Roughly two hundred and fifty miles an hour."

"Right. Have one on standby."

The adjutant glanced at Harry, then said, "Yes, sir. How soon?"

Alexander looked at Harry.

"I need to fly approximately three thousand miles," Harry said.

35

The adjutant gulped.

"And the aircraft will have to get back," Alexander commented. "Let's have a look at a map, Carpenter."

One was produced.

"This is top secret, Carpenter," Alexander said, "as the file indicates. Major Curtis needs to be put down in northern Algeria. The additional mileage is of course necessary to swing south of the battle zone. So, the aircraft will have to be refuelled. Show me where we can do this."

"Ah . . ." Carpenter bent over the map. "The Free French hold Chad. There is an airstrip on the north side of the Tibesti Mountains, and a fuel dump. Or at least there was, when last we were in contact. It could refuel there."

"If the dump is still there. Have a message sent to the local commander, informing him of our requirements. We will need to top up on the way out, just in case of trouble, but the aircraft will need to fuel on the way back as well. Now, from here to Tibesti is about four hours flying time, right?"

"Approximately, sir."

"Then a couple of hours refuelling, then another six hours to the drop zone. When do you wish to be there, Curtis?"

"Thursday evening, sir."

"Then you will need to leave not after the crack of dawn that morning. That gives us two days. Organise the machine and the fuelling, Carpenter."

"Yes, sir."

Alexander stood up and shook hands. "I don't know what you're at, Curtis, but on the evidence of that file and what you have told me, I'd say it's pretty important. I'll wish you good luck."

"Thank you, sir. Are we going to win the battle?"

"Oh, yes," Alexander said, and gave a quick smile. "It's our intention to be in Tunis before any Americans."

"Is it still on?" Simmons was anxious, as indeed was the entire squad, given the coming and going of their commanding officer. The enlisted men appeared to have gone for a walk about the historic city, and only Simmons was waiting in the barracks they had been temporarily assigned. Mustafa had apparently gone with the men.

"It is still on," Harry assured him. "We will move down to Cairo this afternoon, and we leave on Thursday morning."

"Cairo. Yes, sir."

"Don't you want to visit Cairo?"

"Oh, no, sir. It's just that . . . well, this fellow, Mustafa . . . we may have been wrong about him."

"That's good news. And he knows Alexandria, does he?"

"Well, sir, he sort of intimated . . ."

"I'm sure he knows people in Cairo as well. Are you trying to tell me these are female acquaintances?"

"Well, sir, he seems to know this house . . ."

"Oh, dear God!" Harry commented.

He did not suppose he could blame his men for seeking some sexual relief. They were on a mission of which they knew nothing save that it was highly dangerous. And before then for several weeks they had been cooped up in an all male environment. As for the risks they were running . . . even if they all contracted syphilis, that usually took about a fortnight to come out, and in a fortnight they would have completed their mission, and either be heroes or dead.

"And you let them go?" he inquired.

"Well, sir, you hadn't given me any orders . . ." He sounded reproachful. "And they were restless, and nervous . . ." He paused, hopefully.

Harry sighed. The boy was very young. But Mustafa . . . "I'd like a word with that gentleman," he said. "Is he at the brothel with the others?"

"I believe so, sir. Shall I go fetch him?"

"You know where this house is, is that it?"

"Ah . . . well, sir . . ."

"What about this girl back home?"

"I haven't seen her in two months, sir," Simmons said sadly.

"Well, just remember that if you get clapped she probably won't want to see you again, ever."

Simmons considered this. "With respect, sir, do *you* have a girl back home?"

"No," Harry said. "Not in the sense you mean. I have a friend, with whom I am very close. But we only expect to hear from, or see each other, when it happens. That is the only emotional way to run a war. Now go and fetch Mustafa."

"Yes, sir. And . . ." He flushed.

"Oh, stay if you must, if only to bring them back. I want them all present and correct, here, by three o'clock this afternoon. We leave for Cairo at four."

He supposed he should thank God they had only another twenty-four hours in Egypt.

The Desert

Mustafa was all flushing embarrassment. "They wished this, Major," he protested.

"I'm sure of it. And you knew where to take them. How did you know that? Have you been in Alexandria before?"

Mustafa looked more embarrassed yet. "It was some years ago."

Harry frowned. "Just how old are you, Mustafa?"

"I am twenty-eight years old, sir."

"Good God!" He had put the Algerian down as younger than himself. "And what were you doing here?"

"I was on a ship, sir. I was the steward."

"I see. And how many other Mediterranean seaports do you know intimately?"

"Oh, all of them, sir. I know the Mediterranean from Marseilles to Istanbul." Mustafa rolled his eyes. "This is a good house. Very clean. No clap."

"I hope you're right," Harry said. "And just how much of what we are doing have you told the men?"

"Only what I know, sir. That we are going into the desert to raid the enemy communications."

"And the whores?"

"I would not tell the whores anything, sir. I am a loyal Gaullist." He gave an ingratiating smile. "You wish one, sir? I know the very one."

"Thank you, Mustafa. Not right now."

The men were actually brought home by half a dozen MPs, several of whom were carrying bruises. One had a prominent black eye.

39

Alan Savage

"We can throw them in the hut for the night, sir," the sergeant volunteered. "They've been drinking rotgut."

"I'll take care of it," Harry said.

The sergeant looked doubtful, but he accepted the wish of the officer. "I'm going to have to put them on a charge, sir," he said. "There was a bit of punch-up."

"Do your duty, Sergeant," Harry said. "My men will answer to the charges when they return to Cairo."

Supposing they do, he thought.

The men stood to attention, somewhat sheepishly and somewhat unsteadily as well. At least, Harry thought, they looked better than their captors.

He stood in front of them, Simmons to one side. He still didn't know if Simmons had indulged, but at least he had not been arrested, and he appeared to be sober.

"Drinking, and whoring, in the midday sun in this climate," Harry told them, "is a short cut to a heart attack. God knows what else you've been exposed to. You're supposed to be Commandos, the best fighting men in the world. From here on, you'll bloody well act like the best fighting men in the world." He threw out his arm, pointing to the west. "Out there, just sixty miles away, your comrades are fighting, killing and being killed. You are about to have the opportunity to join in that fight. I expect you to take that opportunity with both hands. Now there's a bus waiting. Get on it."

The men filed out, humping their equipment.

"I really am most terribly sorry, sir," Simmons confided as he and Harry sat together in the front row of seats. The bus slowly rumbled out of Alexandria, actually driving west, towards the battle, and in the midst of an unending caravan of vehicles, before swinging south down the road to Cairo, which ran beside the Nile.

"These things happen," Harry said. "Just make sure they don't happen again. You're my deputy. When I'm not there, you make the decisions I would have made, and stick with them."

40

"Yes, sir." Simmons brooded out of the window. He was on the right hand side of the bus, and was looking at the desert rather than the river. "All that sand . . . have you ever read a novel called *The Lost Patrol*?"

"Can't say I have," Harry admitted.

"It's set in the last war. About a patrol in the Mesopotamian desert, in 1916. Right at the beginning of the book, the officer in command is shot by a Turkish sniper. And he was carrying the orders in his head. So the patrol is left without a leader, without orders, without even any knowledge of where they actually are. They manage to reach an oasis, but there they are surrounded by the Turks, or Arabs, or whatever, and systematically killed, one after the other. All because they had no orders."

"Sounds grim."

"Yes, sir. What I mean is, well . . . you are carrying our orders in your head, aren't you? There's nothing in writing."

"That's correct, Lieutenant. I will, however, give you, give you all, our orders and our objective, before we take off on Thursday morning. Then, if I happen to be killed, you can take command. Right?"

Simmons gulped.

Cairo was in a state of considerable agitation. People stood on street corners and muttered at each other, uniforms were much in evidence.

Ash had driven down separately, but he was waiting to show them to the barracks which were to be their overnight accommodation.

"I'm afraid things aren't going very well," he said. "We were supposed to be through the enemy minefields by now and out in open country, where our superiority in armour and in the air can be made to tell. But we're still bogged down."

"But we will win?" Harry asked.

"I suppose so, old man. But there are whispers. Now, these roughnecks of yours – I have received a report that they were arrested in Alexandria, this afternoon."

"I'm afraid that is true. It seems to have been a routine MP raid on a brothel, and my people were inside."

"Good lord! A brothel? At such a time?"

"They are about to fly off on a mission which may very well result in their deaths, Ash. I think a man in that situation is entitled to a last fling."

"Well . . ." Ash frowned, and pulled the end of his moustache. "You weren't with them, were you, old man?"

"Sadly, no. I was visiting the Commander-in-Chief."

"Ah. Well . . . you know you have a full twenty-four hours before take-off. Can I assume that you will, ah . . . keep your men in hand?"

"I shall do that," Harry promised him.

Harry reckoned the best way to keep his men in hand during their day in Cairo was to keep them busy. So he commandeered a car and drove them out, firstly to look at the Pyramids, of which they had caught a glimpse the previous evening, and into the real desert beyond the great tombs. Here he stopped the car and let them get out and feel the sand beneath their feet.

"It's not all like this," he said. "Tell them, Mustafa."

"This is sandy desert," Mustafa said. "But the Sahara is not all sand, as the major has said. Much of it is rocky and stony. But it is all barren. When you are in the desert, survival is the key. You see that small ravine? That is a *wadi*. A long dry water course. But you see . . ." He led them to the edge of the *wadi*, pointed down. "There, you see? Those flowers."

They gazed at the small, multi-coloured little flowers which sprouted out of the sand.

"That means there is water down there," Mustafa explained. "Maybe six, maybe twelve feet."

"With respect, sir," asked Private Evans, "are we going out into the desert to dig for water?"

"Hopefully not," Harry told him. "But it pays to know how to survive if something goes wrong."

The nine of them were utterly alone.

"Now," he said, "I will tell you what we're going to do." He outlined the scheme. The men listened in silence, but he could tell that none of them were entirely happy.

"When do we put on our French uniforms, sir?" asked Private Graham.

"Not until we're ready to go into Algiers. Up until then we stay in battledress. Thus if we happen to be captured, we're prisoners of war and not spies."

"But if we are taken in Algiers, wearing French uniforms . . ." remarked Sergeant Le Boule.

"We will probably be shot," Harry agreed. "It is our business not to be captured."

"You say we are to kidnap Admiral Darlan, sir," Simmons said. "How do we get him out?"

"We will have to play that by ear," Harry said. "But when we do get him out, into the desert, we will be able to contact the air force who will come in and pick us up."

He did not like having to lie to them, but he dared not tell them about Torch, just in case any of them *was* captured. Fortunately, no one thought to ask how, if they were being parachuted in, an aircraft was going to be able to land to take them out.

"What do you think of it, Mustafa?" he asked.

Mustafa's eyes gleamed. "To go in, and snatch Darlan . . . that is brilliant. But it would be simpler to kill him, Major. Safer for us."

"We want him alive," Harry told him. "Let's be getting back. And incidentally, no one will leave the barracks tonight."

"There's something I don't understand about this business, sir," Simmons said after dinner.

"Tell me."

"Well, sir, kidnapping Darlan . . . how is it going to help us win the war?"

"I'm afraid that is something you will have to ask the brass, when we get back to England," Harry said. "We just obey orders, Lieutenant."

Next morning at dawn they were driven to the airport. Their pilots were cheerfully uninquisitive, they were doing a job of work, and this first stage of the journey was undemanding. They flew south-west over endless desert.

"What a place to come down," Simmons remarked.

"Not if it's full of wild flowers, sir," Sergeant Le Boule suggested, determinedly optimistic.

Harry felt they were gradually forming a team, and hopefully he would have a few more days to play with.

It was after the third hour that they saw the mountains of Tibesti in front of them, and shortly afterwards, four hours after their departure from Cairo, as Alexander had calculated, they put down at a small airstrip north of the heights, to be greeted by a weather-beaten Free French commander and his equally well-worn, sun-browned men.

"Just remember," Harry told Mustafa. "No chat."

"You go to Rhodesia?" asked the Commandant.

"Ah . . . perhaps," Harry said.

"But this aircraft is returning here, I am told. For more fuel."

"Well, it has to get back to Cairo, you see," Harry explained.

"I have not that much fuel," the Commandant complained. "What I have should all be for our own people."

"But you don't have any aircraft," Harry pointed out. "You're not going to put aircraft fuel in tanks, are you? Come to think of it . . ." – he looked around the small base – ". . . you don't have any tanks, either."

"They are all up north, fighting the Nazis."

"And so they should be. And you know what, Commandant: I don't think this time they are going to be coming back for fuel."

"The battle is won?"

"The battle is going to be won, one way or another," Harry assured him.

They were given a good meal in the local mess, and then Harry told them to siesta. It was very hot, there was not a cloud in the sky and the sun was like a brass ball. He couldn't blame the Commandant, stuck here on a more or less permanent basis, for being petulant.

But now he had to tell the pilots what he wanted of them.

"Our orders are to fly you wherever you wish to go," said Flight-Lieutenant Pope. "After we leave here."

"Right," Harry said. "Let's have a map."

This was unrolled before them.

"There," Harry said.

"Ghardaia," Pope said. "There's an airstrip."

"No airstrip," Harry said. "That's hostile territory."

"The whole of Algeria is hostile territory," Flight-Sergeant Lustrom pointed out.

"So we get in, and you get out, hopefully without detection. They're not expecting anything from the south," Harry said. "Show us where, Mustafa."

Mustafa tapped the map. "Twenty miles south of the town."

"That's open desert," Pope objected.

"The drop zone will be marked with a light."

"A light?"

"Perhaps two."

Pope scratched his head. "You happy with this, Major Curtis?"

Harry shrugged. "It's the set-up, Mr Pope."

"Okay. So we drop you, and get out of there. That's a two-thousand plus mile round trip." He looked at Lustrom.

"It'll be a damned near-run thing, sir."

"Well, you squeeze in every last drop of petrol," Pope said. "When do you want to leave, sir?"

Again Harry had to look at Mustafa.

"They will expect us between eleven and one in the morning," Mustafa said.

"Okay," Pope said. "We take off at eight. That way it'll be dark the whole way. And back," he added with some satisfaction.

"I reckon we should get some sleep," Harry told Mustafa.

At dusk they ate, and Harry watched the very last drop of fuel, as Pope had required, being pumped into the aircraft.

"Just tell me something, sir," the Flight-Lieutenant said. "How are you meaning to get back out?"

45

Alan Savage

"I imagine it will have to be on foot," Harry said.
Pope scratched his head. "Some distance. Even to get back
here . . . well over a thousand miles across the desert?"
"It's all been calculated," Harry assured him. "I'm just wor-
ried about you. Think you can make it?"
"As long as there are no problems along the way," Pope said.
Harry said goodbye to Commandant Le Marchant.
"You are the fortunate ones," Le Marchant said. "Rhodesia,
eh? And then Cape Town. Out of the war."
"Yes," Harry said. "We are the fortunate ones. But you're
pretty well out of the war yourself now, down here."
"For us," Le Marchant commented, "the war never ends. If it
is not the Boche it is the Arabs. I will wish you good fortune."
But he, and his men, turned up to watch the Commandos
donning their parachutes in total mystification.
"I do not understand," he remarked. "You mean to parachute
into Salisbury?"
"Makes a change," Harry said, and boarded the aircraft.
It was already dark when they took off, flying now to the
north-west.
"I hope there are no more mountains in the way," Simmons
quipped. The moon had not yet risen, and there were only the
stars above them, while below them was pure black.
"There is some high ground," Mustafa said. "North of the
Hoggar Plateau, but we will be past that in a couple of hours."
"These lights," Harry said. "What is the pattern?"
"There is not much," Mustafa confessed. "It will be a quad-
rangle, about a quarter of a mile in area. Four lights."
"What are they?"
"Flashlights, Major."
"Shit," Le Boule commented. "They won't be easy to see."
"We will see them."
"Suppose it's raining?"
"Ghardaia is in the desert, Sergeant. It does not rain. Well, not
very often."
"Suppose it does, tonight?"

46

"You must ask the Major," Mustafa said.

"We go in, regardless of the weather," Harry told them.

He went forward, to sit with the pilots. "Any problems?"

"Not so far."

The instrument panel glowed reassuringly, the various levels all correct, the compass showing them the way. But in front of them it was utterly dark. Harry had actually only dropped into combat once before. That had been outside Calais, on the raid on the German Communications Centre at Ardres. Then they had gone in on the tail of an RAF attack, their way clearly delineated. This was a new experience.

"What time will we reach the drop zone?" he asked Pope.

"We shall be twenty miles south of Ghardaia just after midnight," the pilot said. "A lot depends on how soon we spot those lights. A lot," he added thoughtfully, thinking of his fuel situation.

"And if there is any French air defence system in the town," Lustrom added.

"Mustafa says not."

"But it's over a year since he has been there, sir. Things may have changed."

Harry went aft to sit with the guide. "Was there any military activity in Ghardaia when you were last there?"

"There is usually a small garrison, sir. Foreign Legionnaires. Ghardaia is on the road across the desert, you see. But the protection is against the Touaregs, you know. There was no expectation that the British would ever get there, or the Free French from Chad. A thousand miles is a long way."

Now they could only wait, as the hours ticked by. At half-past eleven Harry went up to sit behind the pilots, and look out. Still the moon had not yet risen, although the clear sky was filled with stars. But below them the ground continued to be shrouded in darkness.

It was midnight when Pope said, "See over there!"

Harry looked at the horizon, and the glimmer of light.

"Ghardaia," Pope said.

"How far?"

"Thirty to forty miles."

"So we're pretty near there."

"I'd say." He peered at his fuel gauge, which was showing two-thirds full; but the long flight back to Tibesti was still ahead of him. "Where the hell are those lights?"

They held their course for another five minutes, and the distant glow of Ghardaia became brighter.

"Think they can hear us?" Harry asked.

"Not yet. And we can't go any closer, anyway. I reckon we're over the drop zone, Major."

The aircraft banked steeply as he circled, and again.

"This has to be it," Pope said. "You either drop blind, or we abort and return to Chad. There's been a foul-up. But in another ten minutes I'm not going to have sufficient gas to get back."

"Right," Harry said. "Then we drop blind." He went aft. "Positions."

The despatcher was already waiting by the door, and the Commandos assembled, each man attached his harness release to the overhead line.

"Have we got the markers?" Simmons asked.

"No. But we're going down anyway." The light winked as the aircraft assumed an even keel. "Let's go."

He was first out, floating down through a surprisingly cold night. He couldn't see up above his canopy, but after a few minutes the sound of the engines faded as the aircraft turned back for Chad. Now he had to worry about what was beneath him – to break a bone would be a disaster. He stared into the darkness beneath him, and suddenly saw a light, and then another.

One of the torches picked him up, and then flickered down so that he could see beneath him. The ground looked flat enough, although there were several bushes. He came down with the usual jolt, immediately rolled over while he got his parachute under control and saw the rest of his squad similarly land safely.

There were several people waiting for them, and of these at

least half were women, their *haiks* fluttering in the slight breeze.
They seemed apprehensive of the burly Commandos, as well they
might be, Harry thought, and then one shrieked, "Mustafa!" and
they surrounded the guide, embracing him and chattering away
in a mixture of French and Arabic.

Harry let them get on with it while he discarded his chute and
made sure none of his men had been injured in the fall.

"Bit of luck, what?" Simmons asked. "Falling in with friends.
I suppose they *are* friends, sir?"

"They're certainly friends of Mustafa's," Harry said. "And
I've an idea they were waiting for us."

Mustafa now came towards them, followed by the six locals.
"You see?" he said. "No problem, eh? This is my mother."

Harry shook hands with the handsome, middle-aged Arab
woman, who seemed embarrassed.

"My mother hates the French in Vichy, but she is happy for de
Gaulle," Mustafa explained.

"Great," Harry agreed.

"And this is my sister, Marguerite."

Marguerite looked very like her brother, but was somewhat
older, Harry estimated. Which would put her past thirty.

"My sister hates the French," Mustafa confided.

"But she goes for de Gaulle," Harry suggested.

"That is right, sir. This is my sister's husband, Philippe."

Harry peered through the gloom at the tall, thin man. He was
definitely not half-Arab.

"I also hate the French in Vichy," Philippe said. "I support de
Gaulle."

"Of course."

"Philippe has a hotel in the town," Mustafa explained. "This is
where you will stay until it is time to go to Algiers."

"You go to Algiers?" Philippe inquired.

"We will talk of it later," Mustafa said, aware that he had
made a slip. "This is my brother, Lucien."

A younger edition of Mustafa.

"Don't tell me, you hate the French," Harry said.

"But I am for de Gaulle."

"Naturally."

"And this," Mustafa said proudly, "is my wife, Yasmin."

Harry was taken entirely by surprise.

"Your wife?"

"You did not know I am married, Major? I have been married for seven years. But we do not see each other too often, what with the ships and the war."

"But now you are home," Yasmin cooed, linking her arm through his. She was a pretty and decidedly buxom little woman, and if not as clearly possessing as much French blood as her husband, still had some, Harry reckoned.

"Briefly," he said, foreseeing stormy times ahead as she discovered her husband was engaged on a highly dangerous exercise. "I assume you hate the French, Mrs Le Blanc?"

"Of course."

"But you support de Gaulle."

"Of course."

"And this is my sister-in-law, Raquyyah," Mustafa said. "The sister of Yasmin."

Harry shook hands. "And you hate the French too, madame?"

"She is not married," Mustafa explained.

"I was married," Raquyyah protested. "But my husband left me."

She was a good deal prettier than her sister.

"And you hate the French?" Harry inquired, politely.

"I do not hate anybody," Raquyyah said. "Except my husband."

"I am to take you into Ghardaia," Philippe said, "and board you at my hotel. But I cannot do this if you are wearing British uniform. People will talk."

"At the very least," Harry agreed. "What do you recommend?"

Obviously wearing French uniforms in a small place with a small garrison, every man of which would be known to every other and to most of the locals as well, would not work.

50

"You will wear Arab clothing," Philippe said. "We have some here."

"Can we not just change into civvies?" Simmons asked.

"No," Philippe said. "If you appear as Europeans there will be questions asked about where you have come from. But Arabs coming in from the desert, that is not a problem."

Simmons looked at Harry, who shrugged. "We are in their hands, Mr Simmons."

They undressed to their underwear, watched with interest by the women, and put on the various *jibbahs* provided, together with a fez apiece.

"You reckon these things are clean?" Evans inquired. "Or will they have bugs?"

"They are clean," Mustafa assured him.

They certainly smelt clean.

Their own clothes were placed in several bags, and the women hurried off and returned with two camels, which had apparently been hobbled in a *wadi* a little distance away. More bags were produced, and into these were loaded their tommy-guns and grenades and spare ammunition, as well as their belts and helmets.

"And those," Philippe said, pointing at their revolvers.

"I think we'll keep these," Harry said. "Just in case."

Philippe looked as if he would have argued, then shrugged in turn. "But you must keep them concealed: we are not allowed to carry arms. Now, my family and I have been here for three days. For the French, we left Ghardaia three days ago to visit my wife's mother's sister in Ghadames: she is not well. Now we are returning, eh? You and your men are Arabs who joined us on our return journey. It is a long walk to the town, so we had better commence." He surveyed his motley force. "The boots," he said. "You cannot wear boots. Arabs do not wear boots."

"You're not suggesting we go barefoot, I hope," Simmons remarked. "For twenty miles?"

"You will wear sandals," Philippe told them, and the women produced nine pairs.

"Surely we can wear our boots until we are within a mile or so of the town," Harry protested.

"That is not possible. The legionnaires regularly patrol this road. If they see boot tracks where there should be only sandals they will be suspicious."

Harry had to accept he was right. Exchanging their boots and heavy socks for sandals and bare flesh caused some merriment, but Harry was still concerned with practicalities. "Those white feet will certainly attract attention," he pointed out.

"Not necessarily," Philippe said. "In the first place, we should reach the town at first light, before it is possible to see clearly, and in the second, you will be Berbers. Berbers have white skins."

"Yes, but if they start questioning us, we don't speak Berber."

"Neither do the legionnaires. They will speak to you in French, and you will reply in French. Let us go." He set off at a brisk pace, followed by his friends and relations. The Commandos came behind, awkward in their sandals.

"It is good, eh?" Mustafa asked, walking beside Harry. "It is all like the clock, eh?"

"So far," Harry agreed.

One thing was for sure: they were going to get blisters. Equally, there was no way they could walk the two hundred and fifty odd miles from Ghardaia, through the Atlas Mountains to Algiers. He could only hope Philippe would be able to cope.

"You like my wife?" Mustafa asked.

"Eh? Oh, she seems charming."

"You like my wife's sister?"

"Absolutely."

"You would like to have her?"

The fellow seemed to have a one-track mind. "Shouldn't you inquire into the lady's feelings, first?" Harry asked. "I have a feeling she's rather off men at the moment."

"That rascal let her down," Mustafa agreed. "But you, an English officer and a gentleman . . ."

"I reckon we should talk about it later," Harry said. "When the job is done. Incidentally, with due respect to your family,

Mustafa, none of them are to know why we are going to Algiers."

Mustafa rolled his eyes. "No, indeed, sir. That would be bad." The Commandos were all in a highly trained and superb physical state, but their training had not included walking twenty miles in sandals. They kept getting pebbles lodged inside the thongs and, as Harry had predicted, they all had blisters by the time the minarets of Ghardaia came in sight in the first dawn light. But entry into the city was very easy. There was a legionnaire patrol on the road just outside the town, but these appeared totally uninterested in the small caravan emerging from the desert, and half-an-hour later they were in the Desert Springs Hotel, a surprisingly modern building. The women immediately filled bowls of water, added various herbs, and the eight Commandos sat around soaking their feet.

"If an enemy could see us now," Simmons remarked.

"What about your staff?" Harry asked Philippe.

"You have met my staff, Major. They are all absolutely loyal."

"You mean this really is a family hotel?"

Philippe pulled a face. "It was not always so. Before the war we had much custom, and a big staff. Since the war there is almost no custom, so I do not need any staff. My mother-in-law cooks, my wife and her sister and the other women do the cleaning and the serving, and Lucien works in the yard."

"And you?"

"I am the manager," Philippe said with dignity.

Some things, Harry supposed, never changed. He found the family intriguing, however. "How come you have an Arab name?" he asked Mustafa. "And your brother and sister French?"

"When my father was here," Mustafa explained, "it was arranged with my mother that the first-born would be given a French name, and the second an Arab name, and so on. So, Marguerite was born first, I was born second, and Lucien was third, then my father returned to France."

"Ah. Now, I need to have a serious chat with Philippe."

"Algiers." Philippe stroked his chin. "Why do you wish to go to Algiers?"

"We have business there."

"Business. You mean sabotage?"

"Ah . . . yes, sabotage."

Philippe stroked his chin some more. "What sabotage?"

"I'm afraid I can't tell you that," Harry said. "Can you take us into Algiers? Have you transport?"

"I have a truck, yes."

"Brilliant. How come you didn't use the truck to go to Ghadames?"

"There is no petrol."

"Not so brilliant. Can't you get some?"

"I have enough to go into Algiers. But to come back . . .?"

"What about the black market? Don't tell me there isn't one."

"Oh, it is possible to get petrol. But it is very expensive."

"I will give you sufficient funds to buy enough petrol to get you back here. When we reach Algiers. What else will you need?"

"I will need a pass from the commandant here."

"Will that be difficult?"

"No. I will tell him there are things I need for the hotel. But taking you into Algiers will be very dangerous. If we are caught, I will be shot."

"Philippe," Harry said, "if we are found in your house, you will be shot. All of you. And this way you will be shortening the war."

"Because you will blow up a few petrol dumps in Algiers?" he sneered.

"Take my word for it. Listen, all you have to do is get us into the city. Then you may return here and forget all about us." Harry had already done a re-think on the whole operation. The idea of kidnapping the admiral and getting him out of the city had only been at all practical if it could be done in a very fast manoeuvre, for which Philippe's truck would have been necessary. But if they had to wait while he found a black marketeer . . .

Philippe fell to stroking his chin again. "You will not come back here?"

"It is not our intention."

"When do you wish to go?"

If he was not going to be able to use Philippe, there was no hope of getting out. Thus, once in, they would have to stay, hopefully with Darlan in custody. And the shorter the time they had to stay, the more hope they had of survival. "I wish to be in Algiers on Saturday night."

"That is more than a week."

"You have it."

"And what will you do in the meantime?"

"We will remain here."

"Every minute you are here is very dangerous for me."

"But we are here, old son," Harry pointed out. "So you will have to make the most of it."

Mustafa was mystified. "How do we get out if we are not going to return here?" he asked.

"It has been arranged," Harry told him.

"And I was not told?"

"Why?" Harry asked. "Did you wish to come with us? I thought you were pleased to be back with your wife?"

"Of course I am. You mean, I am not to come with you to get Darlan?"

"Please do not mention that name again," Harry said. "You have carried out your part of the assignment. You are under no obligation to do anything more." He certainly did not wish a complete amateur getting in the way of what would have to be a highly professional mission.

Mustafa brooded on this. Then he said, "When will I be paid?"

"You were paid in London."

"That was half. I was told there will be more."

"There will be. When the mission has been completed."

"How will I get this money, here in Ghardaia?"

"You will get it. You have my word."

"And you are an English officer and a gentleman," Mustafa

55

said broodingly. He wasn't happy, but Harry reckoned they were all in too deep for any treachery now.

The eight days they had to wait in the hotel were probably the most dangerous of the mission, and the most frustrating. But they needed the time to allow their feet to recover, and to prepare themselves for the assault, checking and rechecking their weapons, and going over the plan of government house. "Sentries here, here and here," Harry said. "Not a lot, but then I would estimate that security is light. They have no idea what is coming their way, and what we are about to try. Now here, on the upper floor, are the Admiral's offices, and his private apartment. I believe that more often than not he has a mistress in bed with him. She will have to be taken with him."

"What about the rest of the guards?" Le Boule asked.

Harry nodded. "When we attack, they will be alerted, and we may be sure that some kind of an alarm will be flashed to military headquarters. We may expect the house to be surrounded in minutes."

"And then, sir? How do we get out?"

Harry looked over their anxious, expectant faces. "We don't."

"Sir?" Several of them spoke together.

"Let us say we take and secure the building, and the Admiral, on the Saturday night. We will then be surrounded, but I don't think they'll risk attacking, because of the Admiral – we will threaten to shoot him if they do so. They will then settle down to a siege, hoping to starve us or scare us into surrender, and also to find out what we are about. We will make appropriate demands for a ransom for the Admiral, and they will negotiate. Our price will have to be impossibly high so that they do not just produce the money."

"But they will, eventually, starve us out," Simmons said gloomily. "So what will we have achieved?"

"On Sunday, we will be rescued," Harry said.

Now they stared at him in disbelief.

"Are we allowed to ask how, sir?" Simmons asked.

"No."

"You mean there's to be another Commando drop, on Algiers, sir?" Le Boule asked. "But if they are planning that, why do they need us at all?"

"Our business is to secure the Admiral," Harry said. "And that is what we are going to do. We leave the rest of the plan to those who are going to carry it out."

"But we *will* be rescued?" Simmons was anxious.

"You have my word on it," Harry told him.

He could only hope he was right.

The Admiral

B eing unable to leave the hotel, or even to stand at the windows in case they were seen from the street, the Commandos had to spend their time playing cards or listening to the seemingly discordant Arabic music played on Philippe's radio. For information they had to depend on Mustafa and his family, who came and went. As for Mustafa himself, it was apparently assumed that he had returned to his home, from Algiers, by means of the daily, over-crowded bus, which rumbled into the little town every evening at dusk, and spent the night before beginning its return journey the following morning.

"Would it not be simpler for you and your men to take the bus?" Philippe asked.

"And spend twelve hours cooped up with a lot of Arabs, together with our weapons and equipment? We would never get away with it," Harry pointed out.

The arrival of the bus apart, there was little activity in the town, except for the cries of the *muezzin* at the top of his minaret. The road, such as it was, continued to the south, all the way to Timbuktu on the other side of the desert, but only an occasional French army vehicle ever went down it.

Their only excitement was when the French commandant and two of his subordinates decided to go out for dinner, in the hotel. The Commandos were hastily bundled up to their rooms and told not to move or make a sound until the French officers had left.

"This has got to be the longest, and hottest, week of my life," Simmons grumbled, when at last they were fed.

Harry was inclined to agree with him. There had been days of nerve-wracking boredom when he had lain in a bed in a safe house in Vichy France, waiting for the next move to the south, but at least the weather had been cool. And on Tuesday Mustafa brought them tremendous news.

"The battle in Egypt is over," he shouted. "The Nazis and the Italians have been beaten. They are running all the way back to Tripoli."

"Are you sure?" Harry demanded.

"Oh, yes, it came in on the radio at the *estaminet*."

"Great stuff," Simmons said.

"Does this mean we are now redundant, sir?" Le Boule asked.

"Don't you believe it, sergeant," Harry told him. "One victory doesn't win a war."

But at least Montgomery had done it without the aid of the Americans!

And time *was* passing. He lay in his bed in the stifling heat on Thursday night, reflecting that in just over twenty-four hours they would be on their way, when the door opened. As the hotel was empty, and it had twelve bedrooms, they had each been given a room to themselves. There was no reason for anyone to come into a room in the middle of the night. Very cautiously Harry stretched out his hand and picked up the revolver which lay on his bedside table, while fervently hoping he would not have to use it. With the window open to allow what breeze there was to enter, and the only other sounds to be heard the barking of dogs, the noise of a shot would sound like a bomb going off.

The intruder slowly approached the bed, bare feet no more than a whisper on the mats on the floor. And now Harry smelt her perfume, and immediately know who she was. He waited, his eyes accustomed to the gloom, having to figure out if she was carrying a weapon, but if she was armed, there was nothing in her hands.

She reached the bedside, and he let go of the revolver, leaving it on the sheet beside his thigh, then threw both arms round her waist and pulled her on to him and across him.

The Cause

Raquyyah gave a stifled shriek, and then Harry's left hand had closed round her mouth while with his right he investigated her body. There was more of her than one would have supposed beneath her all-shrouding Arab clothes, but the material was thin, and he quickly ascertained that she did not have a weapon concealed about her person either. Then he released her.

She had not resisted very vigorously while he was exploring her. Now she gasped, "You have raped me."

"Actually, I haven't, although the idea could grow on me," Harry said. "If you didn't want to be raped, why did you come to my room at this hour."

He removed the revolver from beneath them both, while studying her face as best he could in the darkness.

"I wish to go to Algiers."

"So?"

"Philippe will not let me."

"Why?"

"He is afraid I will tell people that he is a Free French agent."

"And will you?"

"I would not do that."

"So why do you wish to go to Algiers?"

"I am stifling here. It is a stifling place."

Harry couldn't argue with that, even if he suspected she wasn't referring to the heat.

"You reckon it will be better in Algiers?"

"In Algiers there are shops, and there is music, and laughter. There is the sea."

"And how would you propose to live, when you got there?"

She made a *moue*. "There are ways of earning money."

"I am sure there are. But none that would do you a lot of good. You're better off here."

She gripped his wrist, her fingers like talons. "I wish to go to Algiers. I wish you to take me with you, when you go."

"I don't think that would be a good idea either. If you are taken, you are liable to be shot."

61

"That would be better than staying here, to grow old and wrinkled, and alone."

He supposed she might have a point there, too.

"I'll talk to Philippe," he said.

"Listen . . ." Her grip tightened. "If you will not take me, I will go to the Foreign Legion, and tell them you are here."

He wondered if she realised that she might just have signed her death warrant?

"I said. I'll discuss it with Philippe. I am sure we will be able to work something out. Now I suggest you go back to bed. Your own bed."

"But as I am here . . ."

"Your bed," he repeated.

It would be quite impossible to enjoy sex with a woman he might just have to execute.

Philippe, as usual, stroked his chin; he had just returned from the Legion office with his pass to drive up to Algiers and back to fetch various items needed for the hotel, and had been feeling reasonably pleased with himself until he heard what Harry had to say. "That woman has always been difficult," he said. "But there is a problem. She is Mustafa's sister-in-law. More important, she is Yasmin's sister. We cannot just execute her. Or even tie her up. Yasmin would object."

"Quite," Harry said. "She will have to come with us."

"You do not think she will betray you?"

"No," Harry said.

Philippe gazed at him for several seconds. Then he said, "You realise that I have to return here?"

"Of course. But I do not think Raquyyah was planning to return with you."

Again Philippe regarded him for some time before speaking. "You will do it?"

"If I have to," Harry said.

Philippe scratched his head.

"You see?" Raquyyah said proudly to her sister. "I am going with the English to Algiers."

62

"That is crazy," Yasmin declared. "You will be killed, or taken prisoner. You know what they will do to you if you are taken prisoner?"

"*Pouf*," Raquyyah said, "what can they do to me that my husband did not?"

"He didn't do it with electricity," Mustafa pointed out, and looked at Harry. "You must not do this, Major."

"The lady is giving me no choice," Harry said, spotting a possible opening. "She is threatening to blow the whistle if I do not take her."

Everyone in the room looked at Raquyyah.

"Well," she said sulkily, "I am not spending the rest of my life in Ghardaia. If you force me to go to the Legion, then it will be you and the electrodes, eh?" Her gaze swept their faces. "All of you."

"Shit," Le Boule commented.

"So, you come with us to Algiers," Harry said. "Now get some rest. We leave at dawn."

Mustafa followed Harry out of the room. "She will have to die," he said.

"She's your sister-in-law."

"I have never liked her," Mustafa said. "And if she is prepared to betray us . . ."

"What about your wife?"

"She must not know."

"Absolutely."

"You mean to execute her on the way to Algiers?"

"I have been considering the matter. She only needs to be put out of action for twenty-four hours. Can we not tie her up and leave her by the roadside, to be picked up by Philippe when he returns?"

"That is not practical, sir. Firstly, as we are going in on Saturday evening, he will not be able to do the bulk of his shopping until Monday, and thus he will not return before Tuesday at the earliest. More likely Wednesday. Quite apart from the risk of the woman being found during that time, if she is not found, she would not survive five days in the desert, bound and gagged. And then, if she is found, or if by some miracle she were still to be alive when Philippe returned for her, she would be so angry she would go straight to the Legion, and my family would be tortured and hanged."

Harry considered. If everything went according to plan, long before five days were up the Americans should have taken control. But things very seldom went according to plan. And of course Mustafa was perfectly right – even one day spent tied up in the desert without water would do for most people.

"I don't suppose we can just go along with her, take her into Algiers, and turn her loose?"

"Can you take that risk, sir?"

Harry sighed. With possibly several thousand American lives at stake, if the French decided to resist the landings, it would be the most flagrant dereliction of duty.

"I will come with you," Mustafa said. "It is best that I do it."

"You?" Harry was incredulous.

"It is a family matter. My family."

How wrong can one be, Harry thought, remembering his first opinion of this remarkable little man.

"Well," he said, "I can't say I'm sorry to hand over the responsibility. I have never had to execute a woman before."

"But you would do it," Mustafa said.

"If there was nobody else," Harry agreed.

"It is not something you can give to your men, eh?"

"No," Harry said. "That is not how we do things in the Commandos."

"Do you think, when you have completed this mission, I could become a Commando?" Mustafa asked.

"Well," Harry said, once again taken completely by surprise. "I see no reason why not."

If we complete this mission, he thought.

They boarded the truck while it was still dark, carrying their tommy-guns and the satchels of ammunition and grenades out of the hotel and into the lean-to garage. But as there was a dusk-to-dawn curfew they could not leave until daybreak, and then they would have to pass through a Legion check point. The eight Commandos were concealed in the back of the truck, under tarpaulins, while Mustafa and Raquyyah sat in the cab with Philippe. Both Mustafa and Raquyyah bade Yasmin a tearful goodbye. Mustafa, of course, claimed he would be returning with Philippe.

Marguerite was more relaxed, as she was quite sure that Philippe would be back, the next week.

"I will write," Raquyyah promised. "As soon as I am settled."

Yasmin burst into tears all over again.

But at last it was daylight, and the truck drove out of the yard and into the narrow street. The *muezzin* was already calling the faithful to prayer, but that apart there was not a great deal of activity in the town as they drove to the main square and then took the road to the north. The checkpoint was where the road left the town, and there was the usual banter with the legionnaires before they were waved through. The Commandos, crouching in the back and sweating, as it was already quite warm, clutched their weapons, knowing they would have to shoot their way out if anything went wrong, but nothing did, and after half-an-hour they were able to throw back the tarpaulin and get some air. By then the sun was already higher, and the temperature could almost be felt to be rising with every moment.

There was little traffic on the road, although they knew the northbound bus would leave Ghardaia in another hour or so, but the truck was the faster vehicle; the southbound bus would only just have left Algiers. In front of them the Atlas Mountains slowly rose out of the horizon. They had driven another fifty miles when Philippe pulled off the road.

"Why do we stop?" Raquyyah asked.

"Breakfast," Mustafa said. "Are you not hungry?"

The Commandos disembarked and stretched their legs. Philippe prepared the food, not looking at anyone.

"What's going on, sir?" Simmons asked, in English.

"We are the witnesses to an execution," Harry told him, in the same language.

Simmons gulped, and looked to where Mustafa was leading Raquyyah away from the group, talking earnestly to his sister-in-law, who was listening no less intensely. Harry got up and followed – he was the officer in command.

They rounded an outcrop of rock and were out of sight of the rest of the party, where Philippe was serving coffee.

"Why you say I cannot go to Algiers?" Raquyyah was asking.

"Because it is not safe," Mustafa told her. "Not safe for you, and not safe for us."

"*Pouf*," she commented, "who is going to arrest me?"

"We cannot take that risk," Mustafa explained.

He had stopped, and now he drew his knife.

Raquyyah gazed at him, and it. "You are not serious."

"I am sorry," Mustafa said.

"You cannot do this." She turned in a whirl of *haik*, to face Harry, standing behind her. He had killed quite a few men in his time, but always in the heat of battle. Now he felt quite sick. "You will not let him do this," she shouted.

"It is necessary," he said. "I am sorry, but there are too many lives at stake."

"You . . . you bastard!" she shrieked. "You slimy thing from the pit of hell."

Mustafa stood behind her, and she heard him. She dropped to her knees. "Wait," she said, panting. "Please. Tell me what I must do. Please . . ."

"You must die," Mustafa said, and put his arm round her neck.

"Please!" she screamed. "Do not—"

Mustafa drew the knife across her neck in one quick, violent movement, in the same instant releasing her so that no blood would fall on his clothes.

The last scream echoed briefly in the morning, and then died. Raquyyah lay in a bloody heap at their feet.

Mustafa and Harry looked at each other, then Mustafa

cleaned both his knife and his hands on the dead woman's *haik*. Together, they walked back round the rocky outcrop and faced the men.

"Holy Jesus Christ," Le Boule muttered. They had all heard the scream.

"She would have betrayed us," Harry said.

The men exchanged glances. Harry supposed they were as tough fighting men as there were to be found in the world, but like him, they were still conditioned to pre-1939 rules of combat, when war had not been made on women.

At least they looked at Mustafa, and their commanding officer, with new respect.

There was little talk after that. They did not stop again, and were at the southern gateway into Algiers just before dusk. The Ghardaia bus never did catch them up, and they passed the southbound bus early in the afternoon. These apart, there were only a couple of military vehicles travelling south.

"Suppose they find the body?" Simmons asked.

"She is well off the road," Mustafa said.

"But there will be vultures."

"There are always vultures, in the desert, because there is always carrion, of one sort or another."

Simmons looked about to vomit.

When they were an hour short of the city, Philippe pulled off the road again, to allow the Commandos to change their battle-dress for the French Legionnaire uniforms. Now Harry, wearing a sergeant's stripes, sat in the front with Philippe, while the "legionnaires" and Mustafa sat in the back.

"From Ghardaia," Harry explained to the sergeant of the guard at the gate. "We have weekend passes, but our vehicle broke down."

The sergeant only glanced at the passes. "Where is your vehicle?"

"About fifty miles back along the road."

"Would you like me to send out for it?"

"I would be grateful," Harry said. "It is embarrassing, eh?"

"Of course. Tomorrow, eh?" The sergeant waved them through.

By tomorrow it would be all over, one way or another.

Algiers teemed at dusk on a Saturday evening. Called the white city because so many of its buildings were of that colour, it occupied the northern slope of a foothill of the mountains, dominated by the great white castle above the houses, and descending through the various levels, with the *kasbah* on the left, to the long moles of the spacious harbour, which had once sheltered the most dangerous pirates in the Mediterranean. The city was far more French than Arab, with its wide boulevards and their pavement cafés while, protected as it was from the desert by the Atlas Mountains, it enjoyed an almost European climate, sufficiently moist for there to be many attractive parks and formal gardens. Here was a kaleidoscope of chicly dressed women, of soldiers and civilians, French and Arab and every conceivable mixture in between, all settling down for an aperitif before dinner and dancing, everyone oblivious to the catastrophe that was hanging over their heads. Quite a crowd had gathered on the Mole, looking out to sea, where there had apparently been gunfire earlier, and indeed flashing lights could still be seen on the horizon.

Harry reckoned that was the Torch vanguard, but to the people of Algiers it was merely the Allies trying to run another convoy through to Malta. Yet the real armada, if it was there, had to be within a hundred miles of the shore by now.

Philippe turned down a side street, braked in darkness. The Commandos disembarked, and took out their various carry-alls containing their weapons. They were all still sombre about what had happened to Raquyyah, had to accept that their commander and Mustafa had been telling the truth.

"I leave you now," Philippe said. "If you are taken—"

"We won't betray you, Philippe," Harry said, and clasped his hand. "You have done very well." He paid him the promised extra money for the petrol.

"I will wish you fortune," Philippe said, and drove towards the bright lights of the seafront.

Harry checked his watch. "Half-past six. The French dine fairly early, but we don't want to be there much before eleven. Let's eat ourselves."

They found a café and had dinner. The Arab waiters were very subservient, and found nothing to interest them in seven Legionnaires dining with a French-Algerian.

At ten thirty, Harry said, "Let's go. Mustafa, we walk slowly towards the Governor-General's residence."

They strolled through crowded streets. Few people paid any attention to seven men wearing Legionnaire uniforms and carrying small bags. That they were on weekend leave seemed obvious; that they were accompanied by an Arab seemed to indicate they were seeking the more seedy forms of entertainment, probably in the *kasbah*. Their principal problem lay with other French soldiers, who wanted to be friendly and were already half-drunk. But these were resisted, and by half-past seven they were in position across the street from the residence, finding themselves places at a roadside café and drinking beer as they surveyed their target.

"Two men on the gate," Harry said. "How many inside, Mustafa?"

"Two more on the inside gate. I do not know how many in the building itself."

"And the barracks?"

"Around the corner from the building."

"Right. Well, I reckon you have done all that you can, old son. More than you were contracted for. I'm going to see you get a bonus. Maybe even a medal."

"You are sending me away?" As usual, he was aggrieved.

"Yes. I think you should go and find Philippe. You have a wife, Mustafa. Who knows, in the course of time you may even have children. If you stay with us you may have your head blown off."

"I will stay with you," Mustafa said. "I fight for de Gaulle, eh?"

"Well . . . just remember it was your choice," Harry said.

Alan Savage

The Governor-General's residence – it could almost be called a palace – was situated in a quiet section of the town, close to the harbour but well away from the bright lights and cheerful weekend crowds of the main boulevards. Whatever the fortunes of war, which had seen their parent nation beaten and humiliated, whatever the titanic struggle going on at the other end of the continent, or in Russia and the Pacific, the Algerians, many of whom, even if they were French by blood, had been born and bred here, conceived that it had nothing to do with them. They lived in one of the more fortunate areas of the earth, they suffered no food shortages, and there was not a German soldier in sight for several hundred miles.

They appeared to have no concept that there might be soldiers of other nationalities watching them, and approaching them, that their happy-go-lucky days might be drawing to an end. Harry wondered how they would react?

But first, the job in hand, hopefully, was to control that reaction. He studied the palace and the walls and the guards. The building looked bigger than it had appeared on the plan. He could not hope to control something that size with eight men. Therefore it would be necessary to seal off only the area he *had* to control – the Admiral's living quarters. He had committed the plan to memory, and knew exactly where to go, but what he did not know of was the strength of the interior walls and doors. He had to chance his arm and believe that as the building was old and had been built for the deys, it would also be solid.

The street was deserted at nearly midnight.

"Le Boule and Evans," he said.

The two Commandos left the shelter of the darkness and strolled along the street, arm in arm, carry-alls dangling from their shoulders. They drew abreast of the sentries, and paused for a chat. Harry hoped they would obey orders and leave most of the talking to Le Boule – Evans spoke French fluently but with a pronounced Welsh accent.

But they only talked for a few minutes before going into action. It was very quick and carried out with the devastating

70

efficiency practised by the Commandos. When both guards lay dead on the pavement Harry waved his men forward. The gates were already open, Le Boule having secured the keys from the belt of one of the murdered men.

Security, Harry thought, was certainly lax.

He led his men inside, and the gates were closed behind him. They stood on a drive, with spacious grounds to either side. The palace was directly in front of them, round a slight curve. There were several lights on, in the hallways, and in the Admiral's apartment on the left. To the right of the main building there was a large annexe, and this, Harry calculated, was where the garrison would be located. Again, he had no information as to how many men there might be, but he had to estimate at least forty to mount the necessary changes of guard.

He waved his men off the drive and into the trees for the advance on the house. As he did so, someone called from in front of him.

"Etienne? Etienne? Is there a problem?"

Damn, he thought. Security had not been that lax after all. Obviously the opening of the gate set off an alarm in the house, either a light or a bell.

"Etienne?" the sentry called again, coming down the steps and unslinging his rifle.

As he did so, a dog barked, some distance to the right.

"That's torn it," Harry said. "We go in. Go, go, go!"

He led the way, tommy-gun thrust forward. The sentry went down in a hail of bullets. Another man, just emerging and silhouetted for a second too long against the lighted doorway, also went down immediately. Harry leapt over his body and ran into the hall. Noise was slowly rising from all around him, at least one dog barking in the yard, alarm bells ringing. The only shots fired so far had been from his own people, who were now all in the entry hall behind him.

"Piece of cake," Simmons gasped.

"Don't believe it," Harry told him. "Upstairs."

They ran for the stairs on the right of the hall. From behind the stairs, where presumably the pantries were, a man appeared,

71

looked at them, and disappeared again. But there were going to be a lot of men here in a few minutes.

Harry ran up the stairs and saw a man at the top. He was in pyjamas, and Harry had to check to make sure he wasn't Darlan himself. That gave the man time to bring up a revolver. A shot rang out from behind Harry, and the man came tumbling down the steps.

"That is one for me," Mustafa said.

Harry bent over the man, briefly, decided that it wasn't the Admiral, and went on up.

Below and behind him, the front doors burst open with a crash, and men spilled into the hall. The Commandos turned round and gave fire, then ran up the stairs behind their officer. There were shouts and screams, and a gasp of pain. Harry reached the gallery and looked down. There were at least thirty French soldiers in the hall, firing indiscriminately. But one of their bullets had struck home; a Commando was draped halfway down the stairs, head lower than his torso.

"Kippings," Le Boule said. "He's dead."

"In there," Harry said, pointing along the corridor. The men behind them gained the top of the stairs, and as they appeared at the head of the corridor Harry, who was now at the rear of his men and had already pulled the pin on his grenade, threw the bomb. The explosion was vast in the confined space of the corridor. Plaster cracked on the ceiling and some of the walls also crumbled. The guards fell back, shouting and screaming. Several of them must have been hurt, Harry reckoned.

At the end of the corridor a door opened. "What the devil is going on?" a man demanded.

This wasn't Darlan either, but as he wore a dressing gown Harry deduced he was a member of the establishment, probably a valet. And he had opened the vital door.

"Don't shoot him," he snapped, pushing his way through the Commandos to gain the doorway.

"Who are you?" the man inquired, gazing at Harry's French uniform.

"Inside," Harry said, presenting his tommy-gun. The man stepped back and made to close the door. But Harry thrust him aside. "Secure it," he told Simmons. "There is another way in, monsieur," he said to the valet. "A second staircase. Show us."

The man swallowed. "I know of no staircase."

Harry jammed the muzzle of his tommy-gun into the man's waist. "Show the sergeant, or he will cut your throat."

The valet swallowed again. "I will show you."

"Go with him, Le Boule. Take one man, and hold it."

"Yes, *sir*!"

"Evans, you and Nichols go round the apartment, and close all the shutters. Simmons, hold here until I return. Mustafa, come with me."

He ran through a small hall and into a lavishly furnished reception room. Then down a corridor lined with classical paintings towards another door.

This now opened to reveal yet another man in a dressing gown. And this was Admiral Darlan.

"Hands up," Harry said, somewhat melodramatically.

The Admiral obviously thought so too. "Are you mad?" he inquired. "What are you doing here? What was that explosion? What was that shooting?"

He was a tall, heavy man with a strong face and a florid complexion. He did not look the least afraid of the tommy-gun pointing at him.

"Explanations later," Harry told him. "Back up."

Darlan hesitated, and half looked over his shoulder.

"We shall not harm either you or the lady, unless forced to it," Harry said.

Slowly Darlan retreated into the bedroom. In the bed the woman had sunk right down, the sheet pulled up to just below her eyes. She had yellow hair, and Harry supposed she was someone else's wife.

"Just stay there, for the time being, madame," he said. From behind him there came a burst of shooting. "Mustafa," he said.

73

"Keep your gun on her. Your gun, mind, not your hands. And don't kill her unless you have to."

Darlan sat on the bed beside his mistress. "You *are* mad. What are you trying to do?"

"All in good time," Harry said. "You come with me."

Darlan hesitated, looked at the woman, then stood up, pulling his dressing-gown tighter. They returned to the reception room, where a very anxious Simmons was waiting.

"They're shooting at the door."

Harry nodded, and listened to several shots from the other end of the apartment. "They're trying the back as well. Are the shutters closed?"

"Yes, sir."

"Do you seriously think you can defend this apartment against my soldiers?" Darlan asked. "With half-a-dozen men? What are you, mutineers? You have *le cafard*, eh? Too much sun. Surrender, and I will do what I can for you."

"All in good time, sir." Harry gestured the Admiral into the front lobby. The valet was standing against the wall, hands to his ears. Private Rhodes stood beside him, revolver aimed at his ribs. Evans and Graham were on the other side of the lobby, also out of the line of fire, but there were several bullet holes in the door.

Simmons had followed him. "What happens if they rush the door?" he asked.

"We must try to persuade them not to," Harry said, and cupped his hands. "You out there," he shouted. "Admiral, I would like you to tell those people to stop shooting."

Another hesitation, then Darlan shouted, "This is Admiral Darlan. Cease firing."

The shooting actually stopped, no doubt in surprise.

"Now you must understand that we hold the Admiral," Harry shouted. "If any attempt is made to rush this door, he will be killed."

"They will hang you," Darlan said.

"That won't do you much good, sir. You out there," he called. "I wish to speak with your commanding officer."

He kept his tommy-gun pointing at the Admiral.

74

"How do you hope to negotiate?" Darlan inquired.

"We'll work something out."

Simmons was as anxious as ever. "We won't hold off a determined assault."

"Exactly," Darlan said.

"You in there," a voice called. "I am Colonel L'Estrange. Are you all right, Admiral?"

Darlan looked at Harry, who nodded.

"I am all right, at this moment," Darlan said.

"And how many men are in there with you?"

Again Darlan looked at Harry, but this time he shook his head.

"I do not know," Darlan said. "But I think there are several."

"What do they want?"

"What we want," Harry said, "in exchange for the Admiral, is twenty million pounds sterling in gold bullion."

There was a moment's silence.

"That is impossible," Darlan said.

"Nothing is impossible, if one puts one mind to it," Harry told him.

"There is not that much bullion in all Algeria," L'Estrange called.

"Then you will just have to get it from France. When you have, come and see me again, and I will tell you what else we need. And please do not attempt to rush the apartment. It is wired with explosives, and you will lose a lot of people. Not to mention the Admiral."

Another brief silence.

"Madness," Darlan commented.

"I will see about getting the money," L'Estrange shouted.

"Good fellow," Harry said. "Now there is one more thing. We will need food sent up and placed outside the door. Enough for twenty-four hours to begin with. It should include some bottles of wine. The bottles should be unopened. Please bear in mind that in any event the Admiral will be required to taste the wine before we drink any of it."

"Admiral?" L'Estrange called.

"Oh, do as the madman says," Darlan said, irritably.

There was some shuffling in the corridor beyond the door, but no further shots were fired.

"Right," Harry said. "Now we settle down to wait. Simmons, I am leaving you in charge of the door with Evans and Graham. Rhodes, you're in charge of the valet."

"It would be simplest to shoot him," Rhodes suggested.

The valet gulped.

"That would be cold-blooded murder," Darlan protested. "And you call yourself Frenchmen?"

"Actually, no," Harry told him. "With the exception of Mustafa, of course. He's the one in your bedroom. The rest of us are British Commandos. As a matter of fact, Simmons, I think now would be a good time to change into your proper uniforms, just in case things go wrong."

"British Commandos?" Darlan asked, incredulously. "In the centre of Algiers?"

"We get around. Go into the bedroom."

Darlan obeyed and Harry followed. The woman was still in bed, the sheet still held to her eyes. Mustafa was seated in a chair, facing her, his tommy-gun on his knees.

"I don't suppose you feel like getting up and getting dressed," Harry said.

"She has nothing on," Darlan explained.

"Ah. Well, she's welcome to stay there. But I hope she won't be embarrassed if I change my clothes." He opened his carry-all. Darlan and the woman watched with interest as he took off his French uniform and replaced it with British battledress.

"Do you think that will save you, now?" Darlan demanded.

"It should. Geneva Convention and all that." Harry looked at his watch. It was half-past midnight. "Now, sir, we do need to talk."

"What do you have to say to me? Do you realise that by tomorrow morning this building will be surrounded by the finest troops France possesses? Do you still think you can get away?

76

Oh, I suppose you will ask for an aircraft to take you out. And no doubt you will take me with you as your hostage. What will you achieve? Does Great Britain so need twenty million pounds in bullion? Or are you acting on your own, without orders? In which case you will undoubtedly be hunted down like the criminals you are."

"I am quite sure the British Government could use twenty millions in gold bullion, Admiral Darlan," Harry said. "But they are not going to get it. Are they?"

Darlan shrugged. "I can end it in a moment, simply by telling that fool L'Estrange to refuse to co-operate. If you then shoot me, well, I am a fighting sailor. It is a risk I have taken before. And whether I am alive to enjoy it or not, I will die knowing that you and your men will also certainly die."

"What a doomsday scenario," Harry said. "However, sir, you will agree that Colonel L'Estrange, and I am sure even his superior officers, will do everything to keep you alive."

Darlan snorted. "A forlorn hope, Captain."

"Major, if you don't mind, sir. The point I am making is that you are their commanding officer. More, I think many of those men consider you the hope of France. Or at least, the honour of France. They surely are not going to allow you to die, if there is the remotest chance of saving your life. Even if you command them to do so."

"Perhaps you are right," Darlan said. "But I will hunt you down, personally."

"Of course you will, sir. Now . . ." Harry again looked at his watch. It was just coming up to one o'clock. He did not think even if everything went entirely wrong there was anything the French could do about the coming invasion with only a few hours to go. He sat down. "I have to tell you that this business of kidnapping you for ransom is a load of hokum."

"I never believed it for a moment."

"Quite."

"So what do you really hope to achieve?"

"My business is to persuade you to be co-operative."

77

"Now I know you are mad. Co-operate with the British? We have gone down that road too often."

"I quite understand your feelings, sir," Harry said. "The people who are asking for your co-operation are the Americans."

"The Americans?" Darlan looked left and right, as if he expected to see them popping out of the woodwork. "What Americans?"

"Well, in a word, I suppose you would have to say Messrs Roosevelt and Marshall."

"What have they to do with me? We are not at war with the United States."

"If you do not play your cards well, sir, you very soon will be. At this moment, off the coast of Algeria and Morocco, and making for the Straits of Gibraltar, there is an armada of some eight hundred ships, ferrying an army of approximately a million men. Its purpose is to take over French North Africa."

Mustafa gasped. The woman also gasped. Darlan merely stared at Harry.

"You expect me to believe this?"

"I hope you do, sir. If it were not true, I would hardly be risking my life in this fashion. That firing you heard out to sea this afternoon was the advance guard."

Darlan looked at the window, but Mustafa had closed the shutters.

"Even if you could see out, sir, it wouldn't do you any good," Harry said. "The armada is still about fifty miles offshore. And the part of the fleet coming here has still to pass through the straits. But it will be there about now, and it is coming."

As if in confirmation, the telephone by the bed jangled.

Darlan looked at Harry.

"Oh, take the call, please."

Darlan picked up the phone.

"Admiral! L'Estrange here. Are you all right?"

"I am all right. Have you arranged for the money?"

"I am in contact with France, sir. But the reason I am calling is to inform you that our agent in Ceuta has radioed a message that

78

a very large convoy is passing through the strait. He says, *very* large."

"When will this convoy be abeam of Algiers?"

"He calculates about dawn, sir."

Darlan looked at Harry again, and Harry shook his head.

"Keep me informed," Darlan said, and hung up. "So you are telling the truth. Well, we will give them a bloody nose. Holding me is a waste of time, Major. Our plans for resisting attack are all made, our men are all in position or easily summoned."

"Do you command a million men, sir?"

Darlan glared at him. "Perhaps not."

"There are several battleships with this task force. Do you have any battleships?"

"The *Jean Bart* is in Oran."

"But she is crippled, and cannot move except by towing."

"Her guns work."

"She will be blown out of the water, Admiral, and you know it. Listen to me. This is a battle you cannot win. You can fight it, and go down with flags flying and guns blazing, but you will still be defeated, and thousands of your countrymen will be killed. What is more, your province will be devastated. Algiers will be laid flat. Whereas if you were to give your commanders orders not to resist the landings, but to welcome the Americans as your friends, as the future liberators of France from the Nazis—"

"You are asking me to commit an act of treachery."

"I am inviting you to take you proper place upon the stage of history."

The two men gazed at each other.

"And if I refuse?" Darlan asked.

"Then I am very much afraid that you will become the first casualty of the invasion."

"You think that killing me will affect the outcome?"

"I think it may, Admiral. But in any event, I am acting under orders. I would, however, again beseech you to co-operate."

Darlan got up and took a turn about the room. Then he stopped, in front of Harry. "You are a very bold young man."

"Thank you, sir."

"But also a ruthless one, eh?"

"I carry out my orders, sir."

"I have no doubt of it. You realise that my forces extend over a very large area. I cannot possibly contact all of them by dawn. Is that when the invasion is supposed to commence?"

"It will commence before dawn, with a bombardment." Harry looked at his watch. "That will begin within another hour."

"My people will reply instinctively. I have told you, there is no way I can contact all my field commanders in an hour."

Harry picked up the telephone and held it out. "You can start now, sir," he suggested.

Part Two
The Island

Never was isle so little, never was sea so lone.

Rudyard Kipling

The Sister

"I do like a good investiture," Belinda remarked. She stood with the entire group of Commandos on the steps of Buckingham Palace while the medals were proudly held up for the waiting photographers: five Military Medals, one Military Cross, and one Victoria Cross – Harry already had an MC and Bar.

The families were grouped a few feet behind their heroes. The Curtises were somewhat apart.

The hand-held cameras clicked, the newsreel cameras whirred, then at last it was over.

"Now you can have the weekend off," Belinda said. "The boss would like you in on Monday morning." She waited.

"I think I should go back to Frenthrope," Harry said.

"Of course." But she was disappointed.

"I don't suppose you'd care to come with me."

"Ah . . . no. I don't think your people really approve of me."

"Um, listen, I'll go up with them now, and come back on Sunday afternoon. How about that?"

"I shan't be in town on Sunday," she said.

Damnation, he thought, she's piqued. But he couldn't do anything about it on the steps of Buckingham Palace. "Well, then . . . Is there any news of Mustafa?"

"I'm afraid not. We haven't been looking very hard. He got caught up in the general mix-up of the invasion and disappeared. I imagine he's gone back to his people. He did a very good job, but it's over and done with."

"He did several very good jobs," Harry said. "But I can't help but wonder if it was him who shot Darlan. I know he wanted to." Belinda shook her head. "It wasn't Mustafa. They've got the assassin. Some deranged student."

"Makes you think," Harry said, "all that time and effort, all those lives, and he was gunned down anyway."

"But not until he had ordered a ceasefire," Belinda pointed out. "That was your job, and you did it brilliantly. I must rush. Monday morning at the office."

She smiled at John and Alison Curtis, and hurried into the throng.

Harry shook hands with each of the Commandos. He had already been to see Kippings' family – fortunately the dead man had not been married.

"Next time you're on a job, sir, please think of us," Sergeant Le Boule said.

"I certainly won't think of anyone else," Harry said. "I'll be in touch."

Simmons was last. "Some show," he said. "That was the first time I'd ever shaken hands with a general."

"Look at it this way," Harry suggested. "That was the first time General Clark had ever shaken hands with a British Commando. Which is the girlfriend?"

"She couldn't get down, sir." He flushed. "I'm to spend the weekend with her people. You will be using us again, sir?"

"You can count on it," Harry told him. "But I have no idea for what." He shook hands. "I'll be in touch."

He thought it was a funny old world, as the train puffed north. It was January, and very cold. The heat of the desert was hard to remember. Yet he felt that a part of him was still there, not so much in Algiers, as in the hotel in Ghardaia, lying on his bed, sweltering, listening to the cries of the *muezzins* and the barking of the dogs. Feeling the woman in bed beside him.

He had been too conscious of being a British officer in the

middle of an assignment. Mustafa had no doubt been right, and it was senseless to send a pretty woman to execution without giving her some pleasure first. That was the old Roman point of view, as he remembered his history, certainly if she was a virgin.

Raqquyah had not been a virgin.

But he would never forget her begging for her life. He knew, had it been left to him, he would have acquiesced. Thus he was neither as tough nor as ruthless as he liked to think – as his superiors did think. And that included Belinda. So, thank God for Mustafa.

He wondered if he would ever see Mustafa again.

Memories apart, he was feeling distinctly out of sorts. Principally because Belinda was playing silly buggers. Of course, he was being unreasonable. She had her own life to live, and she was as good to him as that life allowed: he had spent two nights in her flat since returning from North Africa. And he was the one who had rejected the invitation to spend a couple more. But for his damned sense of duty he'd have taken her up. What was needling him was that she really might be going out of town on Sunday – with another bloke.

He wondered if he was in love with her? Finding that out would have to wait until the curiously unreal world of the war, which had thrown them together without either of them knowing what the morrow might bring, was over, and life returned to normality. But to someone like himself, who had killed so often, or like her, who had had to send men to their deaths so often, would the return of peace bring normality? Or just a huge emptiness?

"Who's in a brown study then?" His mother was seated opposite him.

"Sorry. Yes, I was brooding, I suppose."

"On the past, or the future?"

He grinned. "Oh, the past. No point in brooding on the future."

"Was it very dangerous?" his mother asked.

"Not at all," he lied. "We had excellent ground support."

His mother shuddered. But she was looking at the strip of crimson ribbon on his tunic. "We're so proud of you."

"Did I hear Captain Forrester say you're due back on duty on Monday morning?" his father asked, embarrassed.

"Well, I did have all of Christmas off, Dad."

"So you did," John Curtis agreed. "Are you planning to marry that girl?"

Harry raised his eyebrows. "Belinda?"

"Yes."

Harry grinned. "It doesn't look like it. I did propose once, last summer, and she turned me down."

"Did she give a reason?"

Harry shrugged. "I think she feels one shouldn't get involved in things like marriages in wartime. Besides, she's already married."

"Good heavens. But . . ." His father flushed.

"We are very fond of each other," Harry conceded. "And she's getting a divorce. But these things take time. Longer in a war than normally."

Alison and John exchanged glances. More and more, they thought mutually, this boy was becoming a stranger to them. Far more so than his elder brother, who, as he was in the Navy, they actually saw less often.

"June Clearsted told me that Yvonne may well be home this weekend," Alison ventured.

Yvonne Clearsted, Harry thought, as the taxi from the station dropped them at the Curtis residence. It was late on a cold Friday evening, already dark, and already with a hint of frost in the air making their breath cloud in front of their noses. The last time he and Yvonne had seen each other had been a bitter experience, with her accusing him of unfaithfulness and deceit . . . although it had taken her a few weeks longer to return his engagement ring, as he recalled.

What does one do with a returned engagement ring? Leave it in a drawer to be forgotten. That was where it was.

John Curtis unlocked the front door. "Doesn't the place seem empty, without Jupiter," he remarked, drawing the black-out curtains before switching on the light.

"I'll get him out of kennels first thing tomorrow," Harry promised, and carried his bag upstairs. He drew the curtain, switched on the light, looked around himself at the bedroom. Every time he went away, even if it was only on a trip to London to receive a medal, he was not sure he was coming back to these four square walls where he had spent so much of his life.

In the two months since Algiers he had been home quite regularly, first with his week's leave, and then, when he had resumed training, as the camp to which he had been assigned had been in Wales, he had been able to get home every weekend. When he remembered the utter secrecy and the travel difficulties of the first couple of years of the war it was like looking back through the wrong end of a telescope. Everything had been turned around in a matter of weeks. As the Prime Minister had said, the victory in North Africa was not the end, it was not the beginning of the end, but it was the end of the beginning, of the seemingly endless, mind-deadening succession of defeats and failures, for the Commandos more than anyone else, as they had been the spearhead of every attempt to strike back at the enemy. Now it was the enemy who was in trouble.

Harry was probably under even less illusions than Churchill. The fighting in North Africa was more intense than ever before, as the Americans had no experience of modern warfare and Rommel was proving just as brilliant a general as ever in the past. All realistic thoughts of invading Europe across the Channel before 1944 had been shelved. The Russians were still engaged in a life and death struggle around Stalingrad. And the Americans and Australians still had somehow to get to grips with the immense distances that separated the Japanese strongholds in the Pacific. The difference between January 1943 and even June 1942 was that no one doubted that these matters would be resolved, victoriously. The Germans and the Italians would be driven out of Africa; the Russians would smash the Sixth Army; the Second Front would be mounted; and Japan would be defeated. It was just a matter of how long these things would take, and at what cost in men and money.

Harry took off his greatcoat and hung it on the door, unlaced his boots and kicked them off, then lay on the bed, on his back. He closed his eyes, and hastily opened them again, as Raquyyah's face immediately loomed in front of him. He supposed this was something he needed to worry about, and perhaps do something about. He had supposed himself traumatised by what had happened at St Nazaire – that had been death on a far greater scale than in his little corner of the desert, and it had been compounded by failure and defeat. But because of the very immensity of the disaster, it had been blurred. He could remember the names, see the faces of so many of the dead, men whom he had personally trained and commanded. But there were just too many.

Only Veronica had retained an individuality. But Veronica had been killed by their enemies, and it had been in the heat of battle, or at least, in the heat of their escape. He did not suppose the German soldier who had fired the fatal shot had even known she was a woman, much less a beautiful one who could love with a rare intensity. There had been no personal involvement.

Veronica had not knelt at his feet and begged for her life. It would never have occurred to her to do so, in any circumstances.

Raquyyah he had not even liked, however much he might have admired her as a woman. But it was her face that came back to haunt him, time and again.

It was not a situation he had confided to anyone, even Belinda. Belinda, so unlike any of the other women in his life, was simply too pragmatic. Which was probably why she was still alive and the others were all dead. Belinda would have considered the situation, and undoubtedly concluded that he was no longer mentally fit for combat. And if he was now her superior officer, she it was who still held the power, by virtue of her position as secretary to the colonel, and her access to even more senior officers – she had been in the Commandos, behind the scenes, even before their formation.

And it would probably suit her very well to have him installed behind a desk rather than a gun. That he could not contemplate while there was a war to be won. What he needed to do was be pragmatic himself. He had a mental problem. Get rid of it, without having recourse to a shrink. How? He had supposed Belinda herself might be the answer to that, but to be effective she would have also to be totally subservient, and she was never going to be that. So . . .

There was a knock on the door. "Are you awake, Harry?"

"Just thinking." He got up and admitted his mother,

"You need a shave," she commented. "The Clearsteds have been on the phone. They've invited us over for dinner."

Harry regarded his mother for several seconds. "How did they know we were back?"

"Well . . ." She flushed. "I telephoned them, as a matter of fact."

"Why?"

"I knew they'd want to hear all about it. About the investiture. About . . . well, it's not formal. Just pot luck. Will you come?"

"Did Yvonne come home?"

"Oh, yes," Alison said. "She'll be there."

Harry had a bath and changed his uniform for blazer and bags. He wondered what she would be like, after very nearly a year – and an important year for her, as she had finally left the comfort and security of her home and her job in the library to join the army.

He was pleasantly surprised. They were the same age, and had known each other all of their lives, beginning when they had attended kindergarten for the first time at the age of six. He did not suppose they had ever been friends, as she was utterly feminine in everything, and did not care to watch games like cricket or rugby, both of which he had been good at. Then he had gone away to Sandhurst, and no sooner had he been commissioned than the war had started.

Their respective parents had still pressed ahead with their

plans for the union they had always wanted, to the extent of that ring. But Harry did not suppose it would have worked even without the interference of Veronica Sturmer. Yvonne had always remained firmly committed to the good and the proper things in life, especially the proper. She knew he was a fighting soldier, which by definition had to mean that he had killed or caused people to be killed; he did not think she had ever allowed herself to think about what that actually entailed. She certainly knew he was a man with a strong sexual drive, but here again, she had never allowed herself to consider what that might entail when a man and a woman were alone in a bedroom together. When he had proposed she had allowed him to kiss her lips for the first time, and she had seemed surprised that it had happened at all.

But after several months in the ATS . . .?

"Harry! How good to see you," June Clearsted gushed, as she always did. "And looking so well. Every time you've been home in the past you've been wounded."

"This time they missed," Harry said, allowing himself to be kissed on the cheek.

He shook hands with James Clearsted and faced Yvonne.

She was just as tall and slender as he remembered, and had the same straight yellow hair – presumably she had to wear it in a bun when in uniform. But tonight she was wearing a dress, which certainly gave the impression that she might have filled out a little. Her face was long, and usually solemn, although tonight she was smiling. "Harry!"

Her voice was low and well modulated, although he knew she could shout when angry.

"It is so good to see you," she said, and presented her cheek to be kissed. This he did, while retaining hold of her hand and giving the palm a gentle scratch. He wondered if she knew what that meant, and thought perhaps she did, for although she did not pull away, there were pink spots in her cheeks when he released her.

"And you've got another medal," June Clearsted said. "The big one."

"Well, they have to give them to someone," Harry said.

"Not the VC," James Clearsted argued.

"I've the citation here," Alison said importantly, and took it from her handbag. *"For behaviour above and beyond the normal call of duty, in that he saved the life of a brother officer under fire from the enemy."*

"This was in North Africa?"

"No, no," Harry said. "This was at St Nazaire, last spring."

"But you were part of that Torch business, weren't you?" James persisted.

"In a manner of speaking."

"That really tells us nothing," James complained.

Harry grinned. "It'll all be revealed in due course," he said.

"When?"

"Well, probably after the war."

James blew a raspberry.

"I think we'd better eat," June said.

Predictably, Harry was placed next to Yvonne.

"Was it really very dangerous?" she asked. "North Africa?"

"Not as dangerous as some. We knew the Yanks were coming. I did, anyway."

"But is it true that Hitler has ordered all captured Commandos to be shot?"

"I believe he has. Whether the orders will be carried out is another matter. All the German commanders on the ground know they're likely to be cited as war criminals if they behave like that."

"But still, it means you really can't afford to risk being captured. Just in case the local man does obey the order."

"Yes," he said.

They gazed at each other, and the pink spots were back.

"When are you returning to duty?"

"Sunday night. I'm due in on Monday morning."

"So am I."

"Where?"

"Catterick."

"Now there's a pity. I'm for London."

He realised that the others were listening to the conversation while pretending not to, and hastily changed the subject. But when they were saying goodnight he suggested they might go for a walk together in the morning.

"I'd like that," she said.

"Well," Alison remarked as they got home. "You and Yvonne seemed quite to hit it off, for a change."

"I think she's grown up a bit," Harry said.

He lay in bed in the dark and tentatively closed his eyes, and for a change did not see Raquyyah's face hovering in front of him.

"I actually have to walk up to the kennels and collect Jupiter," he told Yvonne the next morning, when he picked her up. "That all right by you? It's a good couple of miles."

"Do me good," she said.

They were both well-wrapped up against the chill wind, and she was wearing a hood which rather enhanced her features. Harry wore a flat cap.

"How do you find life in the ATS?" he asked.

She considered. "Different."

"I imagine it is. Tell me in what ways, specifically."

"Well . . . I suppose it's being public. I mean, you know, undressing before a bunch of other women, having to share the bathroom, having to . . . well, be intimate, I suppose. I've never been intimate before, with anyone."

She was an only child.

"I can understand the difficulty. So what do you do about it?"

"Grin and bear it."

"I suppose that's an aspect of life we all have to get used to, at some time or other. But the women themselves, with whom you have to do all this sharing . . ."

She gave a little shudder. "They're not my type. They only want to talk about sex. And the language they use!"

"Well, they're trying to be soldiers," Harry pointed out,

wondering if she had grown up as much as he had thought. And hoped.

They walked most of the rest of the way in silence, and reclaimed Jupiter. He was pleased to see Harry, certainly, and they spent some time leaping around before beginning their walk home. By then it was beginning to snow.

"I think this calls for a warming drink," Harry said, and guided them to one of his favourite pubs, where he knew Jupiter would be allowed inside to lie before the fire.

"Is that mulled wine, I smell, Joe?" Harry asked the publican.

"It is indeed, Mr Curtis."

"Then we'll have two mugs."

"Mulled wine?" Yvonne said. "I don't really drink alcohol."

"It'll do you good," he promised, and pulled his wallet from his pocket. "How much is that, Joe?"

"Nothing to you, Mr Curtis. I've been reading about you in the paper."

"Nothing bad, I hope."

"Only that you've been collecting a big gong. I'll bring these over."

"Thanks, Joe." He escorted Yvonne to the settee by the fire. The pub had only just opened for the day and there were no other customers as yet. Jupiter lay at their feet.

Joe served the wine. "Mind out, now," he warned. "That's hot."

Harry sipped. "Excellent. Come on, Yvonne. Try some."

She obeyed, made a face, and then frowned. "It's rather nice."

"It'll warm the cockles of your heart, and a few other places as well." He grinned at her. "But you don't want to talk about sex."

"Harry!"

"But you see, there's not an awful lot else *to* talk about. Do you realise that if you and I had got married last year you'd probably be a mum by now."

She drank some more wine. "You said you couldn't get married, last year, because you were too young."

"Oh, quite. And too junior. Now I'm a major, things have changed."

She turned her head. "Are you asking me to marry you? Again?"

"No," he said.

"Oh. Well, then . . ." She contemplated her three-quarters full mug. He wondered if she was considering just putting it down and walking out, or throwing it at him.

"You are such a confoundedly touchy person," he said. "It's just that, before we rush into permanencies like marriage, I think we should get to know each other first."

"Know each other?" she cried. "We've known each other all our lives."

"Correction," he said. "We have been acquainted with each other, all of our lives. That's not at all the same thing."

"You mean you are propositioning me," she suggested.

"That's about it. What do you say?"

"I should slap your face."

"Not in public, I hope. Wait till we're alone."

"I have no intention of being alone with you."

"What I thought we might do," he said, as if she hadn't spoken, "was go down to town tomorrow afternoon, spend a little time in a hotel, and then . . . what time are you due at Catterick?"

"Monday afternoon," she said without thinking.

"That's splendid. We can spend the night together, and I'll put you on a train first thing in the morning, and you'll be at your camp in ample time."

"And we would have had sex together."

"That would be rather fun, don't you think?"

"And then?" she asked.

"Ah . . . well, then we'd know whether we are compatible, or not. And if we are compatible, as I am sure we shall be, then . . ."

"You'd marry me?"

"I might well do that."

94

"And if we are not compatible?"

"There wouldn't be much use, would there?"

"And I would have lost my virginity for nothing."

"Don't you think you've been hanging on to that a bit longer than necessary? Anyway, you would have had a bit of fun."

"Not if we are incompatible."

"I think, instead of being a girl soldier, you should be studying law. Then I take it the answer is no."

Yvonne toyed with her mug. "I didn't say that. Do you think we could have another of these?"

"As I'm due in the office at the crack of dawn on Monday," Harry told his parents over lunch the next morning, "I'm going to have to take the afternoon train."

Déjà vu. He had had to use this ploy on a previous occasion, when he had been hurrying down to London to meet up with Niki . . . and found only catastrophe. But that was history.

"Oh, what a shame," his mother said. But for her it was *déjà vu* as well. And for all her fears for his safety, she was growing to feel that he would always come back. "About Yvonne . . ." She hesitated. She knew they had taken a long walk together on Saturday morning, but oddly, he had not gone out last night, preferring to remain at home with them, talking and listening to the radio. This was flattering, of course, but it was not in the pattern of things. Unless they had quarrelled again.

"We've agreed to keep in touch," Harry said.

"Oh, I am glad," Alison said.

"Any idea where you'll be going next?" his father asked.

"Haven't a clue. And you know that if I did, I wouldn't be able to tell you, Dad."

"Of course I know that. I just wonder who decides these things."

"My superiors. Lord Mountbatten."

"Who sits in his office, and looks at a map, and says well, we can make ourselves a nuisance *there*, and if a few men get killed, that's war."

"That's about right," Harry said. "But you don't want to forget that Mountbatten was a fighting sailor in his time, and had a ship sunk under him. He's been through the mill himself."

"But he's out the other side," John Curtis pointed out.

Harry grinned. "So will I be, one of these days. Like when the war is over." He cocked his head as the doorbell rang, and Jupiter, asleep beside his chair, sprang up with a bark.

"Who on earth can that be, at one o'clock on a Sunday afternoon?" Alison inquired.

Probably Yvonne to tell me she's changed her mind, Harry thought, although he would have supposed she would telephone. "I'll get it."

He went into the hall, opened the front door, and gazed at Mustafa Le Blanc.

"Good God!" Harry commented, and looked past Mustafa at Yasmin. Both wore western clothes, even if Yasmin's idea of English chic was an ankle length and voluminous skirt, a tight blouse, and a beret cocked over one eye.

"You see?" Mustafa asked his wife in French. "I told you we would find him."

Yasmin simpered.

"And just how did you do that?" Harry asked in English.

"But you are famous, Major. Your picture is in all the news-papers, eh? And where you live. So I said, we go to Frenthorpe, and we ask, and we find. Like so."

"Yes, but . . . hell, I'm not being very polite, am I? Come in, come in. You haven't met my parents. Mother, Father, this is Mustafa Le Blanc."

Both the elder Curtises had risen and left the dining room. Now they did a double-take as Mustafa and Yasmin entered the house.

"And his wife, Yasmin," Harry explained.

"I am pleased to make your acquaintance," Mustafa said, advancing behind his outstretched hand.

Alison shook hands, looking at Harry.

"Mustafa served with me in North Africa," Harry said. "Yasmin?"

Yasmin came forward, nervously.

"She don't speak English," Mustafa explained.

Yasmin curtsied as she shook hands.

John Curtis joined the greetings.

Alison contrived to get next to her son. "They're not meaning to stay here, are they?" she whispered.

"Ah . . . I'm not sure," Harry said, eyeing the two small bags that had been left on the doorstep. "Have you any objections?"

"They're *Arabs*," Alison said.

"Not entirely. And they're on our side."

"Have you had lunch?" John Curtis asked.

"We had . . . how do you say? A snick on the train."

"A snack. Right. But I imagine you could do with some coffee?"

"Coffee. Yes, that would be very nice."

"I'll get it," Alison volunteered, and hurried to the kitchen.

Harry brought in the two bags and closed the door. "Come into the drawing-room," he suggested, gesturing at the door.

"This is very fine," Mustafa said appreciatively, taking in the chintz.

"It's home," Harry said. "Do sit down. *Asseyez-vous, s'il vous plait*," he suggested to Yasmin.

She gave her husband a glance, and received a quick nod. The men also sat. "How did you get here?" Harry asked. "I mean, England."

"I have applied to return, eh?" Mustafa said. "I fight for de Gaulle, and now I am a hero. It took time, but it was not difficult."

"And this time they let you bring Yasmin."

"I am a hero," Mustafa said again. "And now I am to be a Commando."

"Ah," Harry said. "Yes. We'll have to talk about that. But, supposing you do become a Commando, what will you do with

Yasmin? I mean," he added hastily, "where will she live? How will she live?"

"She will have my pay as a Commando," Mustafa explained. "And she has a home."

"A home in England?"

"Oh, yes, her sister lives here. She has lived here for many years. Since before the war."

"I see. Well . . . how are the rest of the family?" He switched to French.

"Oh, they are very sad," Yasmin said. "Did you not know that Raquyyah is dead?"

"Good heavens," Harry said, avoiding looking at Mustafa. "But how on earth . . ."

"Her body was found in the desert, not far off the road," Yasmin said. "Her throat had been cut. She had been there for days. Days! It was terrible." She burst into tears.

The elder Curtises stood by the coffee tray, looking bewildered.

Mustafa put his arm round his wife's shoulders. "So tragic," he said. "The police spoke with me, and I told them how we had taken her into Algiers, and she had gone off by herself. She must have picked up some man, who had her and then murdered her. I warned her. You warned her too, Major Curtis."

"Yes," Harry said. "I warned her."

Yasmin was still weeping loudly.

"Have some coffee, my dear," Alison said, sitting on her other side, cup and saucer at the ready. Her French was quite acceptable, but rusty. "Who was this person, Raquyyah?"

"Her sister," Mustafa explained.

"Oh, dear," Alison said. "Will they catch the man who did it?"

"I do not think so," Mustafa said. "In Algeria, at that time, with the Americans landing, it was all very confused. People were being killed all over the place. I do not think they will find this man."

"I will find him," Yasmin declared. "One day I will find him. And do you know what I will do when I find him?"

"Ah . . . hand him over to the police?" Harry suggested, optimistically.

"The police, *pouf*! I will tie him up, then I will push a sharp stick up his asshole, then I will cut off his balls, then I will cut off his ears and nose, then I will poke out his eyes. I will do these things slowly, while he screams in pain and begs for mercy. Then I will cut his throat."

The Mission

"My God!" John Curtis commented. Alison was looking sick.

So was Mustafa. Harry presumed this was the first time his wife had outlined her plans. But then, he was feeling fairly sick himself.

"Drink your coffee," he recommended. "Mustafa, I'd like a word."

Mustafa followed him into the hall.

"Tell me what you are going to do," Harry said.

"I have told you. I wish to be a Commando."

"I meant, about Yasmin, when she finds out who killed her sister?"

"How is she going to do that, Major? I am not going to tell her."

"For God's sake, Mustafa, every man in my command knows what happened."

"They have reported this?"

"No, they haven't. They have accepted that it was necessary. That's not to say they won't ever speak of it. And what about Philippe?"

"Philippe will never betray us," Mustafa asserted. "He knows it would mean his own life, as well."

"Shit!" Harry muttered.

What could he do? It might have been to everyone's advantage were Yasmin to follow her sister. But this was rural England, not the Algerian desert. And besides, she was guilty of nothing – yet – save a very natural desire to avenge her sibling.

"She must not be harmed," Mustafa said. "She is my wife."

"And you don't believe she means to carry out her threat?"

"I am sure she does, at this moment. But her anger will die, with time."

"Well," Harry said. "Let's hope it's the first thing that does, in this instance. Now, I have a train to catch."

"We will come with you. We have a return ticket."

Harry supposed they had better, as they would have to have an eye kept on them, and he was the only one who could do that until he could get to Bannon.

He couldn't imagine what Yvonne was going to say.

"Well!" Yvonne remarked. She was waiting on the platform when they reached the station, wearing uniform and looking very smart and handsome.

"Friends of mine," Harry explained.

"They're not English!"

"As a matter of fact, no. They're Algerian."

"I am pleased to make your acquaintance," Mustafa said, seizing her hand. "This is my wife, but she does not speak English."

Yvonne gazed at Harry from under arched eyebrows.

"And you are the Major's woman, eh?" Mustafa said.

"The Major's what?"

"This is good," Mustafa said, stepping back to look her up and down. "You have the fine tits and the shapely legs. In Algeria, you see, we do not see a woman's tits and legs. In Algiers, yes. But in the desert, no. I live in the desert."

Yvonne was speechless.

"Here's our train," Harry said.

Fortunately, the compartment in which they found a couple of vacant seats was crammed with people. There were only two seats.

"I sit in one, and you sit in the other," Mustafa suggested. "And the women can sit on our laps. Your woman on mine, my woman on yours."

"Not bloody likely," Yvonne said, revealing that she had picked up certain expressions in the ATS.

"In England, in situations like this, the men stand in the corridor," Harry explained.

Mustafa looked disappointed – he had definitely been taken with Yvonne's legs. And probably her breasts as well, Harry thought.

"I have a better idea," Yvonne said. "You and I will stand in the corridor, Harry, and let Mr Le Blanc sit with his wife."

"It's a long three hours to London."

"I can stand it," she said, definitely.

Mustafa shrugged and sat down as the train pulled out of the station. Harry and Yvonne found themselves against each other in the crowded corridor. Always *déjà vu*, he thought. But as long as it was always with an attractive woman it was rather enjoyable.

"Where on earth did you meet them?" she asked.

"He was my guide in Algeria."

"On this so secret mission."

"That's right."

"So you can't tell me about it."

"That's right."

She shifted her position, enticingly, and then shifted back again as she felt him move against her. "I don't know why I'm doing this."

"Because you're in love."

"I need my head examined. What are they doing in England?"

"He wants to join the Commandos."

"You have got to be joking."

"Size isn't everything. He's a good man with a gun. Or a knife," Harry added thoughtfully.

She shuddered. "And in the dark, I'd say. What about her?"

"Oh, she wants to kill someone."

She tilted her head back to gaze at him.

"Fact. Her sister was murdered. She wants to cut the man who did it into little pieces, slowly."

He gazed into her eyes, wondering if she would ever know the truth of it, and what she would do if she did.

"I wish I could tell when you are pulling my leg," she remarked.

"Wouldn't that spoil all your fun?"

She made a face. "We aren't going to have to see them in town, are we?"

"You aren't," he promised her.

"These trains are very fine," Mustafa remarked when they disembarked at King's Cross. "I come with you now?"

"No," Harry said. "Today is Sunday. Our day of rest. You say you have somewhere to stay?"

"Oh, yes, with my sister-in-law. In Golders Green."

"Right. I don't suppose you have a card. Well then . . ." He took out his notebook, flipped it open. "Write out the address. Is there a telephone?"

"Oh yes, we have a telephone. It is better than the one in Ghardaia."

"You surprise me. Write down the telephone number as well. Thank you. Now go there, with Yasmin, and stay there until you hear from me."

"How long before I hear from you?"

"Not long," Harry promised. He smiled at Yasmin, and then escorted Yvonne to the taxi rank.

"Major and Mrs Curtis." The hotel clerk beamed; he liked to see husband and wife in uniform. "Just the one night, is it?"

"I'm afraid so," Harry said.

A bellhop took them up to their room. When he was gone, Yvonne said, "You used your own name."

"It's a quaint habit I've got into over the years."

"But now everyone will know."

"Darling, be sensible. Do you have any idea how many people there are named Curtis in England? I'd bet quite a few of them are majors in the army, too."

"But the people in Frenthorpe . . ."

"Equally, I would bet there is no one in this hotel who comes from Frenthorpe, or who has any intention of going there in the foreseeable future."

"You've done this sort of thing before, haven't you?" she accused.

"Haven't you?"

"Of course not. I told you . . ."

"That you're a virgin. Shall I tell you a secret? I have never had sex with a virgin. I'm quite nervous."

She glared at him, again uncertain that he wasn't joking. "If you could be serious for a moment . . ."

"I am serious. At least, as serious as I am going to be. Try to get it into your head. I'm in the killing business. Which means that, by the law of averages, I am also in the business of being killed. Now if I awoke every morning and said to myself, I wonder if this is the day, I'd very soon become a nervous wreck of value to neither man nor beast. Or even woman. I simply have to regard life as a black comedy. Can you understand that?"

She flushed. "Yes. I think so. I'm sorry."

"Equally, I can't afford ever to be sorry. Time for that when the killing stops." He unbuttoned her tunic. "Let's see what you have in there."

Belinda was at her desk in the outer office, looking cool and spruce as always. "I hope you had a good weekend," she said.

"As a matter of fact, I did," he said, with perfect truth.

Yvonne had had more to offer than he had any right to expect, and because they had been mutually nervous about her virginity, it had been almost an entirely new experience. As for afterwards, to both his surprise and relief she had wanted nothing more.

"I think you could say we are compatible," he had suggested.

"I'm glad of that," she had said.

"So . . ."

She had shaken her head. "Don't, please."

"I thought you were interested."

"I am. But I need time to think about it."

Relief had become mixed with irritation. They had been on the verge of marriage now for three years!

"Ask me again when we're both back in Frenthorpe," she suggested.

"That might not be for a little while," he said.

"But it will happen," she had pointed out.

He had seen her off on her train at the crack of dawn, after a night of extreme passion, quite uncertain as to whether he had just been thoroughly snubbed or not. But happy enough, in retrospect.

Belinda wrinkled her nose. "I'd say you had some unsuspecting wench."

"And what did you have?" he challenged.

"The boss is waiting for you," she said. "I understand it's urgent."

"When is it not?"

He knocked, and went into the inner office.

"Harry! Good to see you, as always. We have business."

"As always." Harry sat before the desk.

"I take it you've been keeping in touch with what's happening?"

"I know the Sixth Army has surrendered at Stalingrad."

"I was talking about North Africa. I still haven't properly congratulated on your coup."

"It didn't do Darlan a lot of good."

"True. But then I don't think he had a lot of good coming his way even if he hadn't been murdered. The good thing is that you, we, didn't do it. But you know about Churchill's meeting with Roosevelt at Casablanca?"

"Unconditional surrender," Harry said. "Bit over the top."

"It might work," Bannon said. "It's what happens next that matters. I mean, when we have North Africa."

"Aren't you looking just a shade far ahead?" Harry asked.

"You mean because Rommel savaged the Yanks at Kasserine? The fact is, Harry, those doughboys just don't know what it's all about, yet. They'll learn. I hope. But he knows he's licked. The Eighth Army has got to Tripoli and is still advancing. It's only a matter of time, and Rommel knows that too. The question is, what happens next. What you probably don't know is that after Casablanca, the boss went on to Cairo for a long chat with Alexander. When the Germans and Italians finally evacuate Tunisia, or are forced to surrender, the Yanks and us are going to have perhaps the greatest army in history sitting in North Africa, wondering what to do next."

"So the invasion is on," Harry said.

"Not of France, at this time," Bannon said. "Everyone has had to do a lot of thinking since Dieppe. So perhaps that was an ill-conceived operation, and perhaps there was some leakage. As at St Nazaire the Germans certainly do seem to have known we were coming. But the fact is that we learned a lot of very serious lessons. What does an invasion require? Firstly, a lodgement. This requires a two to one superiority of men and armour to the enemy, at least locally. Secondly, it requires to create a perimeter, which needs to be several miles deep, so that more men and munitions can be brought in. This also calls for an enormous initial superiority in forces on the ground. Thirdly, and backing up the first two, it needs total air supremacy. It goes without saying that before the attack can be launched at all we have to be certain of total naval supremacy. Fourthly, with regard to the above, it needs a seaport for the disembarkation of men and material. And fifthly, and possibly most important of all, it requires fuel, for the planes and the tanks and the trucks and even the motor cycles and ambulances, on a continuous and guaranteed scale. All of this across the Channel, where there is always the chance of a sudden storm to leave our men on the other side like cut flowers in a glass."

"You make it sound like an insoluble problem."

"There is no such thing. But some problems are more difficult, and thus take longer to solve, than others. This is one of them. Meanwhile, we have this vast army sitting on its arse. The obvious way forward is straight up the map. But there are strongly differing opinions about how this should be done. What we might call the Italian school reckons it should be there. They argue that the Italians have never proved very successful in the

107

field, that they have huge economic and social problems in Italy, and that Mussolini isn't so popular as he once was. They reckon he might fall, and it might be possible to neutralise the country. Against this is the fact that there is an enormous German presence in Italy, that once we get ashore there our options are limited, by the very fact that it is a peninsular, with a mountain range running down its middle; Kellerman, who commands there, isn't going to have too much trouble working out where our next advance is going to have to come from and where it will have to go.

"But there is another potential weak spot in southern Europe, one which is in fact much weaker than Italy. Greece. This happens to be Churchill's first choice. I imagine he still has thoughts about avenging the Dardanelles campaign, the failure of which, you may remember, cost him his job in the Great War. But it also makes a lot of sense. The Greeks are a conquered people, not German allies. The same goes for the Yugoslavs. They are far more likely to help us than the Italians. There is also the possibility that if we can re-take the Balkans, we can link up with the Russians and make a concerted advance across the Hungarian plain, which is considerably less of an obstacle than the Alps. There would have to be some sort of a deal with the Turks, but this seems to be on the cards – I think it is being arranged now – and, of course, if an invasion of Greece were successful, there is always the possibility the Turks would come in on our side."

"Sounds exciting," Harry said. "So which is it going to be?"

"If we were in this alone, there is no doubt that it would be Greece. Unfortunately, we are rapidly drifting into the position of junior partner, and the Americans have this fixed idea that the European war can only be won in France. They regard even Italy as an unnecessary distraction. It doesn't look as if they'll go for Greece. However, the Germans can't be sure about this. And it is our business to make them even more unsure about where the next blow is going to fall. We have several teams working on it, but you are our number one man, as it were."

"Thank you," Harry said. "Where?"

"Have you been to Greece?"

"I'm afraid not. The war caught up with me before I had the opportunity to do any extended travelling, so I've only been where the army has been."

"Pity. Still, you'd never been to North Africa either, had you? And things went pretty well there."

"I had a guide," Harry said thoughtfully, the germ of an idea beginning to buzz in his brain. "I know the entire Mediterranean," Mustafa had claimed. And it would not only employ him, again, as a Commando offshoot, but it would keep him away from his wife, for a while at least. He wondered if Mustafa spoke Greek?

"Now here . . ." – Bannon spread a map on the table against the far wall – ". . . is the Aegean Sea. A perfect mass of small islands. Now, most of them have small German garrisons, as well. This island here . . ." – he stabbed the map – "is the one we're interested in."

Harry peered at the name, Spetsos. "Has it any value?"

"As a matter of fact it does. It contains a major radar station which covers all the approaches to the islands, and southern Greece. We want that taken out. This would be necessary in any event, should we decide to go in through Greece. However, in the short term, it will assist in making the Germans feel that is what we are going to do."

"And it can't be bombed?"

"The radar scanner is situated in a bunker, and the amount of concrete the Germans have poured on top of it makes it impervious to even a thousand pounder. The bunker is also built into the side of a cliff. We have tried a low level air attack using rockets, but they simply weren't up to the job. It will have to be done from the land. And, of course, a second attack will convince Jerry that we mean business in that part of the world."

"And just how small is this small garrison?"

"Our information is that it consists of fifty men, under the command of a major."

"So how many men do I get?"

"Ah." Bannon returned to his desk and sat down. "You'll understand that after the catastrophe of the evacuation of Greece and then Crete a couple of years ago, the Navy aren't too keen on risking more of their ships in those waters. They will transport you in, or as close as they can, by submarine, and they will pick you up again when you are ready to leave."

"When," Harry said. "And you still haven't given me a figure."

"They can manage eight. Including yourself, of course."

"To take on fifty Germans."

"Garrison troops, Harry. And they won't know you're coming."

"They'll certainly know we're going," Harry said. "Unless we kill them all."

"Well, of course, tactical arrangements will be left entirely up to you."

"Timescale?"

"You will be landed at night. As I say, the sub will get as close as it can, then you will have to use rubber dinghies. It is assumed that you will lie up during the day, and make your assault by night. There may be a delay, or you may need to make a detailed reconnaissance. The sub will return every night and be in position at midnight, looking for your signal. It will do this every night for four nights. If you are not in a position to be extracted after four nights, it will presume that you are lost."

"Right. Now, problems. I don't speak Greek. Have we anyone on the ground?"

"Yes. A certain Efan Konikos. He is the schoolteacher. There is only one school on the island, and he is a very well-respected man. Equally by the Germans. Or so he claims."

"He claims," Harry commented. "I hope this chap isn't married?"

"Well, of course he is married, Harry."

"And has a family?"

110

"I have no idea. Most of these people do have large families."
He grinned. "There's not a lot else to do, in a place like Spetsos."

"Shit," Harry commented.

Bannon raised his eyebrows. "Don't you approve of large families?"

"Not in our business. I have something to tell you."

Bannon listened. "Unfortunate," he commented.

"That's one way of putting it."

"Do you want this woman, Yasmin Le Blanc, put under preventive detention?"

"I'd just like an eye kept on her. I'd also like to take Le Blanc with me."

"He's not a Commando."

"He's a good man in a scrap, and he claims to know the Eastern Mediterranean, including Greece."

"Well, as I said, you're in complete charge of tactics. Tell me what you'll need in the way of equipment."

"That's a bit tricky seeing as how I don't actually know what I'm going at. Do we have a large scale map of the island?"

Bannon nodded, and spread it across the desk. Spetsos made Harry think of a Cornish pastie, in that it was whale-shaped, without the tail, and the rounded back was serrated with ridges and gulleys.

"Aren't there any roads?"

"I'm afraid this is a pre-war tourist map, which is all we have. You'll see the town, village, more properly, is at the east end of the island, where there is a small harbour. Here at the west end, marked with that X, is the radar installation, and the Germans have actually built a road connecting it to the village. The distance is five miles."

"And where we will be put ashore?"

"Here. Just south of the town. Konikos will be waiting for you."

"So he has a radio."

"Yes, but it must be very sparingly used in case the Germans trace the signals."

111

"And the garrison is in the town?"

"No, the garrison is at the radar station."

"Right. Let's have a plan of that."

"I'm afraid we do not have one."

"Would you like to say that again, slowly?"

"There hasn't been time to get one out. This is a recent installation. But I believe Konikos has one."

"Great. The trouble is, by the time I get to see it, I won't be able to change any of my equipment, or add to it."

"I'm sorry, but there it is. Now, uniforms. We can let you have German uniforms."

"Which means we can be shot as spies if captured."

"That will happen anyway, if you are captured, no matter what uniform you're wearing. Hitler's orders, remember."

"So we mustn't be captured," Harry agreed. "Especially as there won't be any Seventh Cavalry riding to our rescue this time. I think we'll stick to battledress. If the garrison is only fifty men, everyone will know everybody else, very well. A strange face will be *kaput*, even if he does happen to be wearing German uniform."

Bannon nodded. "That's good thinking. Harry, I know this is a beastly job, and perhaps the most dangerous you've ever been on, but it has to be done. And you're our best."

"Again, thank you," Harry said. "Dates?"

"How long will you need to get ready?"

"I'll be using the same squad," Harry said. "If I'm only allowed eight, I won't even have to replace poor Kippings. Give me a fortnight."

"What a shitting awful mess," Belinda remarked when he emerged from Bannon's office.

"I suppose you know all the details?"

"Enough."

"I'll be taking Le Blanc with me again. He will have to be paid pro rata."

She nodded. "In cash, as before, I take it?"

"No. This time the money is to be paid to his wife." He gave her the address.

112

"I'll have to have his permission for this."

"I'll get it for you. Meanwhile, I wish you to let him have travelling expenses and vouchers for the training camp in Wales immediately."

She made a note. "So . . ."

"I'm off to Wales, this afternoon."

"Shit," she remarked. "Do I see you again before you go?"

"Could be," he said, and leaned across the desk to kiss her on the nose.

As Belinda had remarked, he thought, as the train rumbled west, this was the closest thing to a suicide mission that he had been given, because always before there had been back-up. This time there was none. That St Nazaire had turned out to be a suicide mission had not been intended. It had been going to be in, strike hard, and out. Well, he supposed this was no different. In, strike hard, and out. And perhaps, with only eight men, it could be done.

But it was also totally blind. In all his previous missions, from the Lofoten Islands to Algiers, he had known in advance exactly what he was going to encounter, physically. When he had commanded the jump at Ardres he had had Veronica Sturmer to guide him into the German Command Centre. Before St Nazaire they had spent weeks poring over maps and plans of the docks and submarine pens they were to destroy. This time he had a bunker, and presumably a barracks complex, but no idea of their shape or size. He had to rely entirely on a man he had never met.

Surrounded by his family, with all the attendant possibilities of betrayal!

Harry had telephoned Mustafa, as he had promised, and told him also to report to the training camp, as soon as he received travelling expenses from Belinda, and he actually arrived the next day – she was a very efficient woman.

"Now I join the Commandos, eh?" he asked, eagerly.

"Not right now. But you will train with us. We're to go on another mission."

"To France?"

"Not to France."

His squad were waiting for him, and were delighted to see him.

"Where to now, sir?" Simmons asked.

"A long way," Harry told him. "For a start, back to Alexandria."

"Oh, Lord, not back into that beastly desert again. I thought that show was being wound up."

"Keep your fingers crossed," Harry said. "Now . . ." He surveyed their faces. "I have to tell you that this is a most dangerous mission, as it involves penetrating enemy lines, and as you may know, if any of us are captured, we will be shot immediately. I must therefore ask you to volunteer. Any man who does not care to volunteer has my permission to withdraw without any change in his status. I am thinking especially about men with any dependents."

He knew none of them were married, with the exception of Mustafa. But no one moved. He had anticipated nothing less.

"Very good, and thank you. Now, as usual, I can give you no details of our destination or assignment, until we are on the spot. Training will continue as usual."

"Are we to replace Kippings, sir?" Le Boule aked.

"Yes. With Le Blanc."

Mustafa grinned happily.

"What about your girl?" Harry asked Simmons in the officers' mess later. "Did you ever get together with her?"

Simmons flushed. "We spent a weekend together."

"Great. But you volunteered."

"Well . . . it's not as if we were married or anything."

"But you're still hoping to?"

"Ah . . . no, sir, I don't think so."

Another man with an unsatisfactory love life, Harry thought.

"I don't suppose you speak Greek?" Harry asked Mustafa.

"Oh, yes. A few words, anyway." Mustafa grinned. "I

114

can buy you a drink, eh, in Greek. Is that where we go? Greece?"

"It's a big country," Harry said. "But . . . no talking."

"Oh, no," Mustafa said. "Not me."

"How are things with Yasmin?"

Mustafa shrugged. "She suspects nothing. She waits for the war to end, so that she can go back to Algiers, and find the man who murdered her sister."

"You do realise that she is almost certain to find out the truth, one day."

Mustafa gave one of his grins. "One day, perhaps. If that happens, we must decide what to do. You and me, together, Major."

Harry reflected that he was busily tying himself to the strangest people. He wondered if untying himself would ever be possible.

Meanwhile, operating blind as he was, he had to determine the equipment he might need. Which depended on exactly what he intended to do. Looked at in the best possible scenario, they would get ashore without mishap in the middle of the night, and Konikos would be waiting for them. He would know where they could hide during the next day, a time when his plan of the radar installation could be studied. The raid would be carried out the following night, and they would hope to be able to rendezvous with the submarine that same night and get away before the Germans could recover from the attack.

If they could not manage that, they were dead ducks, as outside assistance would certainly be called in by the defenders, unless they killed every man of the German garrison. Garrison troops, Bannon had said, with some contempt. But still professional soldiers.

But the only safe way to look at the operation was elimination. Fifty men! The saving clause was that they were bent on total destruction anyway.

He went along to see Jamie Ross, who was in charge of ordnance.

"I need to take out a radar installation, and its entire garrison," he said.

"How many?"

"Fifty."

"Piece of cake. How close can you get?"

"I mean to bust in, through a gate and then a few doors."

"Right. You need a bazooka. Perhaps two. They're fired from the shoulder so getting them about isn't too difficult. They're intended to knock-out tanks, so think what they'll do to a gates or doors. And the men manning them."

"Two," Harry said. "Can they be taken apart for transportation?"

"Ah, yes. But you will need to know how to put it back together again."

"You have a couple of days to train my squad," Harry told him. "What about the station itself."

"Will you be travelling far?"

"Yes."

"Not ideal for gelignite. But it's the best we can do."

"How much? We're talking about a concrete bunker."

"But you'll be blowing it from inside."

"That's the idea."

Ross nodded. "I'll work out the ratios and make you up a parcel. Just remember to keep it dry. Grenades?"

"I reckon. As a back-up to the bazookas."

Ross grinned. "I'd try to keep them dry, too."

They would also carry their normal equipment of tommy-guns, knives and automatic pistols. With the advantage of surprise, Harry thought it could be done. But at odds of six to one surprise was a vital factor.

"Looks impressive," Belinda remarked, surveying the list in her flat later. "You're off on Friday."

Harry nodded.

"So don't tell me, you need to get back down to spend the last couple of days with your squad."

"Only the last night matters."

She raised her eyebrows.

"I have a feeling there may not be too many last nights after this one," he explained.

"Oh, Harry," she said. "Harry, Harry, Harry."

He had almost come to regard her flat as a second home.

"I wouldn't like you to suppose I'm losing my nerve," he said, not really sure whether or not he was telling the truth.

"Not you, Harry."

"It's just that . . . I've been goddamned lucky so far."

"You reckon?" She got out of bed to make them each a drink.

"You've been seriously wounded twice, for God's sake."

He watched her naked body floating around the flat. Oh, to be able just to lie here, and watch that, for the rest of his life.

"And in return, I've done some pretty God-awful things."

"You've been killing the enemy. You're fighting a war, very successfully."

"Killing the enemy," he repeated. "How close are you to Bannon?"

She sat on the bed beside him, gave him his drink, sipped her own. "You have nothing to worry about there. He is devoted to his wife."

"I meant work-wise."

"Well, I'm his secretary. I know what's going on."

"Has he mentioned Mrs Le Blanc to you?"

"He's had a detective assigned to keep an eye on her. As you recommended, right? Do you think she's a security risk?"

"After a fashion."

"Then how can you contemplate taking her husband with you on this mission?"

"To keep him out of trouble. The fact is, you see, he and I killed her sister."

"You did what?"

"It was a pre-emptive execution. She was threatening to betray us if we didn't play her way. We couldn't be sure she wasn't going to do it anyway, even if only by carelessness. And that could have ruined the entire Torch concept, or at least involved the Americans in a full-scale war to get ashore. Having regard to their showing since getting ashore, virtually unopposed, they might still be on the beaches, and we'd have the biggest fuck-up in history."

Belinda blew through her teeth. "So you executed this woman. You?"

"No. Mustafa actually did it. But I was there. I had to be there."

"I can understand that." She clasped both hands to her throat. "I can also understand why you trust Mustafa so much. And his wife doesn't know who did it?"

"Not yet. But she seems to be dedicating her life to finding out . . . and dealing with the culprit in her own fashion."

"Shit," she commented. "But you say you didn't actually kill this sister?"

"I was there. I ordered the execution."

"Shit," Belinda remarked again. "Can't you, well, have her locked up?"

"Bannon suggested that, but we'd have a bit of a problem. She hasn't committed any crime."

"Neither had her sister," Belinda commented.

They gazed at each other.

"I'm not sure you want to get involved," Harry said. "It's just that . . . it's a weight."

"Absolutely."

"Promise me you won't do anything stupid."

"My business is back-up for you fellows," she said. "Whatever needs to be done . . ."

"Listen," he said. "Will you marry me?"

"Listen," she said in turn.

"I'm serious," he said.

"Knowing my lifestyle and all?"

"Knowing *my* lifestyle and all."

"And Jonathan?"

"Is that his name? You never told me. All right, get your divorce through. You seem able to do everything else."

"I do believe you're serious."

"Never more so. When I get back from this mission I intend to get hitched."

"Period."

"To you. I love you, you silly cow."

"You love the idea," she said. "But . . . we'll see what can be done. Just remember to come back."

The Island

This time their journey was far better organised, and they were in Alexandria the day after leaving England. Major Ash was on the tarmac to greet them.

"Not the same lot," he commented. "I do hope you'll keep them in line this time, Curtis."

"When do we embark?" Harry asked.

"I believe tomorrow morning."

Harry confined his men to barracks. They had all been engaged in routine training for the month previous to receiving their decorations, and had had sufficient leave to feel satisfied with themselves.

This also gave Harry the opportunity to tell them what they were going to attempt. The additional training they had been required to do with the bazookas, assembling the rocket-launchers and dismantling them, as well as firing them, had them all in a state of some anticipation. Harry had himself, with Simmons – just in case – take the explosives course. He would have loved to have his old friend and explosives expert Jon Ebury along, but Ebury was on other duties.

"It's very simple, really," he told the squad. "The navy will put us ashore, we will contact Mr Konikos, we will destroy the radar station, and the navy will bring us back here. Any questions?"

"What are the odds, sir?" Nichols asked.

"Approximately six to one," Harry said. "But we will have the advantage of complete surprise."

"And help from the locals?"

"I don't think we can count on any of that," Harry said. "Apart from Konikos, and his help will have to be secret. The locals have nowhere to go when the Germans come in to pick up the pieces. Do you know this island, Mustafa?"

The Algerian shook his head. "I have not been there."

"Right. We will have to place our trust in Konikos. However, Mustafa, you say you have some knowledge of Greek."

"Oh, yes," Mustafa said.

"So you'll listen to everything not said in English, and let us know if it's anything you don't like."

Mustafa fingered his knife. "I will deal with it."

"Not without reference to me," Harry told him.

That evening Harry was summoned to a conference with Brigadier Linton, the local co-ordinator, and Lieutenant-Commander Grayson, who was captain of *HMS Shellfish*, the carrier.

"As you probably know, Major," the Brigadier said, "we have been operating agents, and indeed, Commando units, in the Aegean for the past year. The success rate is high enough to justify their continuation, but the element of risk is also very high, and equally for the agents. Now Konikos, I'm afraid, is something of an unknown quantity, as we have not operated on Spetsos before – it simply is not big enough to maintain any permanent force. However, its small size makes it the more susceptible to a hit and run raid such as the one you are going to carry out. Commander Grayson knows the waters and this island very well. He it was, after suitable recommendation by the Greek government in exile, who made our first contact with Konikos. Commander?"

"I only met him once," Grayson said. "That was when we took him his radio equipment. He seemed very enthusiastic. Since then, we've been in contact several times, but of course these contacts have had to be very limited in time because of German monitoring."

"We have thus set up a series of two or three letter code signals," the Brigadier said. "Konikos knows we intend to put a

Commando force ashore on Spetsos in the immediate future, and is awaiting our signal that the operation is on its way. He does not know the purpose of the raid."

"If the radar installation is the only German position on the island, he'd have to be a bit dim not to have worked out what we're after," Harry said.

"Oh, he knows," Linton said. "But the important thing is that we haven't told him, yet."

"And there's no doubt he is going to co-operate?"

"As far as he can."

"Knowing that there will almost certainly be reprisals?"

"He would hope to convince the Germans that he, and everyone else on the island, knew nothing about the raid. That is why you must not expose him in any way."

Harry nodded. "Point taken. Well, sir, hopefully we'll be back in a couple of days."

"Hopefully," the Brigadier agreed.

"First time I've ever travelled by submarine," Simmons confessed, as they climbed down the ladder from the conning tower into the bowels of the ship.

"Join the club," Harry said, bumping his head on an overhead pipe.

"Bit cramped, I'm afraid," said the captain, who was waiting to greet them. "We'll make you as comfortable as we can." Grayson watched in some alarm as the gear was brought on board. "Is that gelignite?"

"I'm afraid it is," Harry said. "They couldn't think of anything else for us to use."

"As long as it doesn't go off on board my ship," the Commander quipped.

"How long?" Harry asked.

"We'll be off Spetsos tomorrow night," Grayson said. "We'll send the signal tonight, when we surface."

"Is that safe?"

"Oh, yes. The Germans don't have enough aircraft to mount

more than occasional patrols. As soon as that gear is properly stowed, we'll be away."

Harry was invited on to the conning tower as the submarine eased away from the dock and out through the myriad jetties towards the open sea. He had, of course, been to sea with the navy before, both to Lofoten in the very first major Commando raid, back in 1941, and then to St Nazaire. He had the highest respect for it and its sailors, and always marvelled at the extreme precision with which all duties were carried out. Such precision was even more important on a submarine than a destroyer, and he felt very much a supernumary as the sailors and their officers went about their duties.

"Dive," Grayson said into his intercom.

The land was fading behind them, and in response to the command the hull began to slip beneath the calm sea. Harry found it fascinating, and had to be tapped on the shoulder by his host.

"Time to go below, old man," Grayson said.

His men had been found berths in the crew's quarters, and were mostly lying down. There was not much else to do, as the electric motors hummed and all other sound was lost. Simmons was in the tiny wardroom, pretending to read a novel. He seemed relieved to be joined by his CO.

"Everything going according to plan, sir?"

"It would appear so," Harry said.

"What do we do with the next thirty-six hours?"

"Eat and sleep," Harry suggested.

That night they surfaced, as Grayson had promised, and Harry requested permission for his men to come up in relays and get some fresh air. Unlike the submariners they were not used to being cooped up short of air for long periods, and he needed them to be fighting fit when they got ashore. Grayson readily agreed. But the real reason for surfacing, apart from recharging the batteries and allowing air into the hull, was to contact Konikos.

The procedure was very simple. The submariner's telegrapher sent just three letters, CIC. And again and again.

"What do we get back?" Harry asked.

"CO," Grayson said.

They stood above the set and waited. The telegrapher repeated the signal, and again.

"He must be out on the town," Harry suggested.

"He's not supposed to be," Grayson grumbled.

The set clicked.

"CO, sir," the telegrapher said.

"Thank God for that," the commander said.

"Just what have we achieved?" Harry asked.

"The program is for us to signal him the night before you are put ashore. His reply was an affirmative that he will be in position. We can't use more than very brief signals because the German radio station in Athens is monitoring all wavelengths all the time."

"Then they'll have picked up that signal."

"Absolutely. But there's not a lot they can do with it. As we sent several times, they may be able to locate us, but we are obviously a ship at sea, and we're not going to be here if they send a search aircraft to this area. While Konikos was on the air for hardly more than a split second. They won't have had time to trace that."

"Sounds foolproof," Harry agreed. "Save that you told me that Konikos has been in touch with us quite regularly."

"Always for very brief periods," Grayson said. "And he's still about. They haven't traced him yet."

Another submerged, stale-air day followed. But the squad was conditioned to patience after their experience in Ghardaia. And at last it was again dark.

"I cannot stay on the surface for more than a few seconds," Grayson told Harry. "We're right under the nose of that bloody big radar set. So have your people standing by."

Harry nodded, and got his men together, everyone loaded with the requisite gear. The submarine surfaced, and they scrambled up the ladder to the conning tower, and then down the outside ladder to the still wet deck, where several ratings were already launching the two inflatable dinghies.

"Keep close," Harry told Simmons, who was in the second

boat, together with Le Boule, Rhodes and Nichols. Harry had Evans, Graham and Mustafa with him.

Grayson shook hands. "I'll wish you good fortune. When do I see you again?"

"I'm thinking of tomorrow night," Harry said.

"We'll be here."

The boats were cast off, and Harry gazed at the darker darkness of the island, perhaps a quarter of a mile away. There were lights, some quite bright to the left – he reckoned that was the radar station – and a larger general glow to the east, which was the village. He reckoned there was no anticipation of an attack, from any direction. There was no blackout.

As they could not risk the noise of outboard motors, it was necessary to paddle to the shore. This was entirely dark between the two sets of lights, but now a light flashed, and again, which gave them something to aim at.

"Would there be a reef?" Harry asked Mustafa.

"Perhaps. But they will have the passage marked," Mustafa said.

Harry deduced that, while Mustafa might never have visited Spetsos before, he had visited several of these islands, clandestinely, pre-war, almost certainly smuggling.

They dug their paddles into the still calm sea, and a few moments later were in the gentle surf of the beach. Harry looked over his shoulder, but the submarine had disappeared, although he had no doubt that Grayson was still watching them, at least through the periscope.

Now it was time to look ahead. The second boat was immediately behind them. His boat was already in very shallow water. And on the beach in front of them there was a single dark figure.

"Wait for it," Harry said, and stepped out of the dinghy into knee-deep water. He waded ashore, his tommy-gun thrust forward, and checked as he saw the flutter of long dark hair. "Oh, shit," he commented.

"Sir?" asked the young woman, in English.

"I beg your pardon. I was expecting Mr Konikos."

"My father is sick," the girl said.

Shit, Harry thought again, even if this time he did not say it.

"I will take you to him," she said.

"I'd appreciate that." He waved his arm, and the Commandos came ashore, dragging their dinghies behind them. "We need to conceal these," he said.

"There are bushes over there," the girl said.

"And the Germans do not patrol the coast?"

She shrugged. "Sometimes. They will not look in the bushes. But you must try to smooth the sand."

There was no way they could do that properly, although they did their best. Harry was starting to feel lead balls in his stomach.

"You are in uniform," the girl said, having studied them.

"It seemed like a good idea," Harry said. "Are there Germans in the village?"

"Not at this time. But if people see you . . ."

"I thought your people were on our side."

"Some of them," she said, disturbingly. "Maybe they are all asleep. We go up there."

She pointed, and the Commandos humped their gear; they were all pretty heavily laden.

"It should be all right," she confided. "We live on the outskirts of the town."

She would have been an attractive young woman, Harry deduced in the gloom, her long, dark, curly hair surrounding regular features and a full figure, had he been in the mood to associate females with anything other than total disaster on missions like this.

"What is the matter with your father?" he asked.

"It is a stomach upset," she explained.

Which, he reckoned, was more often brought on by nerves than anything else.

"But he answered the radio signal," he suggested.

"I answered the radio signal," she said.

Alan Savage

"Ah. Forgive me, but am I to understand that you know what
we are here to do?"
"Yes."
"Ah," he said again. "May I ask how many there are in your
house?"
"My mother and my two brothers."
Jesus, he thought, shades of Algeria.
"And they all know?"
"My father has spoken of nothing else this past month."
"I see," he said. "So how many people outside of your family
know about it?"
"Oh, no one else," she asserted.
"I'm very glad to hear that."
But sarcasm was lost upon the girl, who now pointed. "The
village, you see."
In front of them were several lights.
"Looks pretty good, so far, sir," Simmons said at his elbow.
"Too good," Harry grunted.
"Now, listen," the girl said. "I will take you in the back of the
property, eh? There is a shed, and that is where you must stay
throughout the day. I will bring you food and drink."
"And your dad?"
"If he can move. Follow me, but very quietly."
The Commandos crept along a fence at the rear of the school-
master's house. This was two-storeyed, and looked solidly built.
There were no lights. They came to a gate, and she opened this.
Immediately a dog barked.
"Down Petros," she said.
The bark became a gurgle, and a moment later they saw the
animal, which was large and of indeterminate breed.
"You have him well trained," Harry suggested, optimistically.
"I will cut his throat," Mustafa offered.
"You will not touch him," the girl said sharply. "In here."
She opened the door, and switched on her flashlight. The
Commandos filed into the shed, which was not very large. It
was used as a storeroom, and there were various gardening

128

appliances on the walls, as well as a mound of high-smelling compost.

Simmons wrinkled his nose. "We have to spend the entire day here?"

"No one must know you are here," the girl said.

"Except you, and your father, and . . . by the way, do you have a name?" Harry asked.

"My name is Zoe. My mother knows you are here, and my brothers. Nobody else. They will not betray you."

"I'm glad of that. Let's have a look at you."

She shone the flashlight on to her face. She had fine features and lustrous dark eyes to go with her long curly hair.

"Just so I recognise you when next I see you," Harry said. "Your father was to provide us with a plan of where we are going."

"The radar station," Zoe said. "Yes, he has such a plan. He will wish to show it to you himself. As soon as he is able."

"We wish to move tonight."

She nodded. "He will be here before then. Now I will leave you. I will bring breakfast at dawn." She went to the door, flicked her fingers, and the dog followed her up the path to the back of the house.

"Bit of all right, that one," Nichols commented.

"I think it would be a good idea to look and not touch," Harry told them. "If she were to take umbrage, we'd be up the creek."

"There's no toilet," Simmons said, having been looking around. "And we're not supposed to go outside."

"Use the compost heap," Harry told him. "It can't possibly smell any worse than it does now."

Another long day stretched ahead. The Commandos slept as best they could until dawn, when Zoe returned with bread and jam and coffee. In daylight she was a most attractive young woman.

"My father will come this morning," she said. "He has the plan."

"How is he?" Harry asked.

"Not good. It must be something he ate."

"Yes," Harry said sceptically, and stood in the doorway, while the dog Petros gazed at him, unwinkingly. "Looks pretty clear. Do you have a forecast?"

She shook her head. "But it will be a good day."

"So, the sooner your dad can come down the better. Can't he send the plan with you?"

"He wishes to discuss it with you. I must go into the village, anyway. I will be back to bring you lunch."

Harry watched her walk away. There was no sign of life from the house, but now he could hear the distant sounds of the village waking up.

They spent the morning cleaning their weapons and assembling the bazookas. There was no possibility of washing and shaving. But to Harry's great relief, Konikos appeared just before noon. There was a single window in the shed, and although this was both shut and grimy, they could keep a watch on the back yard between them and the house. It was Evans who warned them of a man approaching.

Harry joined the Welshman at the window. He had no idea what Konikos looked like, but this tall, thin man bore a resemblance to Zoe. The schoolmaster came right up to the door, and brushed his knuckles against it. "Let him in," Harry said.

Simmons opened the door, and Konikos came in, looking around himself in the gloom at the men with whom he was surrounded. They were a pretty desperate looking lot, Harry knew, with their unshaven chins and festooned with weapons. "I am Paul Konikos," Konikos said. His voice trembled, as did his body. His face was certainly pale. This could have been a result of the stomach upset, or it could have been sheer fright.

Harry stepped forward. "Harry Curtis."

"You are in command?"

As always, Harry wore exactly the same uniform as his men, without any insignia.

"I am in command, yes," Harry said.

"And my daughter has looked after you?"

"Very well," Harry said. "Have you the plan of the radar installation?"

"Here." Konikos took the folded paper from his pocket, knelt, and spread it on the floor. The Commandos crowded round.

"This road," Harry said. "It is not on my map."

"It was built by the Germans, last year, to connect the harbour and station."

"Right. Gate," Harry said. "How many sentries?"

"Usually two. But they are in constant communication with the main building."

"Right. Open courtyard . . ." He studied the scale. "Fifty yards. Main building. Steel door. Right. Corridor to the left and the installation chamber. Always manned?"

"Always. Six men."

"Right. Corridor to the right leads to living quarters. Kitchens, mess hall, latrines, barracks . . . officers' quarters?"

"To the left."

"How many?"

"A major and two lieutenants. But one is always on duty in the chamber."

"I'm told there is a total establishment of fifty men. Is that correct?"

"That is correct, on paper. At the present time there are four men sick."

"Where?"

"They are in hospital here in town. It is not serious."

"So, two on the gate, six in the chamber, four in hospital, that leaves thirty-eight in the barracks."

"No," Konikos said. "There is always a patrol on the cliffs overlooking the installation."

These were very roughly drawn in.

"How high?"

"Four hundred feet."

"Looks a pretty good set up," Simmons suggested. "If you happen to be a German."

"Yes," Harry said thoughtfully. "It's going to have to be a

131

frontal assault, as in Algiers. We blow the gate with the bazookas, knowing that the alarm will be given. We must therefore assume that the steel doors will be automatically closed. These too we will blow with the bazookas. Once inside, Le Boule, you and I with you, Evans, will take the chamber. We will waste the duty squad and place the gelignite on a short fuse. We will then withdraw. Simmons, you and the remainder of the squad will open fire with the bazookas and your small arms on the doors to the living quarters. You will keep blasting those until we rejoin you – that should be a matter of ten minutes. The charges will then blow and we will evacuate. We should be able to pin them down long enough to enable us to withdraw, and they will in any event be distracted by the explosion and the ruination of their station. Then we regain the beach and signal *Shellfish*. Any questions?"

"They'll come after us," Simmons suggested.

"They won't, if we do our job well enough. With your firepower, you should be able to cut that garrison in half, certainly if they are sufficiently surprised to expose themselves. The bazookas will just about bring the interior of the building down. With that amount of damage, and that number of casualties, added to the destruction of the installation, I reckon it will be a couple of hours, maybe more, before they have recovered sufficiently to mount any kind of a pursuit, especially as they won't know our strength or dispositions. A couple of hours is all we need."

Konikos was looking distinctly agitated. "Will you need me, sir?"

"No, no," Harry said. "When we leave here, you forget all about us."

"Ah. Yes, that is good. I must return to the house, now. I feel sick."

He certainly looked sick.

"Thanks for everything. I will keep the plan," Harry said.

"Of course. Zoe will bring you lunch when she returns from the village."

He stood up, turned to the door, and checked. Harry had heard the noise also, that of at least one motor car close at hand.

"Is there a road near here?" he asked.

"No. Those cars are in my front yard."

"Shit!" Le Boule muttered.

"Well, you get out of here and send them away," Harry told the schoolmaster.

Konikos was trembling even more, and he was staggering as he went down the path.

"How the hell . . .?" Simmons asked.

"We have been betrayed," Le Boule growled with Gallic gloom.

"But who?" Simmons asked.

"The girl," Nichols suggested.

There did not seem to be anyone else, Harry reflected, however much he didn't want to believe it. But the identity of their betrayer would have to be sorted out later, if there was going to be a later; the car engines had stopped, and he could hear the tramp of booted feet, while now a woman screamed. Would that be Zoe, or her mother, he wondered?

The dog was barking, and there was a shot.

"Shit!" Le Boule said again.

It was time to make a very quick and accurate decision. But it was also a very difficult one. The Germans obviously knew they were there. Did they know how many? They would also know why they were there, because there could only be one reason. They would have to be hoodwinked, and that was going to cost lives. Whose? It would have to be his, and one other.

"I need a volunteer," he said.

The entire squad stood to attention.

"Right," he said. "Lieutenant Simmons, you will take command. I'm afraid you're reduced to six men. We have to make this convincing. But you will take the gelignite and the bazookas. Hurry now. Get out of here and make for the hills. Lie low until tonight, and then carry out the assault. Follow the plan I outlined."

Simmons gulped. "While you do what, sir?"

133

"I will hold the fort, with—"

"Permission to stay, sir," Le Boule said.

Harry shook his head. "Lieutenant Simmons will need you."

"I will stay," Mustafa said.

Harry hesitated. But Mustafa was the obvious choice; he had no Commando training, no knowledge of explosives or close combat. And they shared a dreadful secret.

"But, if you stay—" Simmons protested.

"It will be to let you get on with the job," Harry said. "Clear off."

Le Boule and the remainder of the squad were already loading up with as much ammunition as they could carry. Nichols and Rhodes had the bazookas in their arms.

"Well, sir," Simmons said.

"Carry out the plan," Harry said. "Don't let me down, Lieutenant."

"I won't, sir."

"Will they get away?" Mustafa asked.

"We have to hope so," Harry stood at the window, watching the house. There was as yet no sign of any Germans, but there could be no doubt that they were there.

"What's the plan? Do we shoot it out?"

"Only for a few minutes. We need to convince them that we're desperate, but also we need to convince them that it's just us, and that means we have to be taken alive."

Mustafa swallowed. "That will mean—"

"Yes," Harry said. "That we will be interrogated. But these are regular troops. It won't be so bad." He hoped.

He found the absence of any movement on the part of the Germans disconcerting. But then there came another scream from inside the house.

Suddenly it occurred to him that something was wrong, or grotesquely right. The Germans *didn't* know they were in the shed. They couldn't, or they would have moved down here long ago.

He wondered if he and Mustafa had the time to get out – but of course they couldn't do that: their business was to make sure the Germans did not go after the main body. In any event it was too late – men were appearing behind the house, armed with tommy-guns.

Mustafa stroked his own gun; it was his pride and joy. "Do we fire into them?"

"No," Harry said. "Change of plan."

Mustafa looked puzzled, but he held his fire.

"You in there!" someone shouted in English. "We know you are there. Come out with your hands up, or we will fire into you."

"Let's go," Harry said.

"You mean we just surrender? To have our balls burned? You said we'd shoot it out."

"Only to give the others time to get away. They've done that now," Harry told him. "Now we co-operate. Remember, there is just you and me. We have come ashore to reconnoitre with a view to launching a raid on the radar installation at some time in the future. Just that."

Mustafa swallowed.

"You have ten seconds," the voice called.

Harry laid his tommy-gun on the ground, and Mustafa did likewise.

"Don't shoot!" Harry shouted. "We are coming out."

He drew a deep breath, pushed the door open, and stepped into the sunlight, arms held high. Mustafa followed.

"And the others," the voice said.

"There are no others," Harry said.

This was the crunch. If the Konikos family had given a number . . .

The Germans advanced, some twenty of them, weapons levelled. The officer came right up to Harry and peered at him, then waved to his men, who also came closer. Two of them went into the shed and looked around.

"There are weapons here, Herr Hauptmann," one of these said.

Harry spoke German fluently.

135

"For how many men?"

"I would say two, Herr Hauptmann."

Once again the captain peered at Harry. "Two men?"

"We are a reconnaissance party," Harry explained.

"We shall see," the captain said. "Take off those pistols."

Harry and Mustafa obeyed.

"Now come."

He gestured at the house, and Harry and Mustafa went up to it. More soldiers waited at the back door, and these held it open for the prisoners to enter the kitchen. They were gestured through into a comfortably furnished lounge, where the Konikos family was gathered. Mrs Konikos was a middle-aged woman with a dignified face which had dissolved into tears. Harry reckoned she was the one who had done the screaming. Her two sons, young teenagers, were standing together, shoulders touching, looking equally frightened. They all appeared unhurt. But Konikos was slumped in a chair, his face bruised and bleeding where he had been hit several times.

To Harry's relief, there was no sign of Zoe. But to his concern, there was another man in the room, and this man wore the dark coat and slouch hat of a Gestapo agent.

"So," he now remarked, in English. "The boy was telling the truth."

"I am sorry, Major," Konikos mumbled. "I would not have told them."

"I told them," one of the boys said. "I could not allow Papa to be beaten."

Harry wished he could ask the boy just what he had told them.

"A major," the Gestapo agent remarked. "What a good day we are having, eh, Erlich?"

The captain had followed them into the room.

"A day of good fortune, Herr Meissinger," Erlich agreed.

"You will tell me who and what you are," Meissinger said to Harry.

"My name is Henry Curtis, I am a major in the British army, and I was born 2nd August 1921."

"Very good. Your outfit?"

"I am not obliged to tell you that."

"You English, and your rules of war," Meissinger said contemptuously. "I know that uniform, Major Curtis. You are an officer in the Commandos. That means that you have no rights. I have the right to shoot you now, for what you are, a murdering dog."

"Because your *fuehrer* says so," Harry agreed. "What you want to remember, old son, is that your *fuehrer* isn't going to be calling the shots very much longer. Then you will have to answer one or two questions of your own."

Meissinger glared at him, then turned to Mustafa. "And you?"

"Mustafa Le Blanc. I am a soldier with the Free French. I was born 3rd January 1915."

"You are also wearing the uniform of a Commando."

"I am seconded," Mustafa said proudly.

"Then you too will be shot."

Mustafa gulped.

"Now tell me what you are doing in Spetsos," Meissinger said.

"I have told your captain," Harry said. "We were put ashore here to reconnoitre the radar installation, with a view to a raid being launched in the near future."

Meissinger studied him for several seconds. "What is so important about the radar installation?"

"Well," Harry said. "If it were to be operational when we decided to move into these islands . . ."

"This is what you intend?"

"It's a strong possibility."

"I see. How were you put ashore?"

"I am not obliged to tell you that."

"Obviously it was by submarine, Herr Meissinger," Erlich said.

"Obviously. And when is this submarine coming back for you?"

"I am not obliged to tell you that either," Harry said.

"You will, you know," Meissinger said. "Now tell me what

you were doing in Konikos' garden shed. This was arranged by
radio, eh?"

Konikos rolled his eyes in desperation.

"Sheer chance, old man," Harry said. "We needed somewhere
to hide, and this shed was very convenient. On the edge of town,
you see."

"You are lying," Meissinger said. "Why do you suppose we
are here at all, Major? We have been monitoring radio calls from
this island for some time, and have at last succeeded in pin-
pointing their source. This house. It stands to reason that these
calls, which have been in code, have been to your people either in
Alexandria or at sea, and that it was Konikos who set up this
reconnaissance, as you claim it is. Why do you not admit this?"

"Well . . ." Harry checked, as there was a noise from outside.
A moment later the front door was opened and two soldiers
thrust Zoe in.

She stared around her with her mouth open, and muttered
something in Greek as the bag of food she was carrying dropped
to the floor.

"Well, well," Meissinger remarked. "What a pleasant surprise.
I presume you speak English, Fraulein?"

Zoe licked her lips, and glanced from her bruised father, to her
mother, and then to Harry and Mustafa.

"I also presume you know these gentlemen," Meissinger said.

Another quick flick of the tongue. She was trying to decide
how much might already have been given away.

"I don't blame you for being surprised, Miss . . . Konikos, is
it?" Harry said. "I am trying to make this gentleman understand
that my colleague and I, having landed here unknown to anyone
on the island, took shelter in your father's garden shed, where we
were unfortunately discovered. It seems entirely by chance."

"You are a fool," Meissinger said. "Do you suppose you can
hoodwink me? You land on this island, and purely by chance you
take shelter in the house of a man who possesses an illegal radio
transmitter? And this business of being a reconnaissance party.
You British have been raiding these islands for months, but never

before have you used a reconnaissance party beforehand. You have relied on the support and the information from the local inhabitants. Like these people."

"I assure you that you are mistaken," Harry said.

"Bah! We will soon find out the truth." His gaze swept the assembled people, but predictably came to rest on Zoe. "A pretty girl," he remarked. "It is always a pleasure to question a pretty girl. Strip the bitch."

"I must protest, sir," Erlich said.

"What about?"

"Well . . . we are supposed to be officers and gentlemen."

Meissinger pointed. "You may be an officer and a gentleman, Erlich. I am a representative of the Reich that is trying to win a war. Let me remind you again. These two men are Commandos, and by orders from the *Fuehrer* are to be shot on sight. I will let you attend to that later. These people are guilty of aiding the enemy – that carries the death penalty. They have absolutely no rights. Now, if you have not the stomach for the seamy side of our business, you may leave the room."

Erlich stared at him for several seconds, face crimson, then saluted and left the room. That left five soldiers, as well as Meissinger. But the soldiers all carried tommy-guns. Three of these were levelled into the room at the people, the other two had been slung as two men started to manhandle Zoe. But as everyone else was unarmed, the odds were simply too long, Harry reckoned. They would all be cut down in a matter of seconds.

He glanced at Mustafa, whose face was working, in a mixture, Harry supposed, of anger and fear. The little man had half-turned, so that his back was to the wall, no doubt the better to see what was happening to Zoe.

She gave a little shriek as her blouse was torn from her shoulders, while her skirt was dropped past her thighs. Her family stared at her with quivering expressions, but they too could think of nothing to do that would not result in all of their instant deaths.

Zoe's drawers were pulled down to her ankles. She made an

abortive attempt to cover herself but her arms were gripped by one of the soldiers while the other pulled the drawers right off.

They looked at Meissinger.

"Put her in that chair." He pointed at a straight chair by the window, close to where Mustafa was standing.

Zoe was made to sit, facing them. She was panting now, her breath coming in great gasps while tears rolled down her cheeks.

"Bind her," Meissinger said. "Use the table cloth."

The tablecloth, richly embroidered and obviously a family heirloom, was torn into strips, and used to bind Zoe's arms behind her back, and then her ankles to an upright each.

"What an attractive sight," Meissinger remarked. "Now, Major, and you, Herr Konikos, I do not intend to waste any time. I wish to know, firstly, how you two Englanders got here, and how you propose to leave. And I wish to know why you are here. Please, do not give me any more rubbish about a reconnaissance. Are you going to tell me these things?"

Konikos licked his lips. Harry kept his face impassive, while his brain raced, but only round in circles. Mrs Konikos burst into tears. The two boys also looked close to tears. Zoe continued to pant.

"Very good," Meissinger said. He grasped Zoe's right breast, and she gave a gasp of pain and embarrassment. "I am going to cut this off. And then the other one."

"Please," Konikos begged.

"Yes?"

Harry stared at the schoolmaster, whose entire face was trembling.

"Very good," Meisinger said again. "Hans, go into the kitchen and bring me back a large knife. It does not have to be very sharp."

Hans clicked his heels and left the room. They were down to four. But still the odds were too heavy, for the two men who had stripped Zoe and tied her up had now unslung their guns.

"Please," Konikos said again. "You must forgive me, Major Curtis. I—"

He was about to tell all, including the presence on the island of Simmons and the other five members of the squad.

Harry sighed. "All right, Meissinger. You win. We are here to blow up your radar station."

"Two men? With what are you going to blow up the station?"

"Well, actually, there are twenty of us," Harry said. "The others are already in position. With their explosives. You should hear the bang any moment now."

Meissinger ran to the door. "Erlich!" he shouted. "Erlich! Take your men and get out to the radar station. It is about to be attacked."

"That cannot be possible," Erlich protested. He had been waiting in the kitchen.

"It is possible," Meissinger shouted. "The island is crawling with Commandos. Use your radio. Call Captain Meiten. Then get out there yourself."

Erlich appeared in the doorway for a moment, looking first of all at Zoe, then at Harry.

"I'm afraid it's true, Captain," Harry said.

Erlich swore under his breath and left the room, blowing his whistle.

"Well," Meissinger said. "That is very satisfactory."

The soldier named Hans had returned from the kitchen, carrying a large knife. His tommy-gun remained slung.

"Please, sir," Konikos said. "Will you now release my daughter?"

"No, no," Meissinger said. "She is going to amuse us. Let me have the knife, Hans."

Hans gave him the knife, and Meissinger tested the blade.

"Just about right," he commented. "Where do you think I should begin?" He held Zoe's nipple between thumb and forefinger, pulling it away from the breast. "I can remove this, for a start. And then the other one, eh?"

Zoe screamed, a wailing, high-pitched sound.

"Oh, you will have to do better than that."

There was a groan, and Mrs Konikos slipped from her chair and struck the floor with a thud.

"Mama!" shrieked one of her sons, dropping to his knees beside her.

"You have killed my wife," Konikos shouted.

"Nonesense," Meissinger said. "She has only fainted. Hans, some water to pour on that woman. I am going to kill her, Konikos, but slowly. When I have finished with your daughter."

He grasped Zoe's breast again. Hans had again left the room. As Meissinger raised the knife, and Zoe gave another shriek of the purest terror, Mustafa stepped forward, in his hand his knife which had been concealed in the back of his pants, its existence not even suspected by the Germans, and drove the blade into Meissinger's back.

The Assault

M eissinger gave a shriek every bit as loud as Zoe's, and
would have fallen had Mustafa not grasped his shoulders
to hold him up. This confounded the watching soldiers, unsure
how badly the Gestapo officer was hurt, but knowing, from both
in front and behind, that if they fired into Mustafa they would
certainly hit his victim.

For the moment everyone in the room was distracted. Harry
clasped his hands together and swung them with all his force into
the nearest soldier's face. The man grunted, and before he could
recover, Harry had snatched his tommy-gun, dropping to his
knee as he did so, and opening fire. His first shots tore across the
room into the men behind Zoe. Both fell. Then he had swung
back and loosed another burst into the third man, some distance
away. He shrieked and fell backwards, arms flung wide. Harry
used his gun butt to stun the man from whom he had taken the
weapon.

Mustafa now released Meissinger, who slumped to the floor;
Mustafa's battledress tunic was thick with blood. But he was
already round Zoe and picking up the tommy-gun dropped by
the soldier. Just in time, as the door burst open and three men ran
in. But with both Mustafa and Harry firing as the door swung in,
all three were dead on the floor before they had had time to
realise what was happening.

"Mustafa," Harry said. "You are a bloody one-man army."

"We make a good team, eh?"

"Right. Cut that girl loose."

He went to the door, looked out. Erlich had departed, with the

143

motor cars and however many of the men had remained. There were only the eight dead men in the house, and the soldier who had been stunned, but was now sitting up and rubbing his head – his helmet had come off. Mustafa killed him with a single shot, while the Greeks gasped in horror. They had saved their lives, and those of the Konikos, thanks to Mustafa's knife and both of their killing instincts, Harry thought, but there was still a lot to be done if he was going to succeed in his mission. A lot he needed to know.

He stepped back inside. Zoe was regaining such of her torn clothing as she could. Konikos knelt beside his wife, fanning her face. There was blood everywhere. The two boys were huddled against the wall. And Mustafa was carefully cleaning his knife.

Harry looked from face to face: the Greeks were still in a state of shock. "Listen," he said. "I have to know how these people got here."

"They came by a fast patrol boat," Zoe said. She was recovering far faster than her family. "I was in town when it came in, but they moved so quickly I had no time to get back here before them. There were the cars waiting for them, you see, sent from the station. They knew they were coming."

"Because they had tracked down your father's radio signals. And you mean there is a German naval vessel in the harbour?"

She shook her head. "It left immediately, to go on to the other islands. This must be part of a general sweep. It has happened before."

"But it'll be coming back to pick Meissinger up," Harry said thoughtfully. "Would you have any idea when?"

"It usually does not return until the next day," she said.

"There's a bonus. And where would Meissinger, Erlich and their people spend the night, all things being normal?"

"They would sleep at the station."

"Ah. So, after they had finished here, they would go out there. Save that Erlich took both cars. That means someone is liable to return, from the station to pick them up when the initial panic out there dies down."

"What do we do, Major?" Mustafa asked.

144

"We try to link up with Lieutenant Simmons."

"You are still meaning to attack the radar station?"

"That's why we're here, old son."

"But now they know we are coming."

"I never pretended it was going to be easy," Harry pointed out. "Mr Konikos, I imagine the sound of all that shooting has been heard in the town. Will the people come up here to see what happened?"

"Not for a while," Konikos said. "They will be too afraid."

"Right. Now as I see it, you have no option but to get out." He had no idea what Grayson was going to say if he turned up with an extra five people, but he couldn't abandon them. "What you must do is pack up here – I'm afraid you can't take anything with you – and go down to the beach where we came ashore. Do this as soon as it is dark, and wait for us."

And if we don't make it? he wondered. But this whole raid was setting up to be a catastrophe anyway . . . like so many of the others.

"You wish us to leave Spetsos?" Konikos was aghast.

"You cannot stay."

"But . . . you can tie us up, and we will say we know nothing of what you are doing, that you burst in here and killed these people, and then left again."

"Mr Konikos, that simply will not work," Harry said earnestly. "For two reasons. One is that this house has been identified as containing a radio transmitter. That's a shooting offence anyway, isn't it?"

"I will get rid of the transmitter, and deny ever possessing one. They will not be able to prove otherwise."

Harry was tempted to point out that the Gestapo did not often require proof to execute those they suspected of anti-Nazi activities, but decided against it.

"And Erlich? He knows what happened here."

"Are you not going to kill him?"

"I hope to kill a whole lot of them. I can't guarantee that Erlich will be amongst them."

145

Konikos looked at his wife, and spoke in Greek. She replied, vociferously.

"We believe you will kill Erlich. This is our home," Konikos said. "We will stay. Our people will protect us."

"I hope you're right," Harry said. "But if that's your decision . . ." He helped Konikos lift the radio set from its hiding place in an upstairs room, and bury it in the garden. He couldn't believe the Germans wouldn't find it, but Konikos seemed confident enough. "I'm truly sorry to have brought this calamity on you," he told the schoolmaster. "But it will help us win the war." He could only hope he was right about that, too. "Now, we'll drag these bodies outside, so things won't be too unpleasant for you. Then we'll tie you all up. This will enhance your innocence of what was going on, and will also explain why you do not rush into town and raise the alarm the moment I leave. As I said, you can be pretty sure someone will be back from the station this afternoon, and he will release you. At which time you will tell him that you were caught between the two forces and are lucky to have escaped with your lives. Actually, you are. Let's get to it, Mustafa."

They dragged the bodies out of the back door and rolled them down the steps outside. "Now, Mustafa," Harry said, "collect up all the weaponry, and all the spare magazines as well."

Mustafa obeyed, humming to himself. He was having the time of his life. And Belinda, Harry recalled, had described *him* as a natural born killer.

Harry himself went down to the shed where he had seen some rope, and collected enough for what he needed. Then he returned to the house, where the rest of the Konikos family still appeared to be in a state of shock, except perhaps for Zoe, who was again fully dressed. "I'll try not to make it too uncomfortable for you," he said. "But obviously you must be sufficiently well tied up so that you would not be able to escape. Madame?"

Mrs Konikos had been restored to her chair. She was still weeping. Mustafa, having accumulated all the weapons and spare ammunition, started on the boys.

146

"Wait," Zoe said. Harry, bending over her mother, looked up. "I will come with you," she said.

Harry shook his head. "That is not on. We are going to fight a battle, in which we may all be killed."

"But you will kill Germans first."

"That's the general idea."

"I wish to kill Germans. They have humiliated me."

"Zoe," Harry said, with great patience. "All the Germans who have humiliated you are dead." He gestured at the bodies.

"I wish to come with you, and fight," she said fiercely.

Harry and Mustafa looked at each other. Was this to be a repeat of last November? But at least she had said she wanted to fight with them, rather than betray them.

She was watching their expressions. "They killed my dog," she said.

Which Harry reckoned was as compelling a reason as any: he'd certainly want to go after anyone who killed Jupiter.

"Anyway," she said. "You need me. I know the island. You do not. I can take you to the installation without anyone knowing."

"That would be a plus," Harry agreed. "But, young lady, please understand one thing. If you come with us, you are volunteering to be a soldier. That means you are under my command. You will do exactly what I tell you to, when I tell you to, and how I tell you to, without hesitation."

She tossed her head. "Or?"

"Disobedience in the face of the enemy ranks as mutiny, and that is punishable by death."

She glanced at Mustafa. Who grinned. "I am the executioner."

Harry would have supposed that was obvious.

"Stay with us," Konikos begged. "You will be killed."

"I will go with the major," she said.

They finished tying up the rest of the family, then Harry took Zoe outside.

"Have you ever fired a tommy-gun?" he asked.

Zoe shook her head.

147

He gave her one of the captured weapons. "You point it, and squeeze the trigger. Over there."

They were in the back yard. She raised the gun. The violence of the emission caused her to drop the gun.

"You need to hold it tighter than that," Harry said.

She picked it up. "Would I have hit anything?"

"If there was anything there, probably yes. You don't have to be Annie Oakley to shoot this thing."

"Who is Annie Oakley?"

"A female sharpshooter. With a tommy-gun, all you need to do is point in the general direction of your enemy. It doesn't have all that far a range, so you have to be up close, anyway. Now, here's how you change magazines." He showed her, then gave her a haversack with two spare drums. He and Mustafa were similarly equipped, and they also took a belt of grenades each.

"Food?" Mustafa asked.

"We'll stick to our iron rations and water bottles," Harry decided. "It's only going to be a couple of hours, anyway."

They retrieved their gear from the garden shed while Zoe changed her torn blouse and bade a tearful farewell to her family. She didn't say whether she was coming back, but Harry surmised that she had already abandoned them, at least in her mind. She also made up a bundle of food for herself, tied up her hair in a bandanna, and then slung her tommy-gun and haversack.

"I am ready."

"Right," Harry said. "First thing, where will the rest of my men be? I told them to go to ground until tonight."

"I would say in the wood."

"You have a wood?"

"There are two woods on the island. I was thinking of the one nearest the station."

"I think it's more likely to be the one nearest here. They'll be hoping to get some news about what happened to us. Is it far?"

"About a mile from here."

They moved cautiously across country. To their left now was the road, but this was deserted in the early afternoon heat haze.

Beyond that, to the south, as they topped a low rise, was the sea, sparkling blue. And somewhere under that sea was *Shellfish*, he hoped. To the north, but at some distance, were several more islands. Spetsos had been chosen for the site of the radar station because of its comparative isolation, looking to the south and west, from whence any possible allied move through the Aegean was to be expected.

The ground was stony, broken with little ravines, and studded with bushes, and at the top of the rise they looked down a slight valley before the next low ridge. Up there was a cluster of trees. Harry stroked his stubble. Anyone in those trees would not be able to see the road. Therefore it was extremely probable that Simmons had no idea Erlich and his men had driven along it. And he had no idea how many men Erlich actually had.

Mustafa touched his arm, and pointed. A flock of sheep was wandering slowly down the valley. The shepherd followed, moving even more slowly.

"Shit!" Harry muttered. It was obviously going to take several hours for the flock to disappear again.

"It is all right," Zoe said. "That is Buldros. I know him well."

"But he doesn't know us, at all."

"I will tell him it is all right. He will not betray us."

Harry looked at Mustafa and shrugged.

They stood up and made their way down the slope. Both shepherd and sheep regarded them with some astonishment.

Zoe spoke to the shepherd in Greek. He rolled his eyes, but seemed to understand what she was saying. Then Zoe waved her arm. "Let us go."

"Can you ask him if he has seen any other men dressed like us?"

Zoe asked the question, and listened intently to the answer.

"He says no. But he thinks there are people in the wood."

"How does he know that?"

"He saw the birds fluttering."

The oldest giveaway of all, Harry thought – something they had been taught to look out for in the training.

"Well, then," he said. "Thank the old boy, and we'll be on our way."

Zoe allowed the shepherd to embrace her – Harry wondered just how well she *did* know him – and then they passed through the sheep and climbed the slope towards the trees. They had almost reached them when the other Commandos emerged, weapons at the ready.

"Am I glad to see you, sir," Simmons said. "But how?"

"It's a long story," Harry said. "Let's take shelter."

They did so, and Rhodes brewed up some tea while Harry outlined what had happened.

Simmons gave a low whistle. "So it's off."

"Not on your nelly."

"But if they know we're coming . . ."

"Let's decide just what they do know. They know there is a Commando squad on the island, intending to attack the radar station. As it hasn't happened yet, as I told them it would, they'll assume we've decided to wait for darkness. They do not know the size of the squad – I gave them the impression that it was considerable. They do not know that Mustafa and I escaped, or that Meissinger and his people have been killed."

"They'll find out, when they send someone back into town."

"That won't be before this afternoon. Late this afternoon, I would say, when they have concluded there isn't going to be an attack in daylight. As far as they know Meissinger has everything under control, and their primary business is to defend the radar station. Then when they do discover he and his people are all dead, while they'll figure that I will have linked up with you, what are they going to do? To mount an island-wide hunt for us will weaken their forces, and they certainly won't want to be caught in relatively open country at night by a bunch of trigger-happy Commandos. My guess is that they are just going to sit tight and wait for the attack, at least until tomorrow."

"They'll have radioed for help," Le Boule said.

Harry nodded. "Not for defending the station, they'll be confident of doing that. But they'll want assistance to hunt down and destroy any of the Commando force that survives the assault. This assistance will have to be assembled, and then got here. As there is no airstrip, they will have to come by boat. A lot will depend upon how far they have to come, but I don't think they will get here before tomorrow either."

"What about the boat that brought the Gestapo?"

"It has left again. Apparently they're doing a sweep of several islands, picking up suspects. It isn't due to return here until tomorrow morning to pick Meissener up. By then we'll have done the job."

"How?" Simmons asked. "If they know we're coming?"

"We have two advantages they don't," Harry said. "They don't know how many we are. And they don't know we have the bazookas. What we need to do is mount a diversionary attack. I need two men to climb up that hill overlooking the station, and start hurling grenades and firing their tommys. This will certainly bring a reaction. Hopefully, Jerry will assume that is the attack he's expecting. Then the rest of us will carry out a frontal assault as planned."

"Save that the garrison will be out and about instead of tucked up in bed."

"So our medals may well be posthumous," Harry said. "We were given a job to do, and by God we're going to do it."

Simmons swallowed.

"So we'll make a fresh division of forces. Sergeant, I want you on the hillside. You'll have to get down as far as you can to make more of an impact. How far can you throw a grenade?"

"I can throw a hundred yards," Le Boule said proudly.

"Right. Then you must try to get within a hundred yards of the compound before starting. You'll have the young lady with you."

Le Boule looked at Zoe, somewhat doubtfully.

"All she has to do is hurl grenades and fire her tommy," Harry explained. "*She* doesn't have to be within range."

"Yes, sir."

"Will this kill Germans?" Zoe asked.

"Hopefully, lots and lots. Once the garrison is engaged on the ground, Sergeant, you will beat a retreat."

"To join you, sir?"

"If that is at all practical. If not, make for the beach. You will go to the beach anyway, Zoe, and signal the submarine."

"I would prefer to stay with you."

"Remember what I told you about obeying orders. Now for the rest of us. I'll take Mustafa as my back-up. As the garrison will be out and about, Lieutenant, you and the squad will have to lay down sufficient covering fire to allow the two of us to gain access to the building. With the bazookas and your tommys and grenades you should be able to make a bit of a mess while we get inside, lay the charges, and get back out again."

Simmons scratched his head. "You propose to cross an open yard with a bag full of gelignite, under fire?"

"Yes. If I am hit, the mission can be aborted and you will withdraw to the beach."

Another gulp.

"Right," Harry said. "We'll get going as soon as it's dark. You'd better get some sleep."

Harry didn't suppose many of them would. But he selected a soft-looking piece of ground and lay down with his helmet tilted over his eyes. In a few minutes Zoe had seated herself beside him.

"Are you asleep?" she asked.

"Not now," he pointed out.

"I am sorry to disturb you. I wished to ask you, are we going to die?"

"It's extremely probable."

"And you can lie there so calmly?"

"I'm trained for it. You can still get out, you know. Go home. No one will know you've been out here with us, save your family. And that shepherd. But you say he is a friend."

"I have known him since I was a little girl."

"Ah."

There was a brief silence. Harry closed his eyes again, felt her lie down beside him.

152

"Have you had many women?" she asked.

He opened his eyes. "One or two. Have you had many men?"

"I am a virgin."

"Ah."

"Do you think it is right for a woman to die a virgin?"

"Lots of them do."

"I would not like to have that happen to me."

He turned his head to look at her, pushing the helmet away.

"I would be most grateful," she said.

Holy shit, he thought. How do I get into these situations?

She rose on her elbow. "You have seen me naked. Do you not like me?"

"I think you are quite beautiful," he said. "But I am the commanding officer of these men."

"And you cannot have sex in front of them. We will go further into the wood."

He remembered that night in Ghardaia, when he had thought that he could not possibly have sex with a woman he might have to execute. This was a girl he was in all probability sending to her death.

But she had volunteered, both for the dying and now for the living. She wanted that, if only for a few moments. And did he not want it as well? Oh, how he wanted it. Because he was almost certainly going to his death.

Odd, he thought: he had never really felt that before. Even lying on the beach at Dunkirk, scared stiff as the German aircraft zoomed overhead, bombing and strafing, he had always felt it was the bloke next door who was going to be hit. At St Nazaire, when the Germans had opened up on the river with everything they had, and his launch had burst into flames, he had never doubted he would make the shore. But this time . . .

Zoe got to her feet. "Will you come with me?"

Harry got up as well. Presumably every man in the squad knew where he was going and what he was going to do, but no one moved or even turned a head. Being top gun did have some advantages, he reflected.

Zoe was a warm mixture of embarrassed eagerness. Obviously, what had happened at the house had affected her deeply. Harry felt that she was as much trying to exorcise the memory of Meissinger handling her like a side of beef as looking for a one-off experience. Either way, he supposed that if she were to survive the night, she was going to be in a fairly fouled-up state.

But that was looking too far ahead.

As for him, there could be no arguing that he wanted it. He was a sexually active man: the adrenalin pumping through his arteries, as was always the case just before going into action, had him wanting it desperately, and this adrenalin, because of the desperate nature of the enterprise, had been pumping now for several days.

He was afraid of hurting her, yet wanted to feel her, know her. She was an intensely attractive girl, with long, hard-muscled legs, tight buttocks, and those splendid, swelling breasts Meissinger had threatened. While she kissed him with an almost savage desperation, reached down to touch him, tentatively at first, and then with increasing vigour, until he supposed it was an even chance that she would hurt him before he could hurt her.

But then she moaned in a mixture of relief and discomfort, and a moment later he was spent.

"I hope you think it was worth it," he said, rolling off her to lie on his back.

"Oh, yes," she said. "Oh, yes."

"One day I'll be CO," Simmons remarked, as they ate their evening meal.

"It was what she wanted," Harry pointed out.

"Absolutely," the lieutenant said. "Are you fit for action?"

"More fit than ever before."

It was growing dark. They had already studied in detail the map of the island.

"How long will you need to be in position?" Harry asked Zoe.

She looked at le Boule, but there was no doubting the sergeant's fitness. "Two hours," she said.

They synchronised their watches.

"Then you leave here at twenty hundred. We'll give you an extra half-hour. You will commence action at twenty-two thirty."

"I do not understand these figures," she said.

"The sergeant will explain them to you. For the time being, they mean you will leave here at eight o'clock, and begin firing at ten thirty. Now, how long will it take us to get into position?"

"You do not have any hills to climb. An hour and a half."

"Right. So we will leave here at twenty forty-five, and be in position just after twenty-two hundred." He looked round the tense faces. "Any questions?"

He supposed everyone had several, but no one spoke.

By seven thirty – nineteen-thirty – it was utterly dark. There was no moon and sufficient cloud to minimise the stars. Harry always found that at times like this he seemed to be suspended in space. In only six hours he would, literally, be suspended in space, or he would be drinking coffee in the submarine's ward-room. For those six hours it was a matter of convincing himself that it didn't matter which – he could only pick up the pieces of his life again after he had taken that first sip of coffee.

He looked at his watch. "Time to go," he told Le Boule. "Good luck."

"And to you, sir." Le Boule slung his haversack, laden with munitions, and stood up.

Zoe stood also, gazing at Harry. For a moment he thought she was going to kiss him, then she too slung her haversack, picked up her tommy-gun, and followed the sergeant into the darkness.

"Do you think she can handle it?" Simmons asked.

"Right now, yes. She has a powerful hate at the moment." Harry drank the last of the coffee. "Get your gear together," he told his men.

He used his compass to lead them across country. It was slow going, and not only because they encountered the flock of sheep again – fortunately the shepherd seemed to have gone home to bed – but because in the darkness they found obstacles, such as the sudden ravines and even a pond of stagnant water they had not suspected to exist. They were also heavily laden, carrying as they were the two bazookas as well as their shells. But by nine-thirty they were had reached the road, and keeping well down beside it, they were in sight of the gate just before ten.

This was the first glimpse Harry had had of their target, and it certainly looked immensely strong. The gate itself was large and solid. To either side a wire fence stretched into the darkness, electrified, according to Konikos. Beyond the fence was the dark mass of the station itself, and beyond that the sea. The radar installation would obviously look out at that. There was just a gleam of light emanating from the building, and behind that, to the right hand side, the hill rose almost sheer, seeming to over-hang the station, as it was obviously intended to do.

He had already toyed with the idea of dividing his force, one bazooka to each half, so as to make it seem the station was being attacked from several positions at once, thus increasing the German apprehension of the Commandos' strength. But he had an idea that might be counter-productive. Once the Germans were under attack, he needed to apply the maximum fire-power possible to force them to keep their heads down while he and Mustafa gained the building, and that could only be applied through the gate.

He also had to anticipate that Erlich had by now sent into town to collect Meissinger and his men, and had thus discovered what had happened at the schoolmaster's house. The station would thus have doubly been put into a state of readiness to resist the coming Commando attack. But he still felt sure that they would be opting for a strictly defensive stand, pending the arrival of massive reinforcements the following morning. Equally, he calculated that by attacking so early in the evening he might just surprise the opposition – the more normal time for such an action was midnight or just after, when the attackers might hope that half the garrison would be asleep.

He checked his watch. "Stand by," he told his men.

The minute hand crept round, then the last second sweep leading to ten thirty. At that very moment there was the explosion of the first grenade. Presumably it had been thrown by Le Boule, with considerable accuracy, for the explosion was immediately followed by a *whoompf* of flame and another explosion – he had hit one of the cars.

Immediately there were two more, less successful explosions as more grenades were hurled, but by then alarm bells were jangling and men were pouring out of the building, some only in their underwear, but all armed with rifles. But as Harry had anticipated, there was also a large body of men, some twenty strong, in place behind the perimeter fence, who turned round to fire at this attack from behind, and were thus distracted from the gate. Officers shouted orders, but there was a great deal of confusion, as there obviously was some doubt as to whether the station was under attack, or one of the cars had just exploded for some unknown reason.

But now the tommy-guns opened up. At a range of over a hundred yards Harry did not suppose they could do a great deal of damage, but they certainly gave the impression of being a considerable force perched up there. The Germans returned fire, the more experienced presumably firing at the flashes, the majority just blazing away into the darkness.

"Go, go, go," Harry said.

The sentries on the gate were also watching what was happening inside the compound, and never stood a chance. One turned as he heard the crunch of boots on stones behind him, and was cut down by a single shot from Simmons. The other ran for his box and no doubt his telephone, but was also shot immediately.

"Bazookas," Harry called.

Nichols and Rhodes were the two experts. They levelled their weapons, and the tank-busting shells smashed into the gate, where the two halves were locked together. They burst open under the impact, and the Commandos were through.

The scene before them was chaotic, with half the yard thrown into bright relief by the blazing car, the other half plunged into deeper darkness. The yard was full of soldiers, most still firing at the hilltop, but some pushing the second car out of the way of the flames. Now some were turning back to face the shattered gate and the sudden intrusion of another enemy force. Closer at hand, the defence squad turned back, but they were still confused, and were cut down by the tommy-guns of the Commandos.

"Take cover," Harry shouted. "Maintain fire. Mr Simmons, take command. Mustafa!"

He ran for the right hand of the two doorways in front of him, while from behind him the chatter of the Commandos' sub-machine guns and the explosive *whoompfs* of the rocket-launchers rose into the night sky. The effect was certainly dramatic. Men fell about in every direction, officers continued to scream orders, the whole night became one vast kaleidoscope of flashing light and searing sound.

Harry had crossed the yard in seconds, Mustafa at his heels. There was a man standing in the doorway, and Harry shot him out of the way with a burst from his tommy-gun. Then they were inside, and charging down the corridor to the radar installation. A man emerged, pistol drawn, and he too went down, while they swept the room with their tommys, sending bodies tumbling to and fro.

"Make sure of them," Harry told Mustafa, and unslung his bag of gelignite. He knew there would be no time to set a proper fuse – he would have to chance his arm.

Mustafa ran round the room, using his pistol to finish off the dying men, then his tommy-gun to discourage some people who appeared at the inner end of the corridor. Harry knelt beneath the huge radar set and inserted the sticks of gelignite, hoping that no stray bullets found their way inside the chamber.

"Go, go, go," he shouted, when he was finished.

Mustafa rolled a grenade along the corridor. In the confined space there was a fearful explosion, followed by the crash of collapsing masonry, some even came down from the ceiling in the chamber. Then Mustafa was on his feet and moving down the corridor, firing his tommy-gun. Harry went behind him. They had been lucky: a hole had been blown in the inner wall.

Mustafa looked back at him. For the moment there was no

firing inside the building, although there was still a battle going on in the courtyard. "Get out," Harry said.

Mustafa climbed through the hole, dropped to the ground. It appeared no one saw him. Harry followed, sitting astride the hole, taking out a grenade. He pulled the pin, rolled it back along the corridor and into the chamber. Then he dropped beside Mustafa.

"Down," he said. "Down. Flat."

It was the best he could think of, and indeed, their only hope. Anyway, there was no time to change their minds before the building went up.

It seemed the loudest noise Harry had ever heard. Masses of concrete were thrown high into the sky, some crashing down the cliff beyond the chamber, others hurled towards the garrison, others falling amongst the assault party, although these, at the gate, were further off. But as he had calculated, hopefully, he and Mustafa, against the stone foundations and below the level of the blast, remained unhurt.

The explosion was followed by complete silence, for several seconds.

"Get out!" Harry bawled. "Get out!"

Mustafa looked at him questioningly, and he realised the Algerian was deaf. But then, so was he.

He pointed at the gate, and Mustafa nodded, and raced across the compound. By the time they reached the rest of the party the shooting had started again. Harry could tell this from various spurts of dust, but he couldn't hear the shots. He couldn't hear what Nichols was saying either, although the soldier was clearly shouting.

He looked left and right, peering into the gloom. Simmons lay on his face, Private Rhodes on his back. He supposed, in the circumstances, casualties had been light. If they could get out.

"Go," he shouted. "Retreat."

The men fell back through the gate, still firing. But the replies were desultory. The Germans were suffering from shock and very heavy casualties.

Harry stooped beside the men who had been hit, but they were both dead. Poor Simmons had never really begun to live, he thought regretfully, just the one weekend with his girlfriend – who would have to be visited. Supposing he was ever in a position to do any visiting.

He scrambled to his feet and ran behind his men, still unable to hear anything. But they were getting away, at least for the time being – the Germans were too disturbed by the destruction of their station and, indeed, their barracks, half of which had fallen in. The Commandos made their way beside the road, while Harry tried to remember the exact way to the beach. And then, to his great relief, two figures loomed out of the darkness in front of him. One had long, curling dark hair.

Part Three
The Victory

. . . every warrior that is rapt with love
Of fame, of valour and of victory,
Must needs have beauty beat on his conceits . . .

Christopher Marlowe

Relatives

"**B**rilliant," Peter Bannon said. "Absolutely brilliant."

"Would you mind speaking a little louder, sir?" Harry requested.

Bannon blinked at him. "What I was saying," he shouted, "is that from all accounts Berlin is going mad. I'm sorry about Simmons and Rhodes. Good men. But really, when you consider what you accomplished, your casualties were remarkably light."

"We also had four wounded, sir," Harry said. "Le Blanc and I were the only two who weren't hit, amazingly."

"But you still have trouble with your hearing, am I right?"

"Well, just a little. A sort of constant background buzzing."

"You'll have to be checked out. It's back to hospital again."

"Is that necessary?"

"I'm afraid it is. We want you absolutely fit for the big one."

"Italy? Or Greece?"

"Those aren't the big ones. Oh, we're going into Italy, just to keep us, and them, busy. But next year is definitely on for Europe. The plans are being drawn up now. It's going to be, as it is going to have to be, the biggest op of all time, and we are going to need every man we've got. So you go off and get fit."

"Yes, sir."

"Now tell me, what about this woman?" Bannon glanced at the note on his desk. "Zoe Konikos."

"Ah. Well, her father, who was supposed to be our man on the ground, turned out to be a bit of a flop. So she took over, guided us, and took part in the assault on the station. Then she retired with us to the beach, and asked to be taken off. I could hardly abandon her, sir."

"You have something of a record of taking women out, Harry."

"Well, sir . . ." Harry grinned. "They seem to go for me, and they can be very useful."

"I'm sure they can," Bannon agreed, drily. "The first one, that woman Veronica Sturmer, turned out to be a spy."

"With respect, sir, we don't know that."

"The intelligence boys seem pretty sure she was the one gave away the St Nazaire plot."

"That can only be a suspicion. She got herself killed saving my life."

"They're an odd lot, women," Bannon said reflectively. "However, this one, you pulled a lot of rank to have her brought to England."

"I could hardly leave her in Alexandria," Harry pointed out. "She had no money, no family, no friends . . . she'd have wound up on the street."

"And where is she going to wind up now?"

"Well . . . she's a refugee. Who has assisted us. It wouldn't have worked without her. At least we can be sure she's no spy."

"Let's hope so. All right, Harry, she'll go to a camp."

"And Mustafa?"

"Who?"

"The Algerian. He really is about the best fighting man I have ever encountered."

"Who is also a murderer."

"Again, with respect, he is an executioner. Whenever, and whoever, he has killed it has been at my command. By the way, is his wife behaving herself?"

"So far as I know. With you both out of the country there has been no need for her not to. So what would you like done with him?"

"He would like to join the Commandos."

Bannon raised his eyebrows. "A half-caste froggie-woggie?"

"I said, the best goddamned fighting man in England, right this minute." Harry was beginning to get annoyed. He had the highest respect for Peter Bannon, and valued his friendship, but he knew that, however much they might deny it, racism was rife in the British Army, certainly amongst the senior officers.

"I don't think we can allow him into the Commandos," Bannon said. "I'm perfectly prepared to accept your evaluation, Harry, but the fact is that our organisation only exists on complete mutual trust and empathy, both between officers and men, and between men and men. The introduction of someone like Le Blanc into the heart of our group would involve mistrust and uncertainty."

"Even if he proved as good a man as any of them?"

"Even if. I'm sorry, Harry, but it can't be done." He tapped his teeth with the end of his pen. "There is a possibility, however."

"Yes?"

"You could take him on as your permanent servant. That means that he would go where you go. If you decided that he should train with you, that would be up to you. Just as if you decided to take him on your next assignment, that again would be up to you."

"But he would not be entitled to wear a Commando badge. It's his dearest wish."

"He would not be able to wear a Commando badge, Harry. I'm sorry. That's the best I can offer."

"And I'll thank you for it."

"I should point out that as he will not actually be a member of HM Armed Forces – that is, he will have taken no oaths of allegiance – you will be wholly responsible for him, should he, shall I say, take a wrong turning. Or indeed, if he has already done so, without your knowing of it."

"I understand that, sir."

"Very good, Harry. Captain Forrester will attend to all the paperwork. I'll be receiving weekly reports as to your health, and we'll have you back at work just as soon as we get the green light."

"You are incorrigible," Belinda told him.

"If you mean, I'm getting quite good at blowing things up, you could be right."

"I mean this habit of being unable to go on a mission without unearthing some damsel in distress, and foisting her upon us."

"Well, as I told Bannon, they always seem to volunteer, and they come in very handy."

She snorted, and began sifting papers and vouchers. "Right. You're for hospital. I have you on a train for Devon first thing tomorrow morning." She looked up. "That allows you tonight in town. If you're strong enough."

"I have dreamed of no one and nothing but you, all the way home."

"If I could believe that, I could believe anything. Even with Zoe tucked up beside you?"

"It was a crowded, and therefore asexual, plane. However, I would like you to change the date on the travel voucher, until the day after tomorrow."

"So, having left my bed, you can bid Zoe a tearful farewell."

"I certainly think I should say goodbye, and try to reassure her, yes. She doesn't know yet if her family has survived, or been slaughtered."

Belinda gave another snort.

"I also have to see, or at least write letters to, the families of Simmons and Rhodes, and, I suppose, Simmons' girlfriend as well. He was very keen, even if he felt he wasn't getting anywhere."

"Um." But this was a sympathetic grunt.

"And then there's Mustafa." He told her of Bannon's plan.

"You've really taken to that little—"

"Please don't say it," Harry requested. "Bannon did, and I nearly punched him on the nose. Yes, I have taken to him. There is no one I'd rather have standing at my back when the chips are down."

"In that case, I'll start cheering for him too. Right. What do you want done with him? Until you're back in action."

"Where I go, he goes."

"Harry, he can't possibly go to hospital with you."

"Why not? I'm only going down for observation. I'm entitled to have my servant with me."

She considered. "I suppose so. Right-ho. I'll make out another voucher, for the day after tomorrow. Where is he now?"

"I sent him home to be with his wife."

"*The* wife?"

"Bannon tells me she's under control."

"Who knows. She gives me the shakes every time I think of her. And you. Tell me something, just how unwell are you?"

"I don't know that I'm unwell at all. You're a little faint, but that's because of this continual buzzing in my ears. But that's surely because I was so close to that explosion. It'll clear away in time."

"Um. What about other things? No internal problems?"

"Well, obviously I have one or two internal problems. Trips like that one always leave the digestion and the regulars a bit churned up. Even mine, and I've done quite a few."

"Hm. I'd say you do need a thorough check-up. However . . . let's see what I can do first."

Spending the night with Belinda was, Harry supposed, the most reassuring thing that could happen to a man, simply because there was no tension, no necessity to prove anything, or to have anything proved. Belinda took everything in life in her stride, sometimes literally. Longevity she enjoyed. In and out with a bang equally seemed to please her. Even the odd moment of impotence, which had to affect any man straight back from the firing line every so often caused her no concern. "There'll be time in the morning," she said.

It was the first time it had happened to him, and what bothered him was that he was still only twenty-two. He knew it was purely psychological. He had been exposed to enemy action probably more than any other soldier in the British Army who was still alive: it was natural that such a continuous battering of his senses and his sensibilities should get to him, from time to time, fortunately only on a temporary basis.

In himself, he knew that nothing had changed. He still possessed what might be called the immortality-complex of youth, still believed it would be the man beside him, as per poor Simmons, who would buy it rather than himself. He was not even overly affected by the men he had killed or caused to be killed – he was fighting a war. But he suffered a succession of images. The woman, Raqquyah, was back, lurking on the edges of his subconscious. Now she was mingled with Zoe, tied naked in the chair. Or with Veronica, a crumpled bleeding heap in the woods outside Poitiers. Too many women, dying for him, or suffering, anyway.

And the others, such as Yvonne, uncertain what she wanted and what she was doing.

In the midst of them all, Belinda was both a reassurance and a certainty that one day there would be a reality which did not involve death and destruction.

"How is your divorce coming along?" he asked.

"Just about there."

"Thank God for that."

"You realise that when I was married, I mean properly, I didn't sleep around."

"I'm glad of that."

"And I didn't expect Jonathan to either. Things started to go wrong when I found out that he did."

"Absolutely."

"What I mean is, I would expect total fidelity from my next husband, and would offer him the same in return."

"Fair enough."

"So it really isn't on while you are constantly producing nubile young women like a magician with a hat full of rabbits."

"Even if it goes with the job?"

"Even if. I also have no desire to be a widow. I therefore consider that we should wait until after the end of the war."

"How long after that?"

"Harry," she said. "If you're serious, I will marry you the day Hitler surrenders."

"Then I'd better see what I can do about bringing that forward."

Rhodes' family lived in Yorkshire, and Harry had to write them a letter. The Simmonses, however, lived in London, so he could call on them personally.

It was a flat, three floors up, in Hammersmith.

"Major Curtis?" The woman was short and grey-haired and wore spectacles. "Do please come in."

Harry, who was wearing uniform, with all his medal ribbons, entered the room. She peered at him. "Isn't that the Victoria Cross?"

"Yes, ma'am, it is."

"For this assignment you have just been on?"

"No, ma'am. Things don't work that quickly. This was for something that happened over a year ago." Harry faced an elderly man who had just propelled himself into the room in a wheelchair. This was going to be far more difficult that he had feared. "Harry Curtis, sir." He shook hands.

"Major Curtis was in command, when Ian died," Mrs Simmons told her husband.

Mr Simmons still had hold of his hand. Now he squeezed it, tightly. "It was good of you to come."

"Major Curtis has the VC," his wife said.

"By Jove," Mr Simmons said. "You must be very proud of that."

"I am, sir."

"He got it a year ago," Mrs Simmons said. "What did you say you got it for, Major Curtis?"

"I didn't, actually. But it was fairly commonplace. I saved the life of a fellow officer, while under enemy fire. One of those things one does without thinking, you know."

"But no one saved Ian's life," Mrs Simmons said, sitting down.

169

"Ah . . . I'm afraid it just wasn't possible," Harry said. "He was hit, and killed instantly."

"The notice from the War Office didn't say where, or when."

"I'm sorry. It was a secret operation. I can't tell you where, or when."

"But you were there."

"Yes, I was, Mrs Simmons."

"Did he die well?" Mr Simmons asked.

"He died facing the foe, and providing covering fire for us to complete our mission, sir. No man can die better than that."

"Will he get a medal?"

"I have recommended him for one, yes, sir. The Military Cross."

"Thank you," Mr Simmons said.

"His body," Mrs Simmons said. "The notice said nothing about where he is buried, or if we will get him back here. We have a family plot, you see."

"I'm sorry," Harry said.

"Where is he buried?"

"I have no idea, Mrs Simmons. You see, we were under fire and we had to withdraw. There were two dead men. We could not take them with us."

"You left him there?"

For God's sake, Harry wanted to say, what did you want us to do? Stay and die with a man who was already dead? He said, "I had a responsibility to the rest of my squad, those who were still alive, to get them out. I'm sorry. But in warfare the living count more than the dead."

"You left him, for the Germans?"

"I am sure they will have given him a decent burial."

"They're Huns," Mrs Simmons said. "God knows what they will have done with the body."

"The men we were engaged with were professional soldiers," Harry said, feeling quite desperate. "They will have regarded Ian as an honourable enemy, and buried him with the full honours of war."

The Cause

"If only I could believe that," Mrs Simmons said. "And you cannot tell us where this happened."

"I'm afraid not. You will be told, as soon as it is practical."

"And his medal?" Simmons asked.

"If my recommendation is accepted—"

"Why should it not be accepted?" Mrs Simmons demanded. "Did he not die, gallantly, so that you and your other people could escape? That is what you said."

"That is what I have put in my recommendation, Mrs Simmons," Harry said. "But you must try to understand. In a war, there are so many men, dying gallantly, that their comrades may survive. They do not all get medals, however much they may all deserve them. As I was saying, if my recommendation is accepted, you will be invited to the investiture, and you will receive the medal on behalf of your son."

"Ah," Mr Simmons said. He seemed more able to accept the situation that his wife.

"Now," Harry said, "I really must go. But I believe Ian had a girlfriend. Would you have her address?"

"What's *she* got to do with it?" Mrs Simmons demanded. "She's not family. They're not . . . weren't, even engaged. He asked her, but she turned him down."

"I still feel she would like to know what happened," Harry said.

"She lives in London," Simmons said. "She's a clerk in some government department."

"She's not even in the ATS," Mrs Simmons said. "One would think she'd be in the ATS."

"Well, you see, Mrs Simmons, we couldn't even begin to fight a war, much less hope to win one, without clerks. They are the backbone of the industry," Harry pointed out.

He obtained the girl's name and address, and fled, to the nearest pub.

He had no desire to see her at work – so far as he knew, she didn't even yet know that Ian was dead – she would have to keep until this evening. He went instead to Golders Green.

171

"Yes?" The woman was short and dark and attractive, like both of her sisters. She was also suspicious.

"I'm looking for Mr Le Blanc," Harry said.

"He is here. You are to do with Yasmin?"

Christ, Harry thought, what's she done now? "No," he said. "I am to do with Mustafa. I am his CO."

"CO? What is this, CO?"

"Commanding Officer."

"You wish to see him?"

Harry sighed. "Yes, Miss . . .?"

"My name is Tasmina."

"And you are Yasmin's sister, right?"

"I am Yasmin's sister, yes."

"Great. Now, may I speak with Mustafa, please?"

"You understand that he is not well. Since Yasmin left."

"Yasmin has left? To go where?"

"I do not know. Nobody knows. She has just left."

"Has this been reported to the police?"

"Oh, yes. They have been here. But they cannot say where she is."

"Look, can I come in?"

"Oh, yes." She stepped back, and he entered the house.

"Is this house yours?"

"It is my husband's."

"Ah. And he is . . .?"

"He is away. He is in the army. Just like you and Mustafa. Everybody is in the army, nowadays."

"May I ask if he is English?"

"Oh, yes. My name is Tasmina Johnson."

"I see. And you were married before the war."

"My husband came to Ghardaia on business. We met, and fell in love. You would like coffee?"

"That would be very nice. But I would also like to speak with Mustafa."

Tasmina stood at the foot of the stairs and shouted, "Mustafa! There is a man here to see you. Your CO." She showed

172

Harry into a small living room. "You wait here. I will bring the coffee."

Harry wandered about the room, looking at framed photographs of various members of Tasmina's family, in which both Yasmin and Raquyyah figured prominently. Presumably Tasmina knew all about the death of her other sister. He wondered what she thought about it? Again, presumably, it had to be along the same lines as Yasmin.

The sooner he got Mustafa out of this house on a permanent basis the better.

But where the devil had Yasmin gone off to? And with whom? And why?

The door opened and Mustafa came in. He certainly looked distraught.

"What exactly has happened?" Harry asked.

"I do not know, sir. Tasmina went out, leaving Yasmin alone in the house. When she came back, Yasmin was gone."

"How long ago was this?"

"Three weeks."

"Three weeks! Didn't she leave a note, or some indication of where she was going?"

"No, sir. Nothing."

"You must be very upset. I really am sorry."

"It is fate, eh? Kismet."

Mustafa looked at Tasmina as she brought in the coffee tray. Perhaps she was the prettiest of the sisters, and now her husband and Mustafa's wife were both away, he deduced that Mustafa might not be above a bit of incest. Or a lot of it.

"Well, I'm sure the police will find her," he said. "They always do."

"And then they will stick electrodes up her ass," Mustafa said dolefully.

"No, no," Harry said. "This is the British police, not the Foreign Legion. They will bring her back here. By the time they do that, I recommend that you are far away, just in case her disappearance had something to do with Raquyyah's death. You are to come with me, tomorrow morning."

Mustafa's face lit up. "I am to join the Commandos?"

"Only in a manner of speaking. You are to be my servant."

"I am to be a servant?"

"My servant. My support at all times, Mustafa. It seems that it is not possible for you actually to become a Commando. But you will serve with me, and where I go, you will go. Does that suit you?"

"I would like very much to serve with you, Major. I will wear uniform?"

He was in uniform now.

"Certainly you will wear uniform. The only thing you will lack will be the badges. But this may be a good thing, if you are ever captured again."

"And now we go on another assignment?"

"No," Harry said. "Now we go to hospital. Tomorrow, meet me at Paddington Station at eight o'clock."

He went to the hostel where Zoe had been installed, temporarily, was admitted by a hard-faced matron, whose gaze softened when she spotted both Harry's rank and his medal ribbons.

"Zoe was telling us about you," she said. "How you brought her out of Greece."

"Partly," Harry said. "Is it possible to speak with her?"

"Of course." She frowned at him. "No hanky-panky, please."

He wondered just how much Zoe had confessed.

"I wouldn't dream of it."

The matron showed him into a waiting room, and a moment later Zoe came in. The matron departed, but ostentatiously left the door open.

"Oh, Major Curtis." Zoe came forward to hug him.

"No hanky-panky," Harry said.

"I thought I would never see you again."

Her eyes were wet, and he gave her his handkerchief. "I'm not that easy to lose."

"What is going to happen to me?"

"They'll find you a billet. That's a family who will take you in as a lodger."

"I have no money."

"The government will look after that. But you will be expected to find a job. Or accept one if they find it for you."

"I could be an interpreter."

"That's a good idea. Although right now there's not a lot of Greek that needs interpreting. I'll see what I can do."

"And you will come to me again?"

"Whenever I can."

He kissed her, and reflected that she hadn't asked after her family, which was a bonus.

At seven o'clock he presented himself at the address given him by the Simmonses. This too was a flat, a walk-up, but the area was good and the hallway clean. He pressed the bell, and the door was opened by a small, dark girl with somewhat tight features and a limited figure, so far as he could make out.

"Miss Hale?"

"No. I'm Jessica. Did you wish to speak with Deirdre?"

"I would like to, yes. May I come in?"

She allowed him in, studying his uniform.

"You're a major," she remarked. "And you've got the VC."

"Right on both counts, Miss . . .?"

"Tudor. My father is a major. In the RASC. You don't get the VC in the RASC."

"It's not impossible. And usually you live longer. One should always count one's blessings."

"Oh, yes. Here's Deirdre."

Deidre Hale was in complete contrast to her flatmate, being tall and slim, with long, straight yellow hair. She made Harry think of Yvonne on a good day. A very good day. This girl was quite beautiful.

"Harry Curtis," he said, holding out his hand.

Her grasp was warm, but quite strong.

"He's a major," Jessica said, importantly. "And he's got the VC."

"Do you think I could speak with you alone, Miss Hale?" Harry asked, his embarrassment growing with every moment.

"Certainly. Jess?" She glanced at her friend.

"I was just going down to the store, anyway," Jessica said.

"Will you be here when I come back, Major Curtis?"

"I may be."

"I'll hurry."

She banged the door behind her.

Deirdre Hale and Harry gazed at each other. As usual, with the black-out curtains drawn, they were shut off from the rest of the world.

"Do please sit down," Deirdre said. "I'm afraid I can't offer you a drink. Except tea."

"Tea would be fine, thank you." Harry sat on the small settee, laying his cap on the cushion beside him. He watched her moving about the small kitchenette. Her movements, quick but graceful, were in keeping with the rest of her.

"Is it to do with Ian?" she asked over her shoulder. "Lieutenant Simmons? You're his CO, aren't you?"

"Did he tell you that?"

She made the tea. "Yes, he did. Shouldn't he have?"

"Our business is top secret."

"Oh." She regarded the pot. "He was very proud to work with you. It is *was*, isn't it?" She glanced at him.

Harry felt a wave of relief coming over him, even if it was tinged with an immense sadness. Ian Simmons had been the luckiest man in the world, up until he had stopped that bullet.

"I'm afraid it is."

"Milk and sugar?"

"Please. Two lumps."

She poured and brought the two cups across the room, sat in a chair beside him. "He always said one day he wouldn't be coming back."

"That goes for all of us."

"Except for you. Ian always said you were indestructible."

176

"Which is not to say they haven't tried. I wanted you to know how sorry I am, and how much I valued him as an officer."

However untrue that was, he was not prepared to say anything bad about the rather over-anxious lieutenant to this girl.

"And he died most gallantly," he added. "Covering our withdrawal."

"I thought he would," Deirdre said. "Die well, I mean. He was profoundly patriotic."

"You are taking this very well. Better than . . . I shouldn't have said that."

"His parents, you mean. I don't know them very well. I don't think they approved of me."

"Why not?"

She shrugged.

"Were you and Ian . . .?"

"We weren't engaged. We had a sort of understanding . . . well, I'm not even sure we had that."

One weekend together, Harry thought, after which she had turned down his proposal of marriage.

"I felt you should know," Harry said. "Ian was very fond of you. He spoke of you a lot."

Her head turned, sharply; there were pink spots in her cheeks.

"I didn't mean to embarrass you," Harry said. "Men do talk, when under extreme pressure, and they're more likely to talk to their commanding officers than anyone else."

She drank her coffee. "So he was just one amongst many," she said, quietly and half to herself.

"He was one of two who got killed," Harry said. "So perhaps what he said was more important than what anyone else said. Can you understand that?"

"Yes."

"Thus I felt that he would have wanted you to know."

"I'm grateful. Would I have been informed anyway?"

"I'm afraid not. You're not actually next of kin, or a fiancée, or anything like that."

"Just a fringe benefit," she said thoughtfully. "More tea?"

"I should be going."

He stood up, and she did also.

"Your duty done," she suggested.

"That's one way of putting it. But it has been a pleasure meeting you. I only wish it could have been in happier circumstances."

"You're very young, aren't you, to be a major?"

"It's the way things turned out."

"May I ask how old you are?"

"In August I'll be twenty-two."

"Good heavens. Ian was twenty-one, and he was only a lieutenant."

"Well, you see, I was a regular before the shooting actually started, so I had a head start. Ian came in after Dunkirk."

"Yes. I suppose that's it." She glanced at him. "I'm twenty-four. Makes me feel like an old woman."

"Not a chance." He picked up his cap.

She went with him to the door. "Are you married, Major Curtis?"

"There hasn't been much time for that."

"But I'm sure you have a girlfriend."

"I think that's reasonable. She's older than me, too."

She opened the door for him. "Well . . . good luck. Keep surviving."

They gazed at each other. He found her interesting, quite apart from her looks and the fact that she had been Simmons' girlfriend, because she was so calm. Belinda gave the impression of being calm, but she was really a very intense person. He could not help but wonder what lay beneath the exterior of this girl.

He reminded himself it was not his business to find out.

"If you're ever around here again," she said. "I would like to see you."

"I'd like that too," he said without thinking.

The Huntress

N ow why had he said that? he wondered, as he took the tube
back to Belinda's flat. He was engaged to Belinda. He had
been engaged to Yvonne, and if that had ended, he rather felt
that the idea might be stirring again. He would have to tell her
about Belinda, and undoubtedly cause a tremendous scene.
Better to write her a letter, even if that revealed a lack of moral
fibre, which everyone supposed he possessed in abundance.

Belinda had made it perfectly plain that she would demand
utter fidelity from her husband, and he quite agreed with her
point of view. So what was he doing having eyeball to eyeball
contact with an extremely good-looking young woman whose
only connection with him was that she had once slept with his
second-in-command? So Deirdre Hale was perhaps the most
attractive young woman he had ever met, at least superficially.
She had none of the rampant beauty of Veronica Sturmer, none
of the massive confidence of Belinda Forrester, and perhaps
none of the innocent anxiety of Zoe Konikos, but she possessed
the calm assurance of a woman who believed in herself and in the
good things in life. Superficially. That was the bright side of the
moon. But wasn't he also attracted by the possibility that her
outward appearance and presentation might indeed be only
superficial? Wasn't it the knowledge that she *had* slept with
Simmons, and presumably found him wanting in some direction
or another, that was drawing him towards her?

In either case, he needed to draw away from her just as rapidly
as possible. Besides, the chances of him ever seeing her again
were remote.

179

"How did it go?" Belinda asked, pouring them each a drink.

"Let's say I'm glad it's over," Harry said.

"Tell me."

He sighed. "The Simmonses are putting up a not unreasonable but quite illogical front. They want their son's body back to be buried in the family plot."

"Won't they be able to do that after the war?"

"Supposing his grave is marked. I reckon the Germans suffered something like thirty per cent casualities in the shoot-out in Spetsos. They'd all have to be buried, and I imagine Simmons and Graham would have been tossed in with them. Even supposing the war ended next year, which it's not likely to, identifying him in that lot could be a bit of a problem."

"Um. What about the girlfriend?"

"She took it very well. But I think in her case the unfortunate Ian was already yesterday's man."

Belinda studied him. "You liked her."

He remembered that in addition to being a nurse before the war she had also taken a course in psychology. Necessary for her man-evaluating job. On the other hand, she couldn't be psychic.

"What makes you say that?"

"Your ears glowed, for a moment."

"Ah. Well, yes, she's a likeable woman."

"Good-looking?"

"In my opinion."

It was Belinda's turn to say, "Ah. How about your friend, Zoe?"

"Pure misery."

"Doesn't she realise that if she'd stayed, she'd have been shot?"

"Perhaps. But right now she's lonely as hell."

"That figures. And Mustafa, I take it, is raring to go."

"Yes, he is. But he has a bigger problem than any of us. The fair Yasmin has disappeared."

"Wasn't she under police surveillance?"

"I thought she was. That is something I would like you to investigate."

She made a face. "They'll tell me how overstretched they are. But how can she just have disappeared? Didn't anyone know she was going?"

"Apparently not."

"What about the sister she was living with? She must have known."

"Again, apparently not. And frankly, I don't think she cares too much. Remember that between Tasmina marrying this fellow Johnson, well before the war, and Yasmin's appearance this year, is a good half a dozen years. I shouldn't think they were in touch more than once or twice throughout that time. Besides, I have an idea she and Mustafa have something going."

"Isn't that incest?"

"Do you know, I'm not sure it is. She's his wife's sister, not his."

"But he's still your favourite man."

"As I said, there's no one I would rather have standing at my back in a fight."

"And as *I* said, as long as you feel that way, he's my favourite man as well. Let's eat."

"Major Curtis," said Sister. "Not again."

"Not so's you'd notice," Harry said. "I'm having this trouble with my ears."

She raised her eyebrows. "Then we'd better get you down to examination." Her eyebrows went even higher as she looked at Mustafa. "What's the matter with him?"

"Amazingly, very little, although we were caught up in the same explosion. He's my batman."

Mustafa gave what he no doubt hoped was an ingratiating grin.

"Well," Sister said. "We'll have to find him some accommodation."

"That would be very nice," Harry said.

There was a new hospital CO. Harry found it both odd and amusing that he should this time be senior in rank to a captain who was obviously at least twice his age.

"Must have been some bang," Clissold remarked.

"It was."

"Did you know it was going to happen?"

"I caused it."

"Ah. Well, your tympanum is damaged, in both ears. One of them in fact is blown."

"You're not saying it's permanent?"

"Well, hopefully not. You're young enough . . ." He glanced down at the file. "Good God!"

"They always say that," Harry pointed out.

"You're only just twenty-two," Clissold observed, half to himself. "Oh, you will recover, well enough. In the short term."

"What do you mean by that?"

"As you, er, grow older, your hearing will fade somewhat sooner than it should."

"How much older?"

"You'll be in your forties before you're properly aware of it."

"That suits me fine. So, may I be discharged?"

"I'm afraid we can't do that right away, Major. There are one or two other matters . . ."

"Aches and pains."

"There is some evidence of internal haemorrhage. When you say, aches and pains, are they sharp?"

"Well, one gets caught up by the occasional twinge. But only momentarily."

"I don't think a week or so in here will do you any harm at all," Clissold said.

"It is a very nice place," Mustafa commented, as they strolled along one of the country lanes together. "Very restful."

"That's the idea," Harry said.

"But you are not happy."

Harry shot him a glance. Not another psychologist, he thought.

"It's merely that I, you, we, have a war to fight, and it's not going to be won relaxing in luxury."

"A little luxury now and then is good," Mustafa observed.

Harry did not suppose *he* had ever known such luxury in his life before.

But before the week was up, mail arrived. There was a letter from his parents, naturally, a brief note from Belinda, a long epistle from Yvonne . . . Harry couldn't make up his mind whether or not to bin it, unread, as he had done on more than one occasion before.

But there was also a letter for Mustafa, bearing an Algerian stamp.

"Not bad news, I hope?" Harry asked.

Mustafa was frowning.

"It is very strange," he said. "This is from my sister Marguerite."

"Keeping in touch?"

"She asks if I have got together with Philippe. He is her husband, you know."

"I remember Philippe," Harry said. How could I ever forget, he thought. "Get together? What does she mean by that?"

"Well, she says that Philippe has joined up. The Free French. And he has been sent to England for training."

It was Harry's turn to frown. "When was that letter written?"

"Two weeks ago. It got here quick, eh?"

"Yes," Harry said. "But does it say when Philippe joined up?"

"Ah three months ago."

"Three months? And when was he sent to England?"

"Three weeks ago."

"So he would have arrived while you and I went carrying out the Spetsos exercise, or while we were still training for it. And presumably the first time he got leave, he would have looked you up. At your sister-in-law's house."

"That is true. Now that is strange," Mustafa mused. "Tasmina never mentioned him to me."

"I'm afraid that is because she never saw him," Harry said.

"Eh?"

"I would say that when Philippe called at Tasmina's house, she was out, and Yasmin was alone at home."

"And you think they went off together? I do not believe it. That would be incest."

"No it wouldn't. Reprehensible, maybe, but not incest. And the pot should never call the kettle black."

"I do not understand this," Mustafa said.

"It's an old English saying. Philippe is married to your sister, not Yasmin's sister. Unlike Tasmina."

"Well . . ." Mustafa looked embarrassed. "She is a lonely woman. And with Yasmin gone, I am a lonely man."

"Did Yasmin know of it?"

"Oh, no, no. It only happened after she had gone. With Philippe," he said bitterly.

"Then it is just as serious as I feared," Harry said.

He got on the phone to Belinda.

"You are saying this man Philippe was in on the murder . . . oops, the *execution* of Mrs Le Blanc's sister?"

"He didn't actually take part in the execution, but he was driving the truck. He knew what had happened."

"And you think Mrs Le Blanc found out?"

"I'm afraid she did. Then she either persuaded Philippe, or allowed herself to be persuaded by him, to go off together."

"I see. Quite a family they seem to be. Right ho. You want me to contact Scotland Yard and tell them they are now looking for a man and a woman. I'd better have a description of the man. I suppose he's wearing Free French uniform."

"I don't think we are now looking for a man and a woman travelling together," Harry said.

"But you just said . . ."

"I said they left the Johnson house together. I don't think they stayed together very long."

"Shit!" she commented. "You don't mean . . ."

"I've an idea that is what I do mean."

"He could just have gone back to his unit."

"Well, that's the first thing you need to do. Get hold of

someone in the Free French organisation, pull rank, and find out of Private Nuyet, recently arrived from North Africa, has gone AWOL. If he has not, and is all present and correct, we are back to square one. If he has, then what the police are looking for is the dead and probably mutilated body of the said Nuyet, and a murderess. That should make them get their fingers out."

Belinda gulped.

It was a relief to get down to Wales and back to the serious work of training. The remainder of the squad were also there, as well as the usual batch of recruits, although of course none of these were tyros in the art of soldiering or warfare – they were all volunteers from line regiments.

The new camp commander was Colonel Morrison, who Harry had not met before, but who knew all about *him*.

"Glad to have you back, Major," he said. "So, what's next on the agenda?"

"I wish I knew. But I have an idea it's to be Europe."

"Which will be some show. Are you looking for a squad, or just training in general?"

"I expect it will be a squad. Your know we lost two in Spetsos?"

Morrison tapped the file on his desk. "I have the report. That means you're short an officer."

Harry nodded.

"In your assessment, before Spetsos," Morrison said, "you came across as not entirely happy with Simmons."

"I wasn't," Harry agreed. "I picked him for the Algiers job simply because I had to have a French-speaking officer and he was the only one available. He did well enough there for me to keep him in the team, and of course he died in action in Spetsos."

"But you always had doubts."

"He got a bit shaky under stress."

"Well, we'll see if we can do better this time. I'll have a hunt through the files. But I suppose you would like another French speaker."

"I would. In view of what could be coming up, it would be a help if he spoke German as well."

"That could be a tall one. But, as I say, we'll see what we can do. Now what about this—"

"Please don't say it," Harry requested. "Unless you were going to use a word like batman."

Morrison regarded him for several seconds. "He is not a Commando."

"No he is not. He's my personal servant."

"But you wish him given full access to our training methods. That is classified, you know, Major."

"Sir, Mustafa Le Blanc has already been on two Commando missions, in both of which he distinguished himself. He is also a serving soldier with the Free French. The fact that he is not, and apparently can never be, a fully-fledged Commando, is irrelevant when set alongside his value to me, personally."

Morrison was looking at the file. "And Colonel Bannon has already given clearance. You do realise, Major, that should any questions be asked, the matter may well have to be referred to a higher authority."

"I'll take my chances on that," Harry said.

His men were delighted to have him back in their midst, and also to welcome back Mustafa. And it was a pleasure to get back to serious training, even if his ear problem meant that his balance wasn't quite all it should be. He was also pleased with his two replacement recruits, Private Adamson, a true north country-man, bluff and determined, and Lieutenant McIntyre, a Scot from Aberdeen, with all the dourness usually associated with that city, but already highly trained and possessing a pragmatic character which believed in taking tomorrow as it came, quite the opposite to Simmons, who had always been trying to anticipate, unhappily. He also spoke German, fluently, and had a few words of French.

"It is an honour to serve with you, sir," McIntyre said, eyeing Harry's medal ribbons, to which had been added the DSO for his raid on Spetsos.

The Cause

"Let's hope you hold the same opinion after our next mission," Harry suggested

He had no idea what that was going to be, except in a most general fashion. No one could be unaware that Great Britain was slowly being turned into one vast armed camp as more and more American troops and matériel were poured across the Atlantic. The Mediterranean had become a sideshow, although Alexander's men had invaded Italy, forced the collapse of Mussolini's regime, and were slowly working their way up the peninsular in the face of determined German resistance.

Which meant that the raid on Spetsos, and all the other Commando activity in the Aegean, had been a waste of time and several lives. Harry would have liked to be able to persuade himself that the attack on the radar installation had diverted German minds from Italy, but he couldn't do it. The whole thing had been part of the waste side-effects of war.

His desire to be doing something was accentuated by a visit from Belinda, in the late autumn. She came down armed with a sheaf of secret orders for Morrison as well as other section commanders, but her real purpose was a private session with Harry.

"The police actually found the body of a man, two days after the disappearance of Yasmin Le Blanc," she said.

"For God's sake, that was damn near six months ago," Harry said.

"Exactly. But you see, the body was naked, and there were no identifying marks. Certainly nothing to indicate that he was a member of the Free French forces, or even that he was French. They put him in a morgue and waited for a missing persons report, but there was none."

"Not even from the French?"

"Well, it seems a fair number of their people go AWOL from time to time. So do a fair number of ours, you know. These things aren't publicised, and are dealt with in house, as it were, when the culprit is either apprehended or returns to duty. Philippe Nuyet never did. I understand that inquiries were eventually made of Tasmina Johnson, as she was known to be a sister-in-law of his, but this was after you and Mustafa had already gone down to Devon. Tasmina naturally said that she had never seen Philippe, or even that she knew he was in England. So there we have a couple of dead ends that should have crossed, but didn't. Philippe was duly buried, and the case was closed. It wasn't until I told them that the man they were looking for might well have been mutilated, either before or after death, that they perked up. It seems this corpse *had* indeed been mutilated, before death, in the most horrible possible fashion. Far too horrible for them to discuss it with me. There are some things a lady should not know, the inspector said. Pompous twit. So I told him. Castration, injury to anus caused by insertion of sharp object, eyes poked out, ditto, ears cut off, tongue cut out, throat cut. He nearly had a fit. They had put it down as a homosexual sex session gone wrong."

"But now they're looking for Yasmin."

"Ah . . . no."

"Come again?"

"They say, and I'm afraid they're correct, that there is absolutely no shred of evidence to connect this man with Yasmin Le Blanc. The wheels of justice have to turn very slowly, it seems. In the first instance, they are exhuming the body next week, and I have here an order for Mustafa Le Blanc to be given sufficient leave to travel to Nottingham, which is where the body is buried, to make a formal identification of it as his brother-in-law."

"After six months in the ground?"

"It won't be pleasant. But apparently his fingers hadn't been cut off, and on one of them there is a wedding ring. A plain gold band, but they feel perhaps Mustafa may be able to identify it. Once they have got positive identification they have promised to take it from there."

"What about his teeth? Dental records. Or did she knock all of those out too?"

"No. But there is no prospect of a breakthrough there. His dentist lives in Ghardaia. To obtain those records will take until the end of the war. Mustafa it will have to be. He can travel back with me."

Harry gave her a quizzical look.

She grinned. "He really isn't my type."

"I'm glad to hear it. And meanwhile, that homicidal young woman is free. How the hell is she existing?"

"I imagine she sells her body whenever she's hungry," Belinda said.

"Talking about selling bodies . . ."

"Can't be done. I'm sorry. But I'm due back in London tonight."

"With Mustafa."

"I'm to put him on a train to Nottingham."

Harry nodded. "I'd better go get him."

He outlined the situation to the little man.

"Shit," Mustafa commented.

"That's the least of it. Now listen very carefully. Captain Forrester will put you on a train to Nottingham and you will report to the central police station there. Then you will do whatever they tell you to, and when they are finished, you will return here. She will give you all the necessary travel vouchers. But under no circumstances are you to go to Mrs Johnson's house."

"You think Yasmin will be there?"

"I don't know. But there's a strong possibility that she will have been in touch with her sister. This indicates two things, from our point of view. The first is that Yasmin doesn't know where you are, and we need to keep it that way. The second, and far more serious, is that Philippe has been killed because he must have let on to Yasmin what really happened. That being so, Yasmin almost certainly will have passed on that information to Tasmina, which means that we may well have two homicidal women after us."

"Tasmina is not like that," Mustafa objected.

"Would you like to put that to the test?"

Mustafa looked distinctly crushed.

"So go do your stuff," Harry said. "And come on back."

What a mess, he thought. Yet he could have no doubts that he had done the right thing. Raquyyah had been threatening to blow the whole business, and that could have cost hundreds, perhaps thousands, of American lives. If he had worried about the possibility of vengeance, it had never occurred to him that those tentacles could stretch as far as England. Of course as long as he, and Mustafa, were in the Commando training camp, they were perfectly safe. But they could not stay here forever. There were furloughs coming up, and Christmas.

Worst of all was the thought that Yasmin knew where he lived, and that his parents were in blissful ignorance of the possibility of a murderess arriving on their doorstep, hands already wet with blood. Did Arab blood feuds extend to the families of the object of hate? He rather thought they did.

All of these considerations only came to mind after Belinda and Mustafa had left. He went to Morrison.

"I would like a weekend pass. I need to go home, urgently."

Morrison raised his eyebrows. "Trouble?"

"There could be."

The colonel nodded. He was not going to argue with his most decorated soldier.

Harry caught the train that afternoon, arrived in Frenthorpe at dusk, walked the few hundred yards from the station to the house, unable to prevent himself from looking left and right at every street corner. He remembered having this experience three years before, when all of England was looking for Veronica Sturmer – but she had turned out to be on his side. Now he could only remind himself that it was several months since Philippe's murder. Surely if Yasmin had been coming to Frenthorpe she would have done so by now. Yet his parents had to be warned.

Jupiter barked, and Alison opened the door. "Harry! What a pleasant surprise."

He hugged and kissed her, stroked the dog, shook hands with his father, who came hurrying out of the lounge.

"Nothing wrong, I hope."

"There could be. We need to talk."

They sat down, and John Curtis poured them all drinks. "You are making this sound as if this could be rather serious," he remarked. "You haven't come to tell us the invasion is about to happen?"

"No, I haven't, although it is going to happen some time pretty soon, I think. But this is a personal matter."

"You're getting married," Alison said. "To Yvonne?" She clapped her hands. "And she knew you were coming home."

"I'm not with you," Harry said.

"Yvonne's home too. She arrived yesterday. We're going over there for lunch, tomorrow. Oh, I'm so pleased."

Harry drew a deep breath. "Mother, I am not going to marry Yvonne Clearsted."

"But . . . you mean you're not engaged?"

"Ah . . . no. I am engaged to be married, certainly. To Belinda."

"That Captain Forrester person?"

"Right."

"But . . ." Alison and John exchanged glances. Neither of them had ever really taken to Belinda's somewhat authoritarian manner. "I really don't understand."

"It's very simple. I asked her to marry me, and she said yes."

"But didn't you say she's already married?" John asked.

"Her divorce has come through."

"Ah. Yes. I see."

He didn't really.

"But that is not what I've come home to tell you," Harry said.

"What are you going to tell Yvonne?"

"I intended to write her a note, when I had time."

"Dear John," John remarked, and smiled.

"It really will be very unpleasant," Alison said. "I mean, lunch, tomorrow."

"I have no intention of going to the Clearsteds for lunch,"

191

Harry said. "Now, will you please listen. Do you remember that couple who turned up here back in the spring?"

"You mean the Arabs?"

"French-Algerian, actually. And do you remember what the wife threatened to do to the man who murdered her sister?"

"Quite disgusting," Alison said.

"Yes. Well, she's gone and done it."

They stared at him in consternation.

"But the police haven't caught up with her yet," Harry went on.

"You mean she actually . . . cut the fellow up?" John asked.

"For starters, yes."

"Good God!"

He gazed at his wife. This was a world of which they knew nothing.

"The trouble is, Yasmin has got hold of the idea that I was involved," Harry said.

"Good God!" John said again.

"But . . . oh, Harry!" Alison looked ready to burst into tears.

"*Were* you involved?" his father asked.

"I'm afraid I was," Harry said. "In that I was the commanding officer of the squad when Raquyyah died."

"But . . . you said she'd been raped and murdered."

"I know. However, the fact is that she was a potential traitor who had to be executed, and I gave the order that it should be done."

Alison clasped both hands to her throat.

"Now, I don't want you to worry about me," Harry said. "I am totally protected in the army. However, there is a remote possibility that she may come here, as she knows this is where I live. I say the possibility is remote, because she has now been on the run for several months, and I would have supposed if she was coming here she would already have done so. However, it could still happen. So . . . I would like you to be very careful and under no circumstances open the door to anyone who has not clearly identified himself or herself."

192

"And if this woman does show up?" John asked.

"As I say, do not open the door, but call the police."

"She was such a petite little person," Alison mused.

"She still is. That's why she's unlikely to attempt to break the door down. She'll want to get in by stealth."

"Well, we'll certainly keep our eyes open."

"I just don't know what we are going to say to Yvonne," Alison muttered.

Harry sighed. His mother just did not seem able to get into the real world. Or perhaps hers *was* the real world, and it was he, and all the other soldiers and sailors of whatever nationality, all desperate to get at each others' throats, who were really living in never-never land.

For most of them it was just that.

He would have liked to have spent the weekend with his parents, but Frenthorpe was not at that moment big enough for both him and Yvonne. He had been an utter cad there, and was going to have to be more of one. On the other hand, after their night in the hotel he had asked her to marry him, and she had refused.

Just like Deirdre Hale, after her night with Simmons, he thought. He had immediately supposed the fault had been Simmons'. Fuck it.

He only knew that, having done his duty and no doubt further estranged himself from his parents, he had to get out. Dinner was a strained affair, and so was breakfast.

"I have to get back," he said, as soon as the meal was finished.

"So quickly?" his father asked.

"I only came up to have this chat, put you in the picture."

"Of course," John said.

Alison wasn't talking. No doubt she was trying to come to terms that her younger son was a man who had the power, and the will, to order a young woman to be executed. Mother, like Yvonne, had never had the capacity to look beyond the superficial aspects of life, which was no doubt why they got on so well together.

193

He wondered if he would ever come home again. He wondered if he would wish to.

But he still had a full day's furlough before having to return to Wales. He supposed it was another moral blight that, although a much-decorated major with a wealth of fighting experience and the presumed nous that went with it, he could still feel like a schoolboy playing truant when he had a day off.

He reached London in mid-afternoon, having lunched on the train. The city was full of soldiers, a large proportion of them American GIs. They were looking for a good time on a Saturday afternoon. He knew where there was one, for him. But when he got to Belinda's flat, the door was locked and as there was no reply to his ringing on the bell, she clearly wasn't home.

He felt totally frustrated, both because he wanted to have sex with her, and because he had made no alternative arrangements. He went to the office.

"Captain Forrester, sir? She said she was taking the afternoon off. She'll be in tomorrow, I imagine."

Harry could not resist looking at the closed inner door, even if he had no desire to see Peter Bannon at that moment.

"The Colonel is off as well, this afternoon, sir. Saturday, you know."

You'd hardly believe there was a war on, Harry thought. Could they, for all her fine talk about fidelity, have gone off together? She had certainly had a relationship with David Lightman, when he had been the CO.

He was aware of feeling quite angry, without the slightest positive reason. They were both probably doing their own thing. But what was Belinda's own thing? Apart from men?

The corporal was looking anxious. "Is there anything I can do for you, sir?" he asked. "I could try a hotel."

So that I can lie in bed in solitary splendour, Harry thought. "No, thank you, Corporal," he said. "I'll find somewhere for myself."

He knew exactly where he was going.

"Major Curtis?" Deirdre herself opened the door. She was

wearing shorts, and her legs were entirely in keeping with the rest of her. "What a pleasant surprise."

"I just happened to be in town," he said.

She looked at his overnight bag. "And all the hotels are full," she suggested.

"If you'd like me to go . . ."

"I wouldn't. Come in."

She stepped back, and he entered the flat. "Your friend . . .?"

"Jessica. She's away for the weekend."

"Ah."

"There's a coincidence," Deirdre said. "I'm afraid there's only tea." She smiled. "As usual."

"We could go to an off-licence."

"I suppose. What would you like to buy?"

"How about champagne?"

She had her back half turned to him. Now she turned round to look at him.

"Again, if you'd like me to leave, I will," he said.

"And again, I wouldn't like you to leave."

"So?"

"I'm not really that sort of girl," she remarked.

"I didn't think you were."

"But you think I'll keel over for you. Is it lust, or pity?"

"I'm afraid it's lust. Combined right now with a high level of loneliness."

"I wouldn't have thought a man like you would ever be lonely. Is there some curiosity involved?"

"There always is."

"I meant, because of Ian."

"I know that's what you meant," Harry said. "Perhaps. I remember thinking, as I left here the last time. Ian Simmons must have died happy, if he felt he had you to come back to."

"Only he didn't. And you told me he knew this."

"He suspected it, and it made him unhappy. Will you tell me why?"

She gestured him to the settee, and sat beside him. "Immaturity, I suppose. His immaturity."

"Oh, quite. Are you telling me that you regard yourself as mature?"

"I think I am. More than Ian, certainly. He was also upset because I wasn't a virgin."

"I imagine he was."

"Ian came from that breed of Englishman who feels every woman should be a virgin until she's married."

"It's not an uncommon aim."

"Which you do not hold?"

"I didn't come here to ask you to marry me."

"Absolutely. You came here to fuck me, because you felt I was fuckable. Right?"

"You are ninety per cent right, Deirdre. But I also came here because I am a little bit distraught and, as I said, very lonely. I wanted a shoulder to cry on. I also need a bed for the night." He grinned. "You're sitting next to a right mess."

She leaned forward, and kissed him on the nose. "I'm not that mature. So tell me, do we go out and buy the champagne now, or afterwards?"

"Definitely afterwards," Harry said.

The Spearhead

D eirdre had, as Harry had suspected, hidden depths. But if she was prepared to give all, she also wanted all in return. Perhaps this was where Simmons had disappointed her.

"Will I see you again?" she asked, as they lay in bed the next morning.

But it was less a question than a demand.

"I'm afraid I can't answer that," he said. "I go where my superiors send me. And they don't tell me in advance."

"I would very much like to see you again," she said.

"Snap. I will, whenever I can, I promise."

"But you have other calls on your spare time."

"I do," he admitted. "One could say that I'm in more of a mess than before." He kissed her. "But I wouldn't have missed spending the night with you for anything in the world."

"That was a nice thing to say. Even if you didn't mean it."

"Ah, but I did mean it."

"A romantic man," she mused.

"Don't you think men can be romantic?"

"I'm sure they can. The trouble with men is that they put sex first, and hope that romance will follow."

"And women are different?"

"Of course. Women put romance first and hope that sex will follow."

"And I don't suppose that will ever change. Now I have to be getting along."

"It's Sunday morning. Can't you spend the day?"

197

Presumably Belinda was back by now. But he didn't know that. She might well have gone for the weekend.

Besides, he didn't actually want to see Belinda right this minute.

"All right," he said.

He wondered if it was possible to be in a bigger emotional mess, simply because he couldn't keep his hands off a pretty woman. He was sure that wasn't the case. It was because there were so many lonely, pretty women who, because of the traumas induced by the war, craved the comfort of a pair of strong arms around them, and who found him more attractive than most men because of his fighting record as much as any personal ambience, and because he craved an equal comfort . . . again no doubt because of his war record which, for all his exterior insouciance, had him permanently trembling on the brink of a nervous breakdown.

He regained the camp only an hour after a badly shaken Mustafa.

"It was terrible," the little man said. "To think that my wife could do things like that. I had always thought she wouldn't hurt a fly."

"You mean it was definitely Philippe?"

"Oh, yes. There was no doubt about it."

"And no sign of Yasmin?"

"There was something, only a month after Philippe's disappearance. Two prostitutes were sharing a room, and one was found with her throat cut. The other had disappeared. No one knew her real name, but she was described as small and dark. But the police did not suspect her of the crime, you see. They supposed a john had turned nasty and attacked the dead woman, and the other had done a runner. You know how it is, in war time. There are so many people with no fixed abode, coming and going . . ." His shoulders hunched. "My wife, a prostitute!"

He seemed to find this just as difficult to accept as the fact that she was also now a serial killer!

The Cause

Harry telephoned Belinda, but she had already been brought up to date.

"They're keeping an eye out for her, and they're keeping a sort of watch on Mrs Johnson's house . . ."

"Sort of watch?"

"Well, Harry, there is a war on. And we're preparing for the invasion. There are so many people coming and going and getting in each other's way, so many jobs for the police to be doing with millions of soldiers wandering around, they simply don't have the manpower to concentrate on a single case. Anyway, you'll be out of it soon. I mean the frying pan. You'll be going into the fire. The Boss wants to see you tomorrow."

"Would you believe that's the best news I've heard in weeks. By the way, did you have a good weekend?"

There was a brief silence. "A lonely one," she said.

"Ah."

"Just what do you mean by that?"

"I happened to be in London, on Saturday. But you weren't."

Another brief silence. "What were you doing in London?"

"Actually, looking for you. I'd been up to see my folks, and on leaving them, as I had a day to spare, I thought I'd drop in. But I seem to have missed you."

"And you thought I was having it off somewhere."

"Were you?"

"Bugger off," she said. "You're expected in the office tomorrow morning."

She was clearly furious. At being suspected? Or at being found out? In either event, he didn't have a leg to stand on.

He was prepared to be conciliatory when he arrived at the office, but she was not. "Colonel Bannon is waiting to see you," she said, coldly formal.

There were several other Commando officers present, seated in the Colonel's office.

"Gentlemen," Bannon said. "The show is definitely coming off next year. I am not going to give you the date, or the location, but D-Day is fixed for just as soon as the weather can be

199

guaranteed. As I am sure you realise, an invasion on this scale is only practical if we can get everything we need across the Channel, and maintain a bridgehead until it can be built up sufficiently to ensure success.

"But of equal importance is the disruption of the German infrastructure. The RAF is our main weapon here, and they are already bombing selected German targets in France. However, there is a problem: the civilian population. We are fighting to free France from German occupation, as much as a first step to invading Germany itself. We do not wish to destroy French civilians if we can avoid it. So indiscriminate blanket bombing is out. What we need are individual groups operating behind the enemy lines, in conjunction with the Maquis, the French resistance forces, to destroy and disrupt the enemy lines of supply and communication.

"Now, when the show comes off, the main body of Commandos will be used as a spearhead, being parachuted into position immediately in advance of the ground we need to take and hold on the first day. It will be their job to control vital river crossings until they are joined by the main body. I am asking you to volunteer for special services well before then. In this regard you will be working with the Special Air Services, who have been very successful at infiltrating and working behind enemy lines. I may say that there are also Belgian and Free French special services who will be carrying out similar duties. However, they need all the help they can get, and we have been invited to give them that help. This will involve operating behind enemy lines for perhaps several days or even weeks. I do not have to point out the dangers of this. In addition to ordinary combat risks we know that any Allied soldier captured in France, certainly before D-Day, and whether in uniform or not, will be immediately shot. That is an order from Hitler himself, and we have some evidence that it is being obeyed. However, as I say, you will have the assistance of the Maquis."

"Of what value are they?" someone asked. "As a fighting force?"

"If you mean, in the context of what might historically be

called the line, they are of no value at all. They have no military training, no discipline, very little infrastructure and no organised command. They are also very ill-equipped. However, they have had some success at planting explosives and eliminating German personnel. They also, of course, know the areas in which they operate, and this will be invaluable. It is felt that with a stiffening of Commando or SAS personnel they could be very useful."

"Are they trustworthy?" asked someone else.

"All organisations like the Maquis have their share of traitors," Bannon said. "When these are discovered, they are executed. You will have to rely on your relationships with the commander on the ground in this regard. Are there any other questions?" He looked over the faces in front of him.

There was no reply.

"Very good. Now, I know that some of you have your own picked squads with whom you have worked for some time. You will obviously maintain these. Those of you who have no such squads will have to create them, just as quickly as possible. Starting now, I will see you all separately. Obviously, where you are going, and what you are intended to do, is top secret to each individual commander, so that in the case of capture, you will not be able to divulge any information to the enemy that could harm any other squad. I don't want to be macabre about this, but I don't want any of you to be under any illusions about the German ability to make you tell them anything they want to know, in the event that you *are* captured, no matter how strong-minded you are, or how high your pain threshold. Harry, I'll start with you."

The other officers filed out.

"I assume you and yours are all ready to go?" Bannon inquired.

"Absolutely."

"And that you will take your little Algerian friend with you?"

"Yes, sir. Is that important?"

"It could be. Come over here."

Bannon went to the huge map of France pinned against the

wall. "You have of course operated behind the lines in France before. Once in the raid on Ardres, and once while escaping following the St Nazaire disaster."

"Yes, sir."

"And all of your people speak French?"

"They can get by. But my sergeant *is* French. And I have Le Blanc."

"Excellent. Now . . ." He used a wand to touch the map. "You and your people will be put down here, in the open country south of Lisieux. It is well-wooded, and there is a strong Maquis presence. Your business will be to blow up the Paris-Caen railway line, the most important link between the capital and the coast, which seems to have escaped several RAF raids, and also to demolish an arms depot situated near to the village of St Etienne Dutoit . . . here. Any other damage you can inflict upon the enemy will be a bonus, but those are your main objectives. Carried out successfully, they will not only disrupt communications and troop movements between the capital and the coast, but they will hopefully distract a considerable number of men to look for you. You are not expected to take these people on head to head. Instead you will conceal yourselves and call for extraction. This will be done as rapidly as possible. Any questions?"

"Two."

"Well?"

"Firstly, whatever damage or disruption we manage to cause will be put right in a matter of days, probably hours, by the Germans."

"Exactly. Therefore it needs to be blown more than once. I mean, in separate places. Sufficiently to keep it out of action for a week. Once our people are ashore, Jerry won't have either the time or the men to repair it. Our estimation of events is that Jerry will consider the first attacks, on the line, as the work of the Maquis, but after the second, on the dump, he will realise there is a Special Forces Section working the area. This will bring him out in force, and suitably distract him from what may be happening on the coast."

"So I would be right in assuming that the landings will take place in the Bay of the Seine?"

"You may assume what you like, Harry. I am not going to tell you. It is equally likely that you are merely going to carry out a large diversion."

"Then may I ask what is our survival plan if Jerry is *not* distracted by events on the coast?"

"Should that be the case, as I have said, you will call for extraction."

If there are any of us left to extract, Harry thought grimly.

"Your Code Name will be Cut Flower."

"That sounds remarkably appropriate."

"However," Bannon went on, "you are not, under any circumstances, to use your radio to contact us, *except* to call for extraction. We will keep in touch with you via the local Maquis, with whom we are in radio contact, just in case there is a change in orders."

Harry nodded. "All this being when?"

"At present you are scheduled to go in at the beginning of May. This will give you several extra months to bring your men to their peak. Under no circumstances must anyone, anyone at all, know where you are going and what you are going to do. They will of course realise that they will be operating in France, but that is all."

"Meaning that the invasion is scheduled for May."

"Yes, it is. Conditions will be what we require at the end of the first week. But finalisation still depends on the weather, and under no circumstances is that information to go any further."

"It won't," Harry said. "But that raises another question. Suppose the weather isn't right, at the same time as conditions?"

"Then I'm afraid it will have to be put back to the next possible date, which will be the first weekend in June."

"So, do we go ahead regardless? Or will we be warned?"

"Should the op be cancelled, a message will go out on the radio. It will read, 'Star at night, shining bright, all we need is a light tonight.' Can you remember that?"

"Certainly. In which case . . .?"

"You hold everything for another month."

"Staying put wherever we are in France."

"I'm afraid so."

"With the risk of betrayal."

"I'm afraid that too. Keep your fingers crossed for May. You had another question?"

"I assume the Maquis are going to be co-operating with us. If we do manage to stir Jerry up, and are then extracted, what happens to them?"

"There will, obviously, be reprisals. Undoubtedly there will already have been reprisals, for your earlier attacks. These are inevitable, and the Maquis know this, and expect it. In this regard the local commander on the ground is important, and if possible you should bring him out with you. That is why I am glad Le Blanc is going with you. The commander is his father."

"Would you mind saying that again?" Harry asked.

"Frederick Le Blanc, one time resident of Ghardaia in Algeria. Isn't that his father?"

"I should think it is."

"Well, then . . ."

"I think you have forgotten something, Peter."

Bannon raised his eyebrows.

"When we first signed Mustafa up, and discovered something about his background, we learned that his father had abandoned his mother, and her three children, when they were all quite small."

"By Jove, so he did. But these things happen in the best regulated families. People generally get over them."

"Not people like Mustafa Le Blanc. He is sworn to kill his father if they ever meet."

"Good Lord! And you tell me his wife is sworn to kill him, when next they meet."

"I'm afraid she is."

"You do deal with some very peculiar people, Harry."

"Some people might say I'm doing a very peculiar job."

"Touché. Well, I did tell you, when you insisted upon keeping this chap, that he was your responsibility. You are also the commander of this op, both now and on the ground in France. How you handle the matter, whether you decide to leave Le Blanc behind, or deal with the situation, if one arises, when you are in place, is entirely up to you. I know you well enough to be sure that you will allow nothing to interfere with the success of your mission. You'll give Forrester your requirements, and ask her to send Adams in."

Harry saluted.

"One of these days," Belinda said, studying the list, "you are going to blow yourself up."

"I need to make a very big bang."

"I can see that. Well, I don't think this lot can be dropped. You'll have to go in by Lysander."

"Is that practical?"

"I believe so. If he can't set down, there will be a very big bang. Oh, Harry . . ." Suddenly she squeezed his hands, and he assumed that he had been forgiven. "Every time you go on one of these missions . . ."

"I always come back, remember?"

"You're either very lucky, or . . ."

"Very skilful," he suggested. "I prefer to think the latter."

"Did anyone ever tell you that you are the most arrogant bastard who ever walked the face of this earth?"

"I imagine several. But they're quite wrong, as are you. Would you believe I'm scared stiff? I always am."

She regarded him for several seconds. Then she said, "I believe you, Harry. Which makes you about the bravest man I have ever met, in that you still do the job. Usually with brilliant success. But . . . this has to be the last."

"I wouldn't count on it."

"I am counting on it," she said, and kissed him.

"Well, sir," McIntyre asked enthusiastically, "when do we go?"

Everyone knew Harry had been to London for a briefing.

"Not for a while yet," Harry told him. "We have a lot more training to do."

"But it will be France?"

"That seems to be the general idea. Now," he told the assembled squad, "our main business will be to blow up a railway line."

The men exchanged glances. That seemed rather tame after the assault on the radar station.

"So," Harry said, "over the next couple of months I wish every one of you, and that includes you, Mr McIntyre, to become an expert in the handling, placing, and detonating of explosives. The way I detonated the charges in Spetsos is not to be recommended for habitual use."

They grinned appreciatively.

"Experts will be down to train you," Harry went on.

"With respect, sir," Nichols said, "is there any chance of leave? With Christmas coming up . . ."

"There will be leave," Harry told them. "But remember this is a top-secret exercise."

He didn't suppose they would all remember that, but equally he didn't suppose they could do any damage. They were Commandos, the Germans knew the Allies were preparing an assault on the mainland, and there were a very large number of railway lines that could be blown up at the appropriate time.

He set them to work, over the winter, while keeping up their training and the necessary high standards of physical fitness, while he gave some thought to the critical matter of Mustafa and his father.

It was not simply a matter of taking the logical course and leaving the Algerian behind to avoid any risk of friction. A Mustafa left behind when he was so anxious to be a part not only of the Commandos but in winning the war would be a very disappointed and disillusioned man, who might therefore be a very dangerous man. Certainly keeping him away from Golders Green would be difficult.

The short answer would be either to shoot him or have him

locked up for the duration. The first was out of the question; they had shared too much and besides, he liked the little man, and admired both his skill and his courage. Apart from any other considerations, he would be enormously useful on this assignment. The second would be to make him more dangerous yet, because one day – in the not too distant future, the way the war was going – he would be released, undoubtedly believing he had been betrayed by his best friend.

Nor, going back over all of those things to the death of Raquyyah, was it a situation he could discuss with anyone, because of his own involvement. He had not even dared discuss it with Belinda.

Bannon had given him *carte blanche* to deal with the matter as he thought fit. Well, then . . . he determined to leave things as they were, and carry out the assignment with the necessary assistance of Frederick Le Blanc and his Maquis. Mustafa would have to accept that they were essential to the squad's success, and that personal feelings would have to be left to the end of the war. If he could not accept that, *then* it might be necessary to execute him.

But surely commonsense would prevail.

Furloughs remained a difficult problem. Not for the other members of the squad, who were released one at a time for what could well be the last time they would see their families. But he dared not just send Mustafa off. The Algerian had no friends in England outside his few, now very distant, comrades in the Free French, and they were, in any event, virtually sealed off in their camp in the south, awaiting their embarkation orders. That left only Tasmina, but he could not be sufficiently sure of her, or of if she was in touch with her sister.

In the end, he decided to take Mustafa home with him, when he returned for a last time. This was after Christmas. John and Alison was both surprised and shocked, although Mustafa's manners were perfect, and he kept very much to himself. But they could not prevent people looking sideways at them when they took a walk, and John felt constrained to make inquiries.

"You're very fond of that little chap, aren't you?" he asked, when he and Harry were sharing an after dinner brandy. Mustafa, being a Muslim, did not drink alcohol, and was in the other room playing Chinese Chequers with Alison.

"Yes, I am."

John sipped his drink. "Would it be impertinent of me to ask why?"

"As a matter of fact, Dad, it would be impertinent. It so happens that he once saved my life. And he's a damned good fighting man. We also, sadly, share a pretty ghastly secret."

"You mean the woman he killed."

"That's right."

"And now you tell me his wife has quite vanished. So you could say you and Mustafa have a sort of relationship."

Harry gazed at him for several seconds, then burst out laughing. "Not *that* kind of relationship. Did you really suppose that?"

John Curtis was flushing. "Well . . . there is talk."

"Well, you can tell them to bugger off. Mustafa is both my batman and my right-hand man. We fight together, we kill together, and when we die we shall probably die together."

"Are you going to die, Harry? This time?"

Harry grinned. "I wouldn't count on it."

He had to keep them happy.

Those final weeks of training were as difficult as any Harry had known. Morale remained high, although there were some querulous looks and remarks when certain of their comrades left camp, with their officers, and disappeared. Obviously they were being sent to France, while Harry's squad remained in training. Presumably these advance groups were also extracted – or their survivors were – once their missions had been completed, but none of them were returned to the training camp: any recounting of their experiences might have been very bad for morale.

Meanwhile, more and more American troops and matériel were being poured into England, preparatory for the great day, turning virtually the entire southern half of the country into a vast military camp.

When it was his turn for a final furlough Harry felt obliged to go up to Frenthorpe. His parents had seen nothing of Yasmin Le Blanc, but then, neither had anyone else. It was tempting to suppose she might be dead in a ditch somewhere.

As usual, Harry chopped the last day of his furlough to be able to get down to London. This time he had ascertained that Belinda would be at home, and she seemed to have entirely thawed.

"Do you know when you go?" she asked.

"No. Some time next month. Do *you* know when we go?"

"Some time next month. You worried?"

"I told you, scared stiff."

She raised herself on her elbow. "You certainly look distracted."

He pulled her down to kiss her. How to tell her that he was indeed distracted, because his thoughts were in a flat not very far away. My God, he thought, I have fallen in love with that girl. But he couldn't have, he'd only met her twice. And besides, he was in love with Belinda. Wasn't he?

"Oh, how I hate these goodbyes," she said next morning as they dressed. "I'm beginning to sound like a cracked record. It's been going on so long. When is it going to end, Harry? When?"

"Hopefully, it's in sight," he assured her. "Just keep the bed warm."

Then it was time to put her, and Deirdre, and Yvonne, and even poor Zoe, out of his mind as he and his men prepared for the mission. The war, and perhaps the world, seemed to be holding its breath. The war continued to rage, world-wide, but all *sotto voce*, as it were. Alexander's army slowly fought their way up the Italian peninsular, their efforts hampered by so many key men, beginning with Montgomery himself, being brought back to England to prepare for D-Day. The Americans continued to hop from island to island in the Pacific, and in company with the Australians to claw their way through the forests of New Guinea; the U-boats continued to wage their deadly war on the Atlantic convoys, though they had by now been all but defeated as an offensive force; the Russians continued to push the Germans back towards Poland, with enormous losses of life on both sides . . . but it was the imminence of D-Day that filled everyone's mind.

At the end of April Bannon came down for a final word. "All set?"

"All set," Harry told him.

"Right. You go the day after tomorrow. As usual, you'll be on the tail end of a raid, so hopefully no one will pay any attention to you."

"So the big one is still on for May."

"Hopefully. The long range weather forecasts aren't too good. As you may know, we need the juxtaposition of two things: a big tide just before dawn and a full moon. A full moon usually means a big tide, but to get the timing right is another matter – it only happens about once a month. So if it happens to be blowing a gale over those few days, *kaput*."

"And then?"

"As I told you, the next possible date is June."

"But we go ahead regardless."

"You have to. Le Blanc is expecting you tomorrow night. As I say, if the op is cancelled, you will be informed and you will sit tight for the next month. However, if the going gets really sticky, you request extraction and you will have it. But I know you will do the maximum harm to the enemy before that."

"We will certainly try," Harry said. "There's just one more thing: does Le Blanc know that Mustafa is in my squad?"

"Le Blanc knows nothing at all about your squad, Harry. Save your name. I considered it best to play it this way. I don't know, and I don't want to know, what decisions you have come to regarding the Le Blancs. That is entirely your business. All I can do is wish you good fortune . . . and I look forward to meeting up with you again in a month or so."

"Snap," Harry said.

The tension was so great it could be felt as the squad climbed into their truck for the drive to the airport. This was well to the south, and therefore in the generally restricted area, and there was a great deal of stopping at checkpoints to show over-anxious MPs their passes. In many places the road surface was quite rough, and the Commandos eyed the stacks of gelignite bouncing beside them in the enclosed rear. But they were all experts now, and knew it would not explode without a detonater.

The Lysander waited for them on the tarmac outside Exeter.

"We're going in *that*?" McIntyre asked. "There's only one engine."

"And only one pilot, too," Le Boule observed.

Mustafa merely grinned.

"It'll get us there," Flight-Sergeant Reynolds promised them. "And me back."

"I'm afraid there's quite a load," Harry told him, as the gelignite was carefully stowed, together with their arms and ammunition, and their haversacks and kitbags.

Reynolds nodded. "As long as we can get airborne."

This was something of a problem. Reynolds gunned his engine for some time before attempting the runway, and there was an agonising moment of perhaps a second after he had pulled back the yoke before the aircraft actually lifted off.

Harry wiped his brow with his handkerchief.

Above them, the night sky was filled with aircraft, heavy bombers these, with their fighter escorts.

"Do we go above or below?" Harry asked.

"Below, I'm afraid, Major," Reynolds said.

Harry gulped, as he thought of one of those monsters coming down on top of them.

Reynolds could tell what he was thinking. "Chance in a million," he pointed out.

They were over the Channel now, flying at only a few thousand feet, looking down at the whitecaps, visible even in the darkness. Above and in front of them the aircraft continued to zoom along. There was no moon, but also little cloud, and the sky was bright enough to reveal the enormous armada.

Then the French coast.

"This is the tricky bit," Reynolds commented, as the anti-aircraft guns opened up. "These fellows aren't aiming at us; I doubt they even have us on their radar screens. But they can see the chaps above us."

To decrease their chances of being seen he went lower yet and the noise of the Lysander's engine was drowned in the huge noise all about them. But now they were so low they could feel that the flashes of the anti-aircraft guns were within a few feet. Then one of the bombers was hit, and came soaring downwards, flame belching from its starboard wing. Harry could see the crew bailing out, while the Lancaster continued on its way to the ground, so near Reynolds had to bank steeply.

Even the flight-sergeant gave a little whistle. "Close," he remarked.

"Too bloody close," Harry muttered.

Then suddenly there were no more flashes, and they were flying, by themselves, low over an apparently deserted country-side. It wasn't, of course: every so often there was a dull glow to indicate a village or even a town, but the houses were all blacked out. The aircraft themselves had disappeared to the north-east.

"Ten minutes," Reynolds said.

Harry looked over his shoulder at his men.

"Thought we'd bought it," McIntyre said.

"Join the club," Harry said. "But we're just about there. Have you landed here before?" he asked the pilot.

"No, sir. But I've been into France before. They usually choose a pretty good field."

Harry thought of the gelignite in the back. But that was surely the least of their problems.

"There," Reynolds said.

Harry peered through the windshield. "There's only one row." He counted six lights, in a relatively straight line.

"So we take that as our middle marker," Reynolds said, checking his altimeter.

Now there were trees. To many damned trees, Harry thought,

as they slowly descended. The row of lights remained in front of them, at about a mile's distance, he estimated.

Lower yet, until he felt he could lean out of the window and pluck away a branch. Then the trees were gone, and they were passing over a hedge, with the lights directly in front of them. Reynolds reduced speed, and a moment later there came the first bump, then a whole succession of bumps. But these were all minor, and a few moments later they had come to a halt.

"Tell me something," Harry said. "Do you get a medal for each flight?"

"Sadly, no, sir."

"You certainly deserve it."

"I'm afraid we have to hurry, sir."

"Oh, quite. Sorry." He looked back at his men. "Everybody out."

The door was opened, and they dropped on to the ground, to find themselves surrounded by people, men and women, clad in dark jumpers and berets. These began getting into the aircraft as the Commandos were getting out, to pass down the baggage.

"Easy with that stuff," Harry said. "It's mostly gelignite."

"You are Major Curtis?" a man asked.

It was easy to deduce that he was Mustafa's father, even in the dark: he was short and had the same intense features, even if he was considerably the heavier man.

"Yes," Harry said.

"Welcome," Le Blanc said. "I am—"

Harry grabbed his arm and led him away from the plane. "Frederick. I know."

Le Blanc peered at him. "Frederick Le Blanc."

"Yes," Harry said. "But for the moment, I'd like to stick to Frederick, if you don't mind."

He certainly couldn't risk a crisis here in the open, with their gear only half unloaded.

Le Blanc considered for a moment. Then he said, "As you wish. You are in command, no?"

"I am in command, yes," Harry agreed.

The plane was empty, the gear stacked beside it. Reynolds leaned out of his window. "Good hunting, Major," he said.

"Get home safely," Harry said.

The engine had been ticking over, the propeller idly turning. Now it came to life. They watched the aircraft turn before bouncing across the field. Free of its very heavy load it was airborne in seconds, soaring into the darkness.

"That is one hell of a brave man," Harry said. "All right, Frederick, where do we go?"

"It is not far. Two miles."

"Do you have transport?"

"Nothing we can use at night. There is a curfew. My people will carry your gear."

They seemed willing enough, men and women.

"You're the rearguard," Harry told McIntyre.

The lieutenant nodded and called the squad to order, while Harry went to the front with Le Blanc, still determined to keep father and son separated until they had reached their destination.

The way lay through the wood on the far side of the field, the country sloping down to a small river valley beyond. This part was simple enough, and the stream was shallow enough to present no difficulties, but then they were climbing again.

"You are here as part of D-Day, eh?" Le Blanc asked, beginning to puff.

"A very remote part," Harry said. "We are here to cause trouble for the Nazis."

"All of this explosive . . ."

"Will be put to good use."

"Will you tell me where?"

"In due course," Harry said. "When we have seen how the land lies."

Their destination was a village, as Le Blanc had told him, some two miles from the field. Here, to his consternation, there was quite a crowd gathered to welcome them.

"Can these people be trusted?" he asked.

"Oh, yes, they all live here. They are all with us."

Harry could only hope he was right. But as he looked at the women, some with babies in their arms, and at the several teenage boys and girls, lumps of lead began to gather in his stomach. He couldn't take any of them out.

They were taken to the *estaminet*, where it turned out that Le Blanc was the owner. Here the gear was stowed in the basement, covered with various articles of food and cases of wine.

Harry left McIntyre and Le Boule to supervise the work of concealment while he joined Le Blanc senior in the bar, which was by now full of eager partisans. "Do the Germans come here often?" he asked.

"They search, from time to time," Le Blanc said. "But, on orders from London, we have been very quiet these past few months, so they think we have gone away, or are all dead."

"And they have identified no one in the village as being Maquis?"

"I told you," Le Blanc said proudly. "Our people are all Maquis. We have no traitors here. Only impatience. I have had a hard time these past few months, keeping them quiet. But now . . . the invasion is next week, no?"

"What gives you that idea?"

Le Blanc poured wine. "I use my head. Firstly, the invasion must take place with a full moon and big tide, eh? That is next week. And secondly, you are here. Am I not right?"

Harry reckoned the Germans could work out the conditions necessary for a successful invasion as well as anyone, certainly as well as an innkeeper west of Paris. Their only advantage was that the enemy did *not* know they were there.

"Tell me about the situation," he said. "The railway."

"The main railway line from Paris to Caen passes through Lisieux. You are going to blow this, eh?"

"The night before the invasion."

"That is Tuesday. The best tide is Wednesday. But there is something you should know. Your objective is to prevent the transport of troops from Paris to the coast, eh?"

"That's right."

215

"But there is another line, also from Paris, which is further to the south, and then swings up to join the main line about twelve miles south-west of Lisieux."

"Shit," Harry said. "It's not on my map."

"But it is there, nonetheless."

"Then we will have to blow that as well." And I have only seven men, he reflected. "I will require your assistance."

"Certainly. I have waited a long time for this."

"Now where is the ammunition depot?"

Le Blanc frowned. "You mean to blow that too? You will set the whole area . . . how do you say in English? An ant's nest?"

"I understand. Are your people up to it?"

"Well . . . normally I would say yes. But you see, this depot is right outside the village of St Etienne. And it is a big dump. Much high explosive. If it goes up it could well destroy the entire village."

"That's why it hasn't been bombed," Harry said. "The village will have to be evacuated."

"Under the noses of the Germans?"

"The people will have to leave, very quietly, and in groups of not more than three. If this is done at night, they stand a good chance of getting away with it."

Le Blanc pulled his nose. "There is the curfew."

"We'll be there to take out any patrols."

"And the houses? The belongings? They cannot take those."

"I am sorry. They will have their lives."

"They will not like it."

"Explain to them that this will win the war."

"And afterwards? The Germans will be . . . how do you say?"

"You suggested they would be like a disturbed ants nest."

"They will also be hopping mad. There will be reprisals."

"I'm afraid there will. But there should be nothing to link this village to what has happened, if your people can be trusted."

"They can be trusted," Le Blanc asserted, with some pride.

"Very good. So, you will send a couple of your best people across to St Etienne, tomorrow. They must locate absolutely

216

trustworthy people and tell them they must all evacuate next Tuesday night, and stay away from the village for twenty-four hours. This is because the ammunition depot is to be bombed. They must not know about us."

"I will go myself."

"No. I need you. You and I are going to reconnoitre the railway line."

Le Blanc nodded. "Now, you will sleep here. My girls are arranging beds now."

"Fine. What happens if the Germans search the village following the explosions?"

"We have a secret compartment. Come."

He led the way down the stairs, where the Commandos and the Maquis were putting the finishing touches to the concealment of the weapons and explosives. Several women were constructing camp beds at the far end of the room, watched appreciatively by the men, and not only because of the beds.

Le Blanc led Harry past them, and the beds, to the far wall. Here there was a large dresser. He snapped his fingers, and two of his men came forward to move it, to reveal a blank wall, but in it there was a slight depression. Le Blanc pushed this, and part of the wall swung in. Beyond was darkness. Le Blanc shone his torch into a fairly large chamber, dank and cold.

"Looks like a good place to get rheumatism," Harry suggested.

"If you have to go in, it will only be for a few hours."

"Air?"

Le Blanc shone the torch into the upper right hand corner. "There is a vent."

"Well, I suppose it's better than being shot."

"There is just one thing, sir." McIntyre was standing behind them.

"Yes?"

"Supposing we do have to go in, this piece of furniture will be replaced in front of the switch, right?"

Le Blanc nodded. "That way it is not possible to tell there is anything behind. Apart from the door, the walls are solid. You see?" He tapped the wall beside him. The sound was absolutely flat.

"Yes, but what I am thinking is, suppose all this is done, and we are neatly concealed, and the Germans turn really nasty and arrest you and all your people. How do we get out?"

Le Blanc looked at Harry.

"I would say we don't," Harry said.

"Jesus!" McIntyre muttered.

"It's unlikely to happen," Harry said. "Right. I suggest we get some sleep."

The door was closed, and the dresser pushed back into place. The gear was all stowed, and the Commandos, and their helpers, were waiting.

"Would you like a woman?" Le Blanc asked. "Any of these girls would be glad to be of service."

"I don't think that would be a good idea," Harry said. "We need sleep. There's a lot to be done tomorrow."

"Then I will bid you good night." Le Blanc turned away, and found himself facing Mustafa.

The Winners

"Papa?" Mustafa asked.

He could only ever have seen photographs of his father, but he appeared to have recognised him instantly.

Frederick Le Blanc was clearly mystified. He looked at Harry, but then Mustafa was also looking at Harry.

"Allow me to introduce your son," Harry said. "Mustafa Le Blanc."

The other Commandos had gathered round, intrigued.

"Mustafa?" Le Blanc peered at the little man.

Harry was watching Mustafa's hands, one of which was hovering close to his fearsome knife.

"Mustafa!" Le Blanc said again, and held out his arms.

Mustafa hesitated, looked at Harry, and received a quick nod. He went forward to be embraced, and at the same moment Harry stepped close behind him and plucked the knife from his belt. Mustafa checked, and tried to turn, but was already in his father's arms.

"Mustafa," Le Blanc said a third time. "You dear, dear boy. Oh, how good it is to see you again. After all these years. We have so much to talk about. Your dear mother . . . how is she?"

"Waiting for you to come back," Mustafa said, freeing himself.

"After she drove me out?"

"She drove you out? You abandoned her."

"No, no, it was not like that at all," Le Blanc declared.

"Who is this woman you speak about?" demanded one of the waiting women.

219

"Ah . . ." Le Blanc looked embarrassed, and Harry deduced that *this* woman was probably his current mistress. Then he looked at her left hand, and gulped – she wore a wedding ring. And she was tall and strongly built, ruggedly handsome, with long, curling brown hair.

"We speak of my mother," Mustafa said. "My father's wife."

"Your father's . . ." The woman looked from face to face. "You bastard," she said.

"It was a long time ago," Le Blanc explained.

"You bigamist!"

"Well, you see, with me here, and my wife in Algiers, and then the war . . . it was not practical to obtain a divorce."

"Bastard!" she shrieked again, and ran at him, nails bared.

"Shit!" McIntyre muttered.

Le Boule had grabbed her arms and was holding her, while she panted and fought him.

"I think we have discussed sufficient domestic matters for tonight," Harry said. "What is your name?"

"I am Aimée."

"Aimée Le Blanc. I would have said that was a peaceful sort of name."

"Le Blanc?" she almost spat at him. "How can it be Le Blanc, now?"

"Let's leave it like that for the time being. Now you, everyone . . ." He looked over all their faces, some curious, some astonished, some amused. "Listen to me very carefully. Our business is to win this war against the Boche. Personal feelings have to wait until that is done. I am now taking command here, and you will obey me, and no one else. I need the help of you all, but I will be obeyed. Understood?"

"You are nothing but a boy," Aimée sneered.

"Don't try me, madame. My business is killing people. The enemies of my country, which means anyone who is an enemy of me."

"He is right," Mustafa put in. "He kills people. Like nobody I have ever heard of."

Aimée Le Blanc swallowed.

"So we are now going to have a good night's sleep," Harry said. "I have given Monsieur Le Blanc instructions as to what we need to do tomorrow, and he will pass these instructions on to you. Now, dismissed."

They hesitated, then slowly climbed the stairs.

"You give me back my knife?" Mustafa asked.

"Only if you swear you will only use it as I direct."

"Until after the war, eh?"

"What you do after the war is entirely up to you, Mustafa. Just remember that they still use the guillotine, in France. Now turn in."

"What a shitting awful mess," McIntyre muttered, sitting beside him to take off his boots. "I thought we'd come here to fight Germans, not the local population."

"Par for the course," Harry told him. "The Germans come first."

The next morning the village appeared to be peaceful. Harry left McIntyre in command, and suitably dressed in French peasant clothes and a beret, set off with Le Blanc for a look at the countryside. This was ideal for concealment in the short term, consisting of *bocages*, small fields separated by high hedges and narrow lanes, and interspersed with woods. They saw no Germans, and carefully avoided any of the several hamlets they passed by. It took some time, but by noon when they were ready to sit down to their bread and cheese and paté, and their bottle of wine, all carefully packed for them by Aimée – Harry could only hope that she hadn't taken it into her head to poison them, or at least, Frederick – they were within sight of the railway line.

Harry spread his map on the ground and identified exactly where they were. To his right was a culvert, to his left the railway crossed a bridge over a small stream. The church steeples and water towers of Lisieux were just visible beyond the next hill.

He studied the bridge through his binoculars, watched a sentry walking up and down. Then a train came through, and both the sentry and another man, emerging from the hut on the far side of the track, waved at the driver.

"How many sentries?" he asked.

"Normally two."

"Shifts?"

"Four hours a time. Regular as clockwork. Midnight to four; four to eight; eight to noon; noon to four; four to eight, eight to midnight."

"You are quite sure about this? The times, I mean."

"I have studied them for months. Where will you blow?" Frederick asked. "The bridge or the culvert?"

"Both."

"Eh?"

"And also at the junction. Take me there."

"It will have to be tomorrow. We must be back at the village by dark."

Harry nodded. "All right, tomorrow."

"But . . . you mean to blow the line in three places?"

"Four."

Frederick wiped his brow.

While Harry looked at the sky. They were some distance from the sea, but there were heavy black clouds scudding in from the south-west.

"The weather is not good, eh?" Frederick asked.

"No," Harry agreed.

"Will you postpone the operation, if it is bad?"

"No," Harry said.

Frederick gulped.

All was still quiet at the village. Most of the men were in the fields with the cattle or weeding the cabbage patches; the children were in school; and the women gossiped. The men Frederick had sent into St Etienne had not returned, but there was no reason to doubt that they would do so.

Aimée appeared to be in a better mood than on the previous night, although she still muttered "Bigamist" under her breath when serving Frederick.

"What are you going to do about her?" Harry asked, interested.

Frederick shrugged. "After the war, I will get a divorce from Opryah, and make Aimée an honest woman."

"Well, I think you had better tell her that," Harry suggested.

By Saturday the weather had deteriorated, with low cloud and occasional drizzle. On Sunday the entire village, it seemed, attended church, and Harry thought it a good idea for his men to do so as well. Only Le Boule was a Catholic, but he felt it might be good for their souls. The priest blessed them all – he was apparently Maquis himself.

By then Harry had looked at the line west of Lisieux, and had decided where he was going to place the other two sets of explosive.

That evening he held a meeting with Frederick and three of the leading Maquis, together with Aimée and, of course, his squad.

They listened to the radio at the appointed time, but there was nothing for them.

"Does this mean they're going ahead?" McIntyre asked.

"It looks like it. Now, here is the schedule." He spread his map on the table. "We will operate in pairs, to begin with. We need to take up our positions on Monday night, as they are some distance away. We will then lie low until the following night. Mustafa, you will come with me. Our position will be here." He prodded the map at the bridge. "Sergeant Le Boule, you and Nichols will be at this position, here. Evans and Graham, you will be at the culvert, here. And McIntyre, you and Monsier Le Blanc will take the fourth, here, at the junction. You'll see that these positions are about twenty-two kilometres west of Lisieux, and roughly the same distance back to St Etienne. This is not as I would have liked, but has been forced on us by circumstances. The rendezvous at St Etienne is timed for four o'clock on Wednesday morning. How long will it take you to cover twenty-two kilometres?"

McIntyre looked at Le Blanc.

"I know the best ways," Le Blanc said. "Seven hours."

"That means an early start for you, but perhaps that is all to the good. Right. You will take up your positions, in the woods or anywhere else that promises total concealment, tomorrow night, to be ready to move as soon as it is dark on Tuesday. Lieutenant McIntyre and Monsieur Le Blanc will go first, because they have the furthest to come back. You will explode at twenty thirty."

McIntyre nodded.

"You will then return as fast as you can to the rendezvous, here." He prodded the map, a crossroads about half a mile north of St Etienne. "You must get there by four in the morning. Then you will wait there for the arrival of the rest of the party, supposing we are not already there. Understood?"

"Understood."

"Sergeant Le Boule, you will blow next, immediately afterwards, at twenty forty-five. There will then have been two separate explosions eight kilometres apart. You will then return to the rendezvous."

"Yes, sir."

"Evans, you and Graham go third, at ten thirty. By that time all German interest should be centred on the line west of Lisieux. Your detonation, in the culvert, will focus them back up here again and hopefully have them thoroughly distracted. It will also isolate Lisieux, at least as far as the railway is concerned. Then act as the others. Le Blanc and I will blow the bridge, at eleven. We are going last because we have the shortest distance back to St Etienne. By then the whole area should be buzzing, with all German attention focused on the railway. Hopefully, after the second two explosions coming two hours after the first, they will be looking for other charges before beginning to wonder who did it. Hopefully, also, the guards at the depot will have been distracted by the explosions. They may even have been called upon to lend some aid. If the Germans suppose the blowing up of the track was the work of the Maquis, they will not anticipate any further attacks that night, simply because they will doubt you have the capability, Frederick."

Frederick nodded. "And my people? I have twelve available."

"They will be at the rendezvous by four, and link up with us. We will then enter the depot, place our charges, and withdraw. The civilians will have evacuated the village by then, I hope."

"Yes," Frederick said. "Those of them who have been persuaded to go."

"We can do nothing more than that," Harry said. "The charges will be set to go off at five thirty. By then we must have got a good mile away."

"And then?" Frederick asked.

"At the same time as our explosive goes off, the Allies should be landing in France. This news should spread like wildfire, and will further disrupt the German activities, in every area, but especially where they have just suffered a massive attack. We have been instructed to withdraw to the woods . . ." – again he prodded the map – "here, and wait for our people to reach us."

"And if the Germans come after you in force?"

"They're supposed to be preoccupied. However, if the going gets too rough, I have been authorised to call for extraction. I'm afraid it can only be for us, and perhaps you. What do you expect?"

Frederick shrugged. "There will be reprisals. But as you say, with so much distraction, we should be able to evacuate and get into the woods ourselves. If the Allies are truly coming."

"Then it will be a matter of holding out until they get to us."

"Sounds simple. But it won't be."

"We will do it."

"Right. These reprisals, is there any way of telling who they will be?"

"No. They take people at random."

"And you can accept this?"

Frederick shrugged. "We have no choice."

Monday was tense. Word had spread through the village that the attack was going to take place within the next forty-eight hours, which indicated that D-Day was also within the next forty-eight hours. People gathered on the street corner and muttered at each other, and smiled encouragingly at the Commandos. And still they had not seen a German, although they could occasionally hear the rumble of traffic on the main road, which was only a couple of miles to the south. Déjà vu. Harry had spent a day like this once before, hiding in that farmhouse outside Poitiers, waiting for the Maquis to get him across the border into Vichy France. But those circumstances had been horrendous. He and his companions had still been in a state of shock following the catastrophe at St Nazaire, and they were aware that their presence was known to the enemy. This time he could not believe they were being so fortunate.

McIntyre thought so too. "Bit of a doddle, so far," he said. "You don't suppose we could call London and get a confirmation that it's on?"

"No," Harry said. "Our orders are under no circumstances to use the radio until after we have blown the line and the depot. If the Germans were to pick up our signals and move in and get hold of any of us, it might well ruin the whole invasion plan."

"It's just that it's starting to rain."

"I don't think a little rain will put Eisenhower off," Harry said.

But it was also starting to blow. They listened to the radio at six o'clock, but there was nothing.

"So we go," Harry said. "I'll see you on Wednesday morning, outside St Etienne, at zero four hundred."

They wore uniform. Not that it would do them a lot of good if they were captured, Harry supposed, except in so far that they could claim to be part of the invasion force rather than stray Commandos. But if they were going to die, as was extremely likely, he wanted them to go as proper soldiers.

Then they loaded their gear and set off into a very dark, windswept and wet night. The cloud cover was complete, but they each had a compass and a map, and they had been well-trained in the art of orienteering. He did not doubt they would all find their positions.

He and Mustafa made steady progress across country, and reached their spot just before midnight, which was ideal timing.

As it had taken them four hours to come in, it should take them no more than four hours to get back to the rendezvous, which was actually closer than the village.

They made themselves as comfortable as possible. Each had a waterproof groundsheet, which helped to keep off some of the rain, although the water splashed with disturbing plops on their helmets.

"Do you think we will catch cold?" Mustafa asked.

"I think that's very likely. But not for a couple of days."

"By then we will be back in England."

"Keep believing that."

The rain stopped about three in the morning, although the wind remained strong. But soon after dawn the sun came up, and then the day grew steadily warmer. From their position they could hear the roaring of the express train, as it travelled to and from Caen.

"Will the invasion force have left England yet?" Mustafa asked.

"No," Harry said. "They only have to cross the Channel. They won't leave until dark."

"It is like Algeria, eh?" Mustafa asked. "We knew it was coming, and nobody else did."

"But it was coming," Harry said. "That's the important thing."

He wondered why he was feeling uneasy. He did not remember that in Algiers. But there the weather had been perfect.

They slept on and off during the day, ate their bread and sausage, drank some wine, stared at the clouds scudding across the sky.

"Do you ever think of death?" Mustafa asked.

"Often," Harry said. "But not at times like this."

"What will they do to Yasmin, when they catch her?"

"I'm very much afraid she will be tried and convicted, and then she will be hanged. Although I suppose a good lawyer might get her off for being criminally insane. Then they would lock her up for life."

"That is terrible. Do you know a good lawyer?"

"Not personally. But I can probably find one. It wouldn't be cheap."

Mustafa brooded.

"You really need to concentrate on the job," Harry remarked.

"I am sorry. I should not have raised the matter. I will concentrate."

The day drifted by. Harry could imagine the immense hustle and bustle in the English south-coast harbours, gathering pace as the day drew in. But just before dusk it began to rain again, and the wind seemed stronger than ever.

"Let's go," Harry said, when they had eaten the last of their food, drunk the last of their wine. It was just coming up to eight. They crept through the fields and across the paths, and arrived at a position overlooking the bridge, just as a train came through, whistle blowing, sparks flying.

"Two men," Harry said, studying the bridge through his binoculars. "Stamping up and down. Your daddy was right, Mustafa: they have just been relieved."

He continued to study the two sentries for some time. They paraded together for a few minutes, then one retired into the box, while the other sauntered slowly across the bridge and back again. Harry then studied the country to either side. Lights in the distance – that was Lisieux. Nothing closer at hand. It was too bad a night for anyone to be casually abroad.

There was a flash of lightning, followed immediately by a clap of thunder.

"We will use our pistols," he said.

"Why not my knife?" Mustafa objected.

"Because I do not wish to risk either of us being hurt until after the explosives have been placed. And in this weather no one is going to hear a couple of shots. You can finish them off with your knife. If that is necessary."

Mustafa grinned.

They waited another hour, while another train came through. At a quarter past eight they crept down on to the bank of the shallow stream that ran under the bridge. Harry pointed at the sentry above them. They could hear his boots thudding as they marched to and fro. Mustafa nodded, and climbed the bank again. Harry climbed on the far side of the bridge, towards the hut.

"Hello," Mustafa said.

The sentry turned, and Mustafa shot him in the chest. He went down with a gurgle.

The second sentry ran out of the hut, and Harry shot him in the back. He also went down with hardly a sound, while the noise of the two shots was lost in another clap of thunder.

"They are both dead," Mustafa said, somewhat regretfully.

"Helmets and jackets," Harry said.

They pulled off the wet, bloodstained jackets, and dragged them on. Neither fitted, Harry's was too small and Mustafa's too large. But they did not expect to be closely inspected. The two bodies were dragged to the edge of the ravine and rolled down.

"Piece of cake," Mustafa said.

Harry was already returning to their lair for sufficient of the explosives – the main part he was keeping for the depot. Mustafa joined him and they carried the gelignite to the bridge, heard the distant roar of a whistle.

"On the bridge," Harry snapped.

They scrambled up, put on their coal-scuttle helmets, slung their rifles, and stood on to either side of the track to wave the train through. Then they climbed back below the bridge and set their explosives. Mustafa remained on the bridge while Harry extended the line and the box back a hundred yards. Then he rejoined Mustafa. The time was eight twenty.

There was a pot and crockery and coffee in the hut, and he made them each a cup, grimacing as he drank his – it was definitely ersatz. They both checked their watches, as the minutes ticked away. McIntyre was late. At eight forty another train came through. Five minutes later they heard an explosion from down the line.

"I hope that's your dad," Harry said, wondering how Le Boule was reacting; it was time for him to blow as well, but it was part of the plan for there to be a short time between each explosion. He wondered if anything would ever go exactly according to plan?

Mustafa grinned, and Harry wondered just what were his plans regarding the domestic scene, when the war was over.

They listened to sirens wailing in the distance. But none close at hand. Once again they checked their watches. It was just coming up to nine when they heard the second explosion.

"Now we wait," Harry said.

The area to the west was certainly very active, lights flashing, sirens wailing, even some gunshots. But here, so close to the town, all was quiet – so far.

"There is someone in the stream," Mustafa whispered.

"Shit," Harry muttered. "I'll do it."

He moved to the embankment, looked down. There was certainly someone in the stream, making very little effort at concealment, as he splashed through the water. Except that it was a she.

"Shit," he commented again. "Aimée? What in the name of God are you doing here?"

"I have come to you," she said. "There has been a message on the radio."

"Oh, Christ," he said. "What did it say?"

"Something about a bright night and needing a light."

Harry listened to more sirens, from very close, while his heart pounded and his brain seemed to seethe. He was dealing with catastrophe. But he kept his voice even.

"When did that come through?"

"Just after four, this afternoon. I left immediately to come here."

What a foul-up, he thought.

"You must stop it," she said.

"I cannot stop it, because it's begun. Your husband and my lieutenant are already on their way to the rendezvous. So are Sergeant Le Boule and Private Nichols. And I have no means of getting in touch with Evans and Graham in time."

230

"Then what will you do?"

"Continue as planned."

"Only there will be no invasion."

He nodded. "Not for another month, at least. Listen. Get back to the village, go to bed, and swear you never left it."

She hesitated, and they heard the growl of an engine close at hand, at the same time as they saw the headlights of the vehicle, uncertain in the rain.

"Go," he said. "Quickly."

He left her and scrambled back up the embankment, to join Mustafa, just as the command car pulled to a halt in the lane on the far side of the hut.

"How many?"

"I cannot see. What did the woman want?"

"To tell me that the invasion has been postponed. I assume because of the weather. Tommy-guns. We have to take them all."

"Then what do we do?"

"It's started. We have to finish it, now. And then request extraction, immediately."

As if that would be practical in this weather, he thought bitterly.

They both dropped their rifles, levelled their tommy-guns, and advanced to the end of the bridge. An officer came up the slope towards them, followed by a soldier. Both were armed, but the pistols were holstered. Harry looked past them at the command car; it was an open tourer, but the roof was up because of the rain. He could make out the driver, but not if there was anyone else in the car.

"The line has been blown in two places," the officer said. "Have you seen any suspicious activity?"

Harry cut him down with his first shots. Mustafa dealt with the soldier. There were shouts from the car, as someone in the back fired, and the driver tried to turn the car. Because of this the shot went wide, and Harry and Mustafa fired into the car, which exploded in a gush of flame as bullets struck the petrol tank.

"Down," Harry shouted, and they knelt beside the bridge while debris showered around them.

"If that were to hit the gelignite," Mustafa gasped.

"It hasn't, or we'd both be in hell by now," Harry told him.

"If the invasion is off," Mustafa said, "should we not just blow the line now, and get out of here?"

It was a temptation. But that would leave all the others out on a limb.

"We stick to the plan," Harry said. "At least we know there won't be any more trains out of Caen."

"But there will be more men coming here," Mustafa said.

Harry nodded. "We'll go back to the hideout and the box. We can't do any more good here."

They took off their German tunics and left them with the rifles, then retreated to the trees. Just in time, as a train now came up down from Lisieux, proceeding very slowly, with men in front of it on the track.

"They will find our explosives," Mustafa whispered.

Harry nodded. That part of the plan at least would have to be modified. He watched the train approaching. It was certainly full of men, while the sappers in front were peering at the track with the aid of torches. But visibility was still poor because of the rain. While the minutes were ticking away.

The train had just reached the bridge, and the burned out car. Men were shouting, and quite a few were disembarking. Then there came the third explosion, from the culvert, effectively sealing the line. The Germans became more excited yet, staring along the track, while more sirens wailed and more cars emerged from the rain mist. Now they were hunting around, while others peered at the dead bodies. Then someone looked under the bridge.

"Time to go," Harry said, and pressed the plunger.

The noise was enormous, the explosion devastating, seeming louder than the destruction of the radar station because it was in the open air. Pieces of track, of the bridge, and of men were flung high into the air; some debris even reached close to where Harry and Mustafa were hiding, a hundred yards from the bridge.

"Let's go," Harry said.

The Cause

They gathered up the rest of the gelignite and made their way
through the wood, surrounded it seemed on every side save to the
south-east by screaming noise. But everything was going according to plan – his plan. The Germans were indeed too concerned
about what was happening to the railway, about how many more
explosives might have been planted, to mount an immediate
search for the perpetrators.

But only his plan was working. If there was going to be no
invasion, then they, and their allies, were in the deepest trouble.
He could only call for extraction . . . and leave the Maquis to
their fate. What a shitting awful mess, he thought.

But first, the final task.

They reached the rendezvous at three thirty. The twelve
Maquis were waiting for them, but no one else.

"What happens if none of the rest make it?" Mustafa wanted
to know.

"You ask too many damned questions," Harry told him.

He listened to sounds from the village, and thought he heard a
shot. But the depot guard had no idea what was about to hit
them.

Figures loomed out of the drizzle. Evans and Graham.

"All correct?"

"Went like a song, sir."

Le Boule and Nichols arrived a few minutes later.

"They're buzzing," the sergeant said.

It was five to four before McIntyre and Frederick arrived,
both exhausted. "All systems go?" McIntyre asked.

"On our part, yes," Harry said. "But I have to tell you that the
invasion is off."

They gazed at him in consternation.

"It was cancelled last night," Harry said, "after we were
emplaced. It doesn't seem to have occurred to London that
we would have to take up our positions twenty-four hours in
advance. But there it is. I assume they waited as late as possible in
the hopes that the weather would clear, and it didn't."

"What do we do, sir?" Evans asked.

233

"We return to the village," Harry said, "and call for urgent extraction. But first of all, we blow this dump."

The silence was deafening.

But again everything went like clockwork. As Harry had expected, the Germans could not really conceive that the Maquis had either the men, or the firepower and explosives, to launch another major attack on the same night as they had destroyed the Paris-Caen railway. The sentries were more concerned with listening to what was happening to the north, the officers were on the telephone trying to find out what *was* happening. They were utterly surprised when Harry used his normal tactics of a frontal assault behind a hail of tommy-gun bullets, under the cover of which he set his explosive charges. These did not have to be either large or elaborate, merely placed inside the door of the first storeroom. This was sufficient to set off a chain reaction.

He set the fuse and rejoined his men.

"Casualties?"

"Two dead, sir," McIntyre said. "Both French."

"Damn," Harry said. He had been particularly impressed by the behaviour, and the verve, of the French volunteers, so contemptuously dismissed by Bannon as not being of "line" quality.

"And Sergeant Le Boule, sir."

"He's not dead?"

Harry had become very fond of the burly NCO.

"No, sir. But he's losing a lot of blood."

Harry bent over Le Boule, who was lying on the ground and cursing in French.

"We're taking you out, Sergeant," he said. "It's only minutes. What about Jerry?"

"Several of them are holed up in that barracks, sir. There are six dead."

"Shit," Harry commented. "All right. Get out of here. Make for the village."

He positioned himself just inside the gate, checking his watch. There were only five minutes to go, but that was long enough to allow the Germans time to defuse the detonator, if they had the courage. On the other hand, if they stayed inside . . .

"You in there," he shouted. "Come out and surrender. You have one minute before the place explodes."

There was no immediate reply, and he had waited long enough, if he wasn't to go up with it. He levelled his tommy-gun and fired a burst at the door, then left the gate and ran down the drive. Someone fired at him, but as he heard the shot he knew he hadn't been hit. Then, panting, he hurled himself into a ditch, lying flat, while the whole night kaleidoscoped around and above him. Burning debris dropped beside him, and he clawed it away from his clothes. Then he was on his feet again, staggering to and fro, and realised that he was again deafened, from the continuous rumbling in his ears.

The depot was still exploding, great bangs and screaming firework-like missives hurtling into the air. The whole complex was in flames and, as he had feared, some of the houses in the village, only a few hundred yards away, were also burning from the red-hot debris which had scattered about them.

While as for him . . . his uniform was torn in several places, but he still had his belts and his weapons, and he was still alive, even if cut and bruised. He hurried across country for the village.

He caught the squad and the Maquis up after half an hour.

"Am I glad to see you," McIntyre confessed. "That was some bang."

"How's Le Boule?"

"Not too good. We've bandaged him as tight as we can, but there are several ribs broken, and I reckon the bullet is still in there."

Harry peered at the sergeant, who was being carried on an improvised stretcher consisting of a groundsheet tied to two rifles. It had to be very uncomfortable, and Le Boule was no longer making any noise at all.

"You wouldn't have a doctor in your village, I suppose?" he asked Frederick.

"No. But there is one in Orbec. I will send for him as soon as we get home."

Harry could only hope they would be in time.

It was just growing light when they reached the houses. At that very minute the Allies should have been landing on the Normandy beaches. But they weren't.

People came out of their houses to greet them, and ask questions. Le Boule was carried into the restaurant and laid on a table, while Frederick gave instructions and sent a messenger on a bicycle to Orbec. Now Harry could inspect the wound himself. It was certainly a fearful gash – he could see the splintered ribs through the bloody flesh. And now Le Boule woke up and began to scream with pain.

Frederick gave him a sedative and he subsided again, while people crowded into the room to look at him.

"Will you tell your people how sorry I am about the dead men?" Harry requested.

"They died for France. Their mothers and sisters will know that. But Aimée," Frederick said. "Where is Aimée?"

Nobody seemed to know.

Harry unpacked his own radio, which was more powerful than the resistance machine, as that was intended only for receiving.

"Cut flower," he said. "Cut flower. Extraction required. Urgent."

He had to call three times before he had a reply.

"Cut flower. Map Reference 14Z. Midnight, 11."

"Can't it be tonight?"

"Sorry, old man. Not possible before then. Out."

Harry and McIntyre peered at their coded map. "14Z," Harry said. "There." He used his fingers to lay off the distance. "Seventeen kilometres east. Frederick?"

Frederick peered at the map. "That is good ground. There should be no problem."

"Right. I'm afraid we will have to remain here until tomorrow night."

Frederick nodded. "That will be all right. But listen, Aimée has disappeared."

Harry frowned at him. "What do you mean?"

"No one has seen her since last night, when she left the village."

"She came to see me. She was the one brought the news that the invasion had been postponed."

"What time was this?"

"She came to me about nine o'clock. She told me that I should abort the mission. But I could not. You and McIntyre, and Le Boule and Nichols had already gone into action."

"Then what did she do?"

"I told her to return here as quickly as she could, and say nothing."

"But she did not come here."

"Then . . ." The two men gazed at each other.

"She will have fallen, and hurt herself," Frederick said. "I must go and look for her."

"I will come with you, Papa," Mustafa volunteered.

Frederick nodded, and strapped on his pistol. Harry opened his mouth, and then closed it again. Filial devotion? Mustafa had given his word he would take no action against his father until after the war. And Aimée certainly needed finding.

The two men left, and he could attempt to regroup his command. They all desperately needed sleep. Not only had they had none for forty-eight hours, but they were suffering the downbeat both of the action and the realisation that they were, literally, cut flowers.

He spoke to each man, reminded them that the following night they would be taken out. Then he tried to get some rest himself, in the restaurant, so that he could be close to Le Boule.

The doctor from Orbec arrived in the middle of the morning, having driven over in a horse and cart. By then Frederick and Mustafa had returned. They had been unable to find Aimée, and Frederick was in a thoroughly distraught state.

"The Germans have arrested her," he asserted.

"You don't know that," Harry protested.

"They have," Frederick insisted.

"Why should they do that?"

"She was breaking the curfew."

"Well, surely that is not an execution offence."

"Oh, they will let her go. But they will rape her first, and probably beat her."

"As long as she comes back." Harry went to join the doctor. Le Boule had been undressed and his uniform hidden, while the Commandos were also wearing civilian clothes. The doctor was a gloomy little man, who rubbed his chin and pulled his nose.

"That is a gunshot wound," he pointed out.

"An accident when hunting."

"With a gun? You are not supposed to have guns."

"Are you going to report it?"

Some more rubbing and sniffing. "He must go to hospital, or he will die. And in hospital . . ."

"They will diagnose a gunshot wound."

"That is correct. They will inform the authorities, and the Germans will search this village."

"We don't want that," Harry said. "Tell me this: supposing he does not go to hospital for another twenty-four hours. Can he survive?"

"Perhaps. I cannot promise it."

"Then we'll chance our arm. Leave me all the painkillers you have. And doctor, I am assuming that *you* will not be reporting this to anyone."

"Or you will have me murdered. I understand. You are English."

"However did you guess?"

"Your accent is atrocious. I will wish you success, Englishman."

He gave Harry both pills and liquid, and left. Le Boule continued to groan, but Harry kept him well sedated.

"Think he'll make it?" McIntyre asked.

"Just keep hoping."

It was another of those impossible decisions. He could attempt to save Le Boule's life by letting him go to hospital in France. But as the doctor had pointed out, his wound would be quickly diagnosed, and the village searched by the Germans. Whereupon they would all be shot, including Le Boule. So his life wouldn't have been saved after all. Nor did he have any doubt that this would have been the sergeant's choice, had he been capable of thinking.

"When should we leave?" he asked Frederick, who was still in a thoroughly depressed mood, with the disappearance of Aimée.

"As soon as it is dark. I will guide you."

"How are things with the boy?"

Frederick shrugged. "He is all I have left, now."

"You have a wife and two other children in Ghardaia."

"That was a long time ago," Frederick said morosely.

The afternoon drifted by. The villagers went about their business, milked their cows, stopped at the restaurant for a brandy and to look at Le Boule, muttered at each other. Then one of the young men dashed into the bar, panting. "The Boche!"

"Where?" Frederick asked.

"On the road, and the other road. There is a lot of them. Tanks."

"Where are they going?"

"They are coming here," the boy shouted.

Frederick and Harry looked at each other.

"They have no reason to come here," Frederick said.

"I'm afraid they probably do. Aimée."

"She would not betray us."

Harry had his doubts about that, after the revelation that Frederick had married her bigamously. But he said, "They will have tortured it out of her."

"My Aimée!"

"You said we could hide in the cellar."

"But you will miss your plane."

"We'll have to chance that. Perhaps they won't stay very long." He rounded up his men. By then the clank of tank tracks was very loud.

239

They collected all their gear and trooped down to the cellar, and into the room at the back. Frederick provided them with torches, but nothing could dispel the utter dank darkness of the compartment.

"Christ, to be shut up in here," Evans muttered.

"We won't be," Harry insisted. But he looked at his watch. It was just after five. There was time, if the Germans left in another couple of hours.

He fed Le Boule some more sedative, and raised his head, at the sound of firing, permeating even the inner cellar.

"What the hell?" McIntyre asked. "They're not shooting it out?"

A whole village, Harry thought, prepared to die for France.

The firing grew louder, combined with a large number of other sounds, shrieks and screams and crashes and bangs. Then they heard movement immediately outside the door. They grabbed their weapons and waited, and a few moments later the door was flung open, by Frederick.

Now the noise was enormous. They appeared to be in the middle of a battle.

"Quick," Frederick said. "You must come out."

"What's happening?" Harry asked.

"They are certain you are here. Aimée must have told them. They have not attempted to come in to search for you, they have simply surrounded the village with tanks and are blowing it apart."

"Shit," McIntyre muttered.

"What are your people doing?" Harry asked.

"They are dying, Major Curtis. Dying."

"Come on." Harry led his men into the cellar; even as he did so, the entire building shook, and plaster fell from the ceiling.

"Looks like we've bought it," McIntyre suggested.

"Then we go dearly. Let's have a look."

"What about the sergeant, sir?" Nichols asked.

Harry chewed his lip. "We can do nothing for him now."

"I will see what I can manage," Frederick said.

"Thank you." Harry led the way up the stairs and into the restaurant.

Now he could smell burning, and indeed the restaurant itself had been hit; he guessed the upper floors were on fire. But then so was most of the village, the houses collapsing into blazing rubble. As for the people . . . he gazed through the shattered door, at several corpses, men, women and children, lying on the street. They had clearly been trying to reach the restaurant and the leadership of Frederick to tell them what to do. Even as he watched, more shells crashed into the houses, and the church began to collapse. No doubt there were people in there as well, Harry thought savagely.

It was growing dark, and now the Germans were closing into within a hundred yards, firing at point-blank range. Above Harry's head the ceiling cracked, and he retreated to the stairs just before it crashed in.

"What do we do?" McIntyre asked.

"We sit tight for another hour, until it's dark," Harry said. "And then we shoot our way out."

"Will we make it?"

"Probably not. But we'll take as many of those bastards as we can with us."

"What about the Sergeant?"

Harry sighed. "He'll have to stay put."

"They'll shoot him."

"Yes," Harry said, grimly.

Frederick had joined them. "My village," he wailed. "My restaurant. My people!"

"You can only avenge them," Harry told him, "or die yourself. We'd better get down."

The restaurant was now burning fiercely, and the heat was intense. But the shooting had stopped.

"Do you think they'll go away?" McIntyre asked.

"I don't think they will, until they find our bodies. Listen."

They could hear shouts, and then the sounds of water being thrown on the flames.

"They know where we are," Frederick moaned.

"Right. Now the drill, as soon as the flames are under control, will be to toss several grenades down here before coming in themselves. We must beat them to it. Get your gear. Anything that will fire."

He himself strapped on his pistol, and a belt of grenades, checked his tommy-gun and made sure he had a spare magazine. Then he stood by Le Boule, but the sergeant was unconscious. That was the best way to go, he supposed.

He rejoined his men. "Stand by," he said.

Their faces were understandably tense, but they were all armed to the teeth. Even Frederick had a belt of grenades.

"Now, listen," he said. "We go up, through the last of the flames. Grenades first, to clear a path, then tommy-guns. Then make to the east. We may have to hold them again to keep the landing field clear. But our first business is to get out of here. Understood?"

They nodded.

"Right. Then let's go."

He ran up the smouldering stairs, hurling one grenade and then another as he did so. The explosions were immediate, and he was rewarded with cries of both pain and dismay. Then he was running through a smoke and water haze, and hurling two more grenades. To either side were more explosions as his men charged behind him, he could only hope no one threw a bomb straight at him.

He reached the street. There were soldiers to either side of him, mostly manning a hose, but already in retreat as the Commandos burst out of the building. He sprayed them with bullets and scattered them even further, then hurled two more grenades. One landed on a command car and sent that sky-wards. Then he was down a side street, running as fast as he could, and realising that the tanks had been withdrawn. That was a bonus.

People were firing at him now, and he tripped and fell, uncertain whether or not he had been hit. He felt no pain, but he knew he wouldn't, until the shock wore off. And when he tried to get up, he found he could stand.

Behind him the night was again a kaleidoscope of sound, but he saw Mustafa, running towards him.

"That ditch!" Harry shouted, and they slid into the shallow depression together. For a few moments there was no one else. Then they saw Frederick, staggering towards them, firing to either side, before falling to the ground.

"Papa!" Mustafa cried.

Frederick was lying still.

"He's dead," Harry said.

"Papa!" Mustafa cried again, and got up.

"For God's sake." Harry grabbed at him, but missed. The little man ran towards his father's corpse, loosing a stream of bullets into the figures who were emerging from the houses. "Shit!" Harry muttered, as Mustafa crashed to the ground still firing, and driving the Germans back.

He realised he was the only survivor. Unless he too got up and charged at the enemy. But his business was survival, not heroics. It wasn't as if he could save any lives – even as he watched Mustafa rolled on his back, arms flung wide, one hand clutching his knife, his body a mass of blood. If there were any other survivors, they knew where to go.

Harry crawled into the night.

"Stupendous," Peter Bannon said.

"I lost my entire command," Harry said. "And an entire Maquis village."

"That is very tragic. But you did what you were sent to do. Aerial photographs show the railway line down in four places. It will take them weeks to repair."

"Weeks they now have."

"They'll hardly get it right before we go in. And that munitions depot is just a hole in the ground."

"Do you reckon it was worth all of those lives?"

"Of course it was, Harry. Don't go all morose on me. So

243

maybe a hundred people got killed. The stuff in that depot alone would have done for a few thousand of our soldiers. Listen, go away and have a good rest."

"I'd like to volunteer to be part of the Commando force on D-Day, sir."

"You're a glutton for punishment. I'll see what I can do. But for God's sake put your head down and your feet up for at least a week."

"Good advice," Belinda said. "My God, you look awful. All those scratches on your face and hands . . ."

"And in other places," Harry said. "I had to crawl through varying degrees of ditch and bush for damn near ten kilometers before it was safe enough to get up."

"But you made it. You always make it."

"Thanks to Reynolds. I'm going to recommend him for a medal. Amongst several." He wondered what they could do about Mustafa? Something, surely. But all of those brave, devoted men, who had followed him to hell and back on so many occasions . . .

"You also look extremely depressed," Belinda pointed out. "You'd better let Mother look after you for a day or two."

He could think of nothing he wanted more. With Belinda? Oh, yes. Deirdre was sanity, but no sharing. Belinda was the only woman on earth with whom he could possibly share his experiences.

"I'd like that," he said.

"Then let's go." She put on her cap, gathered up her handbag. "Oh, by the way, they've got your little friend."

"Yasmin?"

"The very one. She made the mistake of calling on her sister at about the same time as a policeman. She's in Holloway awaiting trial for murder."

"And she'll hang."

"I imagine that's likely. She'd need a very good lawyer to get her off."

"Then let's find a very good lawyer."

"You serious? It's you she wants to kill."

"I've sent too many innocent people to their deaths, recently," Harry said. "I need to save one."

"But she's not innocent."

"Compared with me, she is. Let's find that lawyer."

"He won't be able to do anything more than have her certified insane."

"She'll be alive."

Belinda sighed. "I don't understand you at all. Haven't you just asked Bannon to get you in on the invasion? How many people do you reckon you're going to kill then?"

"Not people," Harry said. "Enemy soldiers. We're not innocent."